Kiss Me Every Day

What Reviewers Say About Dena Blake's Work

Perfect Timing

"The chemistry between Lynn and Maggie is fantastic…the writing is totally engrossing."—*Best Lesfic Reviews*

Racing Hearts

"I particularly liked Drew with her sexy rough exterior and soft heart… Sex scenes are definitely getting hotter and I think this might be the hottest by Dena Blake to date…"—*Les Rêveur*

Just One Moment

"One of the things I liked is that the story is set after the glorious days of falling in love, after the time when everything is exciting. It shows how sometimes, trying to make life better really makes it more complicated… It's also, and mainly, a reminder of how important communication is between partners, and that as solid as trust seems between two lovers, misunderstandings happen very easily."—*Jude in the Stars*

"Blake does angst particularly well and she's wrung every possible ounce out of this one… I found myself getting sucked right into the story—I do love a good bit of angst and enjoy the copious amounts of drama on occasion."—*C-Spot Reviews*

Friends Without Benefits

"This is the book when the Friends to Lovers trope doesn't work out. When you tell your best friend you are in love with her and she doesn't return your feelings. This book is real life and I think I loved it more for that…"—*Les Rêveur*

A Country Girl's Heart

"Dena Blake just goes from strength to strength."—*Les Rêveur*

"Literally couldn't put this book down, and can't give enough praise for how good this was!!! One of my favourite reads, and I highly recommend to anyone who loves a fantastically clever, intriguing, and exciting romance."—*LESBIreviewed*

Unchained Memories

"There is a lot of angst and the book covers some difficult topics but it does that well. The writing is gripping and the plot flows." —Melina Bickard, Librarian, Waterloo Library (UK)

"This story had me cycling between lovely romantic scenes to white-knuckle gripping, on the edge of the seat (or in my case, the bed) scenarios. This story had me rooting for a sequel and I can certainly place my stamp of approval on this novel as a must read book."—*Lesbian Review*

"The pace and character development was perfect for such an involved story line, I couldn't help but turn each page. This book has so many wonderful plot twists that you will be in suspense with every chapter that follows."—*Les Rêveur*

Where the Light Glows

"From first time author, Dena Blake, *Where the Light Glows* is a sure winner…"—*A Bookworm's Loft*

"[T]he vivid descriptions of the Pacific Northwest will make readers hungry for food and travel. The chemistry between Mel and Izzy is palpable…"—*RT Book Reviews*

"I'm still shocked this was Dena Blake's first novel… It was fantastic… It was written extremely well and more than once I wondered if this was a true account of someone close to the author because it was really raw and realistic. It seemed to flow very naturally and I am truly surprised that this is the authors first novel as it reads like a seasoned writer…"—*Les Rêveur*

By the Author

Where the Light Glows

Unchained Memories

A Country Girl's Heart

Racing Hearts

Friends Without Benefits

Just One Moment

Perfect Timing

Kiss Me Every Day

Kiss Me Every Day

by

Dena Blake

2020

KISS ME EVERY DAY

ISBN 13: 978-1-63555-551-6

This Trade Paperback Original Is Published By
Bold Strokes Books, Inc.
P.O. Box 249
Valley Falls, NY 12185

First Edition: July 2020

Credits
Editor: Shelley Thrasher
Production Design: Susan Ramundo
Cover Design By Tammy Seidick

Acknowledgments

In life, I try my best to turn a bad situation into a good one and that is no different in my writing. This book is about the choices we make, good or bad, and how they impact the future—ours, the people we love, and those all around us. I sought to spin more lighthearted fun into this one, and hopefully I succeeded. In the end, I think we'd all welcome a do-over once in a while.

I am forever grateful for the Bold Strokes Books team, Radclyffe, Sandy Lowe, and everyone else involved in making my stories go from a very rough draft to a masterpiece in print. Shelley Thrasher, you consistently enhance my writing, give me great grammar tips, and find oodles of repeated words. I cannot thank you enough for your words of wisdom.

My writing family has grown substantially, and is full of loving and talented people who easily share their support. I am so fortunate to be part of this tribe.

Kate, Wes, Haley, and my family. Along with Mom and Dad, you are the ones who have made me who I am today—my roots. I won't ever forget that.

Finally, thanks to everyone who has spent their hard-earned dollars and time on my books, and to all those who have given me support along this journey. Your kind words and encouragement are always felt and welcomed. You make my days brighter.

Dedication

To those who have ever dreamed of having a do-over.
Keep dreaming.

Chapter One

Wynn Jamison sat at her mahogany desk in her ridiculously large corner office on the third floor of the Sexton Technologies IT headquarters building. She spun to face the plate-glass window behind her and stared at San Francisco Bay. She glanced to her left to catch the other stellar view streaming through the floor-to-ceiling windows. She loved having two drastically different views, one of the bay and the other of the city of Mountain View, equally spectacular. The smog had lifted early today, and she was able to see the peaks of the Santa Cruz Mountains rising above the homes blanketing the lower hills of Silicon Valley.

It was a gorgeous area, though admittedly, it would've been even more so without the massive number of business parks scattered across it. The natural beauty of the land was growing sparse as the office buildings and homes became increasingly larger and closer together, filling the land. She wasn't one to complain. Her excessively large home was nestled neatly among them. She enjoyed the sanctity of the mountains along with the close proximity to the city. How she'd love to jump in her Jeep and drive Highway One, get lost in the massive redwoods of Big Basin—hole up there until the impending storm dissipated. Possibly even stop in Half Moon Bay and do some clamming. There was something to be said for a little solitude and mud.

A soft knock sounded on the door, and without turning she said, "Come in."

The door clicked open and someone stepped into the office. "Everyone is where they should be." April's voice was soft, almost somber. "The smaller groups are in the conference rooms, as instructed, and the larger group in the canteen."

Wynn's pulse jumped, which surprised her. She'd made announcements like the one she was about to make before without a bit of regret, but somehow she was different today. Maybe she'd lost her edge and was getting soft—letting the empathy she'd buried deep inside so long ago resurface. She sucked in a deep breath. She couldn't afford a mistake like that right now.

With a manila file folder in her hand, April stood beside Wynn's chair and looked out the window as well. "It's a beautiful day. You don't have to change that, you know."

The statement wasn't completely accurate. The view was breathtaking, almost too gorgeous to leave at this moment, but a raging squall was approaching over the horizon for a lot of people within the company: some who deserved it, and some who didn't. Innocent casualties were a fact of life in the dog-eat-dog world of information technology, and today she was the one chowing down. At least for the time being.

"There's no turning back..." Her words caught in her throat, and she cleared it, replacing any emotion she felt with the outer stone persona she presented at work. That was why she still remained in her position. "Not now. It's a done deal." When had she become such a ruthless bitch?

She stood, straightened her mint-green blouse, and shrugged on the matching jacket to her navy-blue Ralph Lauren slacks before she took the folder from April. She read through the speech she'd prepared and practiced a hundred times this week, then closed the folder and handed it back to April.

She crossed the room to the door. "You can stay up here if you'd like," she said. It was going to be a bloodbath, and April would become a target even though she hadn't been involved in any of the decision-making. That was all left to Wynn. Every large company needed an axman, and she was Sexton Tech's.

April rushed in front of her and opened the door. "Nope. I'm right behind you." She seemed to sense Wynn was struggling today.

She exited the elevator on the ground floor and glanced both ways. The IT complex was so large she had to admit sometimes she got lost. In the past she'd made a point of going to the canteen to mingle with all levels of employees, but now it seemed she never had time. She missed the energy such contact added to her day. Yet considering what she had to do today, it was probably best that she'd stopped.

"This way," April said, and led her down the hallway and into the main canteen.

They worked their way around the room to an area where a microphone had been connected behind a few of the tables. She sucked in a deep breath, and regret stung her as she scanned the room—made minimal eye contact with the majority of people anxiously waiting to find out why they were gathered together. She settled her gaze on Evelyn Cantor, her former boss and mentor, who stood to the right of the tables flanking the group. Evelyn reported to Wynn now and knew what came next. She showed no sign of anger, but the pain in her eyes was clear. Since being promoted to chief operating officer, in an effort to save her emotional sanity, Wynn had learned to detach from the employees, but Evelyn, the current chief information officer, interacted with them daily and saw them as family.

A nervous silence blanketed the room, and everyone stilled. This sort of silence sucked the wind out of people, made the hairs on their arms stand up. Wynn was well aware that her presence had caused it. She glanced at Evelyn again, who flattened her lips. No help coming from her. She calmed the shiver tracing her spine, for this was Wynn's job, no one else's. She'd made the decision—she had to announce it.

"Thank you all for coming this morning. As you know, Sexton Technologies has faced several challenges in the past few months. We've had to cut contractors and temporary employees to the bare minimum, and at this point I'm saddened to say we are having to reduce our workforce even more."

Chatter within the crowd interrupted her focus, but she gathered her thoughts. It seemed they'd suspected, rumors had run through the building like a game of telephone, morphing into new catastrophic misconceptions with each transfer, and now they knew exactly why they had all been gathered here. "You are all in this room because your positions have been eliminated. At the present time we do not have other positions for you. This has been a very difficult decision, made after a painstakingly long review of the options." She paused, trying to keep her composure as some of the employees began to cry, and others shouted obscenities. "Each of you will receive a generous severance package, and Human Resources will work with you to complete your transition." She paused for a moment to manage her body language. "Do you have any questions?"

Multiple questions and comments came from the audience.

"Who made the decision?"

"How am I supposed to pay my mortgage?"

"How am I supposed to support my family?"

"I just bought a new car."

The voices echoed in her mind, and her vision tunneled as the back of her neck heated. She was drenched with sweat. Was it hot in here? The beast of anxiety she'd kept tucked away for the past five years had burst out of its locked cage and was ripping the chains from its limbs. She took in a few deep breaths to calm herself, then focused on her heart. It was racing so fast she felt like everyone could see its rhythm pounding in her chest.

"Evelyn will answer all your questions." That was all she could get out. She couldn't answer any of them because she couldn't speak. Suddenly April was next to her, moving her to the side, and Evelyn took the microphone.

"Leadership at the highest levels in the company has reviewed this decision. Your severance packages are based on the duration you've worked for the company and should help each of you through enough time to find placement elsewhere." Evelyn had taken charge and was handling the situation masterfully, as usual. Sometimes Wynn wondered how she'd gotten ahead of her on the leadership ladder. "Tables have been set up at the sides and in the back of the room that are separated and sectioned alphabetically. Please find the letter for your last name taped to the wall behind the table to receive the information on your packages. HR is available to assist if you have any additional questions." She pointed to several people flanking the tables.

April whisked Wynn out of the room, into the elevator, and back into her office before going back to her own desk just outside the door. Then she stepped back into the office. "Your mom called while we were downstairs. Do you want me to get her on the line?" She always chose her words wisely, never indicating Wynn's panic attack or that Wynn had just shattered the security of so many lives.

"No. I'll call her back in a little while. I need a few minutes to recover." She was an introvert at heart, and company announcements of any kind took a massive emotional toll on her. The magnitude of this one had totally drained her.

April poured a glass of water from the pitcher on the table and set it on the desk in front of her. "I'm right outside your door if you need anything."

"Thank you. I do appreciate you, April." She knew she must look horrible, because that's exactly how she felt.

April nodded and gave her a solemn smile. "I know."

She rotated her chair to the windows, closed her eyes, and tried to relax as April exited the office. Visions of waves crashing the beach played in her head as her heartbeat slowed. She hadn't had to practice meditation in years, but it was the only thing keeping her sane right now.

Her stomach jolted, and she jumped in her seat when the door to her office swished open and bounced against the wall. She spun around in her chair to find Evelyn standing in front of her desk, hands on her hips.

"That speech you gave out there was insufficient." Evelyn's face became redder as the vein in her neck pulsed.

"It's the reality, Evelyn. We discussed this many times, in detail." They had and were always on opposite sides of the argument. Cutting production wasn't an option, so cutting resources had become the fastest way to recover over the past few years.

"How can you be so cold? You just gave twelve hundred people their walking papers."

"It's not personal. It's business." The panic attack told her she wasn't completely sure about that.

Evelyn pointed to the door. "It's fucking personal to them."

She narrowed her eyes as her stomach churned. She knew exactly how personal it was. Not that long ago she herself had been in the same position—found herself on the receiving end of walking papers at the small start-up tech company she'd had so much faith in a few years before. Only she'd been left with nothing when the company folded. "The severance package was excellent. If they have any skills at all, they should be able to find employment before it runs out." She'd done it herself before she came to work for Sexton Tech, and then she'd worked hard, clawing her way to the top.

"When is the last time you actually talked to any of the employees? Actually had lunch in the canteen? When did you turn into such a heartless bitch?"

She bolted from her chair and clenched the edge of her desk. "You're treading on thin ice, Evelyn."

"Am I?" Evelyn stepped closer. "Then drop the fucking pick and crack the ice. Get rid of me. I dare you."

"That's always a possibility." She stood firm. "If you want to go down this road farther, I will."

Evelyn dropped her hands from her hips and looped her arms tightly across her chest. "Got it." She glared for a moment before she dropped her arms, spun, and headed to the door. "I'll be in my office trying to figure out how we're going to run this place without the resources you just fired. So much knowledge is out the door."

The company had taken too many risks, put money into new technology that hadn't paid off. Contractors and temporary employees had already been reduced to the minimum. Return on investment was down, and the company stock had taken a dip. They'd had no other choice but to cut the workforce. They hadn't eliminated a huge number. Considering that the company employed close to forty thousand full-time employees, cutting three percent was a small amount overall. They would get two months' severance, and benefits would continue for six additional months following. After all, she wasn't heartless. Among all that, Wynn had fought mercilessly to keep Evelyn's job from being cut, which she would never tell her.

She picked up her pen and jotted herself a note on the pad in front of her.

Visit canteen for lunch next week.

It would be an attempt at normalcy that she would probably never achieve. Once the company had gone public, they'd decided to make all the food in the canteen free, for full bellies promoted better productivity. It was a small price to pay in the grand scheme of things, but after today's staff reduction it seemed frivolous.

She glanced at the time on her laptop. Twelve o'clock, long enough for the terminated employees to have been escorted from the building. She wrapped up one last email, gathered her things, and headed to the elevator. She would get some support from Jordan, her older sister, who'd called earlier in the week and scheduled her for a late lunch. She hadn't expected the invitation, since Jordan seemed to work twenty-four-seven.

Wynn's mother was babysitting the children of Wynn's oldest sister, Suzanna, and her husband James, who were enjoying a weekend away. Hoping their company would get her mind off this morning's activities, she'd planned to go there later to spend some time with them. Wynn had always intended to have kids in her future, but work had been her sole priority recently, and the idea seemed to have completely dropped off her radar lately.

The only thing brightening her day was knowing she'd be seeing her niece and nephew this afternoon. That wasn't entirely true. She'd also thought that Carly, Jordan's wife, might show up later this evening. She usually had mixed feelings about seeing Carly, who had been with Jordan about a year. But after the morning she'd had today, she was looking forward to seeing her. Maybe Carly could help her make sense of the remorseful feelings bubbling inside. Her chest tightened. Or maybe Carly would be disappointed in her for what she'd done.

Chapter Two

This day was dragging on longer than Carly had expected. She'd wanted to cancel all the remaining appointments on her calendar and go straight to her in-laws' home to swim with the kids, but that wasn't possible today. Her last session this afternoon was with a couple, Sara and Mike, who'd been teetering on divorce. She'd talked them off of the ledge once before but now wasn't sure she'd be able to do it again.

As she glanced from Sara, then to Mike, and back to Sara again, all the signs that they were moving on were there. Minimal to no eye contact, obvious untruths, and arguments that were growing more hurtful by the day. None of that even included the so-called friends they'd each acquired over the past few months.

Her thoughts wandered to Jordan and the conversations they'd had recently about the same subject. Jordan had proposed an open marriage, and Carly didn't know which had hit her first—impacted her the most—the shock or the pain. Would that arrangement help improve the mediocre life she'd been living with Jordan or just complicate it more? She didn't know what she was thinking. An open marriage was impossible for her to even consider in her profession. Her colleagues would crucify her. She was at a loss. Her life with Jordan had changed so much over the past months, she barely recognized whatever they had now as the relationship she'd once enjoyed with her, the one they'd begun together just a little over a year ago. The intimacy had disappeared slowly after their honeymoon, and she wasn't just talking sex. That was lacking too, but mostly she missed the conversations, the embraces, the small gestures people make when they love someone. She especially missed the ones that let her know she was loved in return. They'd both stopped doing any of that several months ago. Clearly she'd rushed into this marriage too quickly.

"She's more than just a friend, and you know it." Sara's raised voice brought Carly out of her thoughts.

"No more of a friend than he is."

They both stopped talking. Carly had been reading body language long enough to see that both of them had fallen out of love with each other, and each of them had most likely fallen into love with someone else. New lovers masked as friends were easy to spot in decaying relationships. The fact that they sat at opposite ends of the couch only cemented that observation further.

They'd married right out of college, loved all the same activities, same kinds of food. It seemed to be a match made to go the distance. But their sexual compatibility lay at opposite ends of the spectrum. She was good with once a week, and he wanted sex all the time. She wanted romance and he wanted release. Carly had been trying to get them to meet somewhere in the middle for close to six months, and while they both had seemed to compromise at first, they appeared to be right back where they'd started. They didn't have any children, so they really had nothing to keep them together except their love for each other and the will to make their marriage work.

Mike looked at his hands and then up at Carly. "I moved into my own place last month."

She raised her eyebrows. This was news to her. "Oh. I didn't realize you were at the point of separating."

"I wasn't. We had an argument, and it just happened."

Sara jumped in. "One minute we were arguing, and the next we were having sex like it was our last moment on earth together."

"After that, I packed a bag and left. Rented an apartment and went back and got my stuff the next week."

She observed Sara's reaction. She didn't seem upset or even confused. "And how did you feel about that?" Carly asked, still wondering about her own marriage. Would she be upset if Jordan moved out completely?

"Honestly, I was relieved about not having to worry about the next argument we'd have." It wasn't uncommon that being concerned about future events would impact a couple's actions.

She looked from Mike to Sara and then to Mike again. "Why didn't you come in or call me?"

"Because I thought you'd try to convince me to stay." Mike didn't lose eye contact. He was probably right. She would've pointed out all the good in their marriage.

Sara glanced at Mike. "And everything between us has been great since then," she said softly. "We talk almost every day."

He touched Sara's knee. "It feels like I have my best friend back."

Sara clasped his hand and smiled widely. "I know. It's like the dead weight on my chest is gone, and I can breathe again. All the anger has gone away."

"Exactly," he said. "You'll always be my best friend."

"And you'll be mine." Sara dropped her head against his shoulder. They'd been high school sweethearts as well. Kids growing up together didn't always make for good couples as adults. Couples who met as adults usually had a mutual respect for each other that wasn't always present in those who met in younger years.

Carly's attempts to set them on a better track to keep them together seemed to have failed. *Maybe some people are better off as friends*. "Well, it appears you've found the best solution for the both of you." She smiled, concealing her disappointment. "Do you think you'll be able to withstand new relationships with others when they develop?" She'd also warned them in the past about the difficulties of finding someone new, but they seemed to have both accomplished that feat already.

They nodded, and Mike said, "It'll take some time before we can actually double-date." They both laughed. "But yes. I'm glad she's found someone who makes her happy. I never wanted to be the source of her unhappiness, and that's what seemed to be happening more and more over this past year."

"Well, okay, then. I guess we don't need to continue counseling, unless you want to come in separately."

Mike stood. "I think we're good."

Sara, on the other hand, only nodded as she stood, making Carly think that maybe she wasn't as sure of this resolution as Mike was.

She waited for Mike to turn to the door before she made eye contact with Sara. "You have my number if you want to call or schedule an appointment."

Sara nodded again and followed Mike out of the office. Something pulled in Carly's heart. It was always difficult when a couple made a final decision and left her care, especially when they took a different road than she'd seen coming. She flopped into the chair, took a swig of Coke Zero, and spun around to gaze at the Palace of Fine Arts. She'd purposely chosen a brownstone in the Marina District because of the gorgeous view. She wanted a serene space that made her clients feel relaxed and comfortable. It also helped her decompress between sessions. She tried to detach from her clients, but sometimes that was difficult. She'd scraped and saved for years to be able to afford the lease on her office, but it was well worth the cost to keep her peace of mind on a daily basis. It didn't hurt that her grandparents owned the building, and she was renting the place for a fraction of the cost. In fact, they owned multiple properties in the city, including this one and the building where she lived in Nob Hill. Her grandparents had told her that when the tenant upstairs moved, she could take over the whole space so she would only have to travel downstairs for work.

Did every couple have to reconcile? Were they better off apart? Would she and Jordan be better off apart? She shook her head. She doubted they could remain friends, and she loved Jordan's family too much to let them go. Jordan's sister Suzanna had been her best friend since college. Not being able to confide in her would put a huge hole in the center of Carly's life. Not seeing her niece and nephew—her godchildren—would absolutely kill her. She loved those kids like they were her own.

Maybe it would be better for her and Jordan to just be friends again. It wasn't like they spent all that much time together anymore.

They'd been on different schedules for a while now. Sex between them was practically nonexistent, and when they did make love, it wasn't all that special. Jordan was always preoccupied, and it seemed rushed, like more of a duty than the feeling of intimacy she craved.

She thought about a recent discovery she'd found while visiting Jordan at her office. Her assistant had innocently said something about how expensive it must be to keep two townhouses in the city. After a year of marriage, Jordan was still maintaining her own place. Jordan had explained the circumstances away perfectly, said it hadn't sold, so she'd planned to sublet it, which still hadn't happened. Carly clearly remembered Jordan telling her it had been sold early on in their marriage. She'd lied about it for no reason. What did that mean? Was someone else living there? Someone Jordan was seeing? Was Jordan just holding on to the place in case their marriage didn't work, or was she actually planning to end it someday?

The big D word popped into her head. Carly had always been such a proponent of reconciliation. How would she explain that outcome to her colleagues and her patients? How would she even convince herself it was okay to divorce? She pushed the thought from her head. She needed to work on understanding her own faulty thinking before considering anything that drastic.

Someone knocked softly on the door. "Come in."

Stephanie, her assistant, stood in the doorway. "That was your last appointment, so if you don't need me, I'm going to take off."

"That's fine." She blew out a breath as Stephanie turned to go and then said, "Steph, wait. Can I ask you a question?"

Stephanie spun around. "Sure."

"What do you think about divorce?"

"That's a pretty broad question. Can you be more specific?"

She smiled. Steph didn't buy in to the typical baiting questions she used on her clients. "One, do you think it's appropriate to divorce if people are better off apart? Two, do you think it's possible for people who divorce to remain friends?"

"One, hell yes. I grew up with parents who should've divorced, and it was miserable. Two, that depends on the people. My parents are happily divorced now, but they're not friends. They don't speak unless I'm the reason."

"Why aren't they friends?"

"The divorce was brutal. Between dividing their belongings, money, and child support, lots of things were said that couldn't be forgotten." Steph shrugged. "They're civil when they end up at the same place or event, but neither one of them goes out of their way to talk to one another."

"Do you think it would've been better if they'd divorced sooner?"

"I was sad when it happened because I liked having them both in the same house with me, but when I look back on it, I do think it might have been better if they'd split sooner."

"Thank you. Your insights are spot-on, as always."

Steph started to leave and then stopped. "Divorce isn't a bad thing. I mean, we're living in the twentieth century. No one brands you with a scarlet letter or anything. People just realize they want different things. They want to be happy." With that, she turned and swept quietly out of the room.

Carly relaxed into her chair, wondering who the better marriage counselor was, she or Stephanie, before she picked up the phone and called Jordan.

Jordan answered after the first ring. "Hey. What's up?" At least she didn't avoid her calls.

"Just wanted to let you know I'm going to your mom and dad's to see the kids this afternoon."

"Cool. Is Suz going to be there?"

"Suzanna and James are out of town, remember?" She could tell she wasn't getting Jordan's full attention. So much for her answering right away. What difference did it make if she didn't listen?

"Right. So, I'll see you at home later?"

"I thought you could come by and see them, take a short swim, and then we could go to dinner from there."

"Right." Jordan dragged the word out slowly. "Where are we going again?"

"You forgot." She couldn't hide the disappointment in her voice.

"Nope. Not at all. I just had my mind on something else—kind of in the middle of something. I probably shouldn't have picked up."

"What could be more important than me?"

"Absolutely nothing. I just have a lot to finish before I can get out of here." Jordan sighed into the phone. "What time is the reservation?"

"Seven."

"I'll try to get to Mom and Dad's as soon as I can, but I'm not guaranteeing it will be early enough to swim."

"Okay. Then I'll let you go." She was having a hard time suppressing her irritation. No matter how much work she had on her plate, she never made Jordan feel she was too busy to talk to her. Just another sign she'd married the wrong person. She took a notebook from the top drawer of her desk and flipped it open. Last month's entry had been a *two*, but that conversation had just lowered the number to a one. Underneath it she scribbled, NO CONNECTION ANYMORE—AT ALL. She flipped the notebook closed and shoved it back into her drawer.

Chapter Three

Wynn walked past the tables and wicker-lined chairs on the bistro's patio and entered the restaurant. She immediately spotted Jordan at her favorite table by the front window. Her sister was a creature of habit. Once she found a place she liked, she continued going there until they screwed something up. Her current choice for lunch was a little French bistro on Baker Street that served the absolute best seafood stew. This place had lasted longer on Jordan's radar than most, so their service must be excellent.

With leather booths and padded, wooden chairs, it had a homey yet elegant feel. Small tables that could be pushed together to create substantial seating for large parties filled the dining room, and window seats provided the opportunity to enjoy the quiet hum of diners chatting inside while also watching the weather and passersby on the sidewalk. The food was a little pricy, but Jordan was buying, so Wynn didn't intend to worry about the cost. In fact, she might just order a bottle of wine as well. She needed something to change her mood. She let the hostess know she was with Jordan and then weaved through the tables to where she was seated.

Jordan stood as Wynn approached the table. "Happy birthday, sis." She gathered her into a hug.

"Thanks." Her birthday wasn't until tomorrow, but this was the only time Jordan could fit Wynn into her schedule this week.

"How old are you this year?"

"Thirty-one." The work she'd had to do this past year as chief operating officer had made her feel so much older. Was the job worth it?

"Still just a pup." Jordan squeezed the two lemon wedges remaining on the plate in front of her into her water.

"She's bringing you a water and more lemon wedges."

"How about a bottle of wine?"

"Really? It's so unlike you to drink in the middle of the day."

"I need a little something to relax. It's been a rough morning."

"I'm all in on that." Jordan waved the waitress down. "Can we have a bottle of the sauvignon blanc?" The waitress nodded and left the table. "What's going on?"

"I just had to lay off twelve hundred people at work."

"Was it unavoidable?"

"It was now. It wouldn't have been if we'd made some better choices last year." There had been a layoff then as well, one that had paved the path that led to her promotion. She should've looked at more options earlier.

"Don't beat yourself up. It happens. It's only business."

That's what she'd been telling herself to get through it, but it just didn't feel that way anymore. "Not to them, it isn't."

The waitress came back with the wine, opened it, and poured Jordan a taste. She drank it, nodded, and the waitress filled their glasses. "Are you ready to order?"

"You go first." Jordan motioned to Wynn. "Order up. It's on me."

"I'll have the seafood stew and a small salad."

"Ooh, that sounds good. I'll have the same, and bring some sourdough bread and butter as well." Jordan collected their menus and handed them to the waitress. "You need to keep your strength up to face the aftermath this afternoon."

"I'm not going back to work. I'm going to Mom and Dad's to see the kids. They're watching them this weekend."

"Right. Carly's going over there later too." She sipped her wine. "Be an awesome little sister and take her out to dinner tonight."

The waitress came back with their salads and a loaf of bread, and Jordan immediately ripped a piece from it and buttered it.

"Why? What are you doing?"

"I need to catch a meeting. It'll also give me a break from the whole 'let's have a baby' conversation." She took a bite of bread and then washed it down with a drink of wine.

"Carly wants to have a baby?" That wasn't surprising. Carly was great with Suzanna's kids and always seemed to enjoy being around them.

"Yep. Started harping on me about it six months into our marriage and never lets up. I'm not ready for kids, at least not my own. Don't know if I ever will be. I'm not sure how I got myself into this mess of a marriage."

Wynn knew exactly how she'd done it. Jordan loved a challenge, and Carly was definitely that. She was knowledgeably witty, the kind of woman who thinks outside the box and voices her thoughts in the best possible way at the best possible moment. Exactly the reason Wynn had been attracted to her as well, not that she wasn't also gorgeous. Jet-black hair and sea-green eyes flashed through her mind, and her stomach jumped. Gorgeous indeed.

"That's an interesting way to think about the love of your life." She broke off a piece of bread, buttered it, and took a bite. She needed something in her stomach before the effects of the wine kicked in.

"Yeah, well, her beauty may have misdirected me when we met, and then the phenomenal sex blinded me."

"And now?" She took a gulp of wine and pushed the thought of Carly and Jordan having phenomenal sex from her head. Not what she wanted to hear *at all*.

"We just don't seem to have the same life goals."

"It's a little late to figure *that* out, don't you think?" She'd suddenly lost her appetite.

"You're not telling me anything I don't already know, and she won't even consider separating, let alone divorce." The waitress brought their bowls of stew, and each of them moved their salads to the side—Jordan's almost completely devoured and Wynn's barely touched. "I should blame it all on you. I have to admit I didn't really notice her until I saw her talking to you at one of my events. She was radiant that night. Still is." Jordan ripped off another piece of bread from the loaf. "It's been nice having someone of her caliber and looks by my side. Too bad we're not moving in the same direction."

Her mind scattered. How could Jordan not want Carly? "Are you kidding me? I totally backed off because you said she was the one."

"Hmm, that's interesting. I didn't know that." Jordan tilted her head. "I would've enjoyed a little friendly competition."

"You're such an ass."

"True. But you've known that since we were kids." Jordan dunked a piece of bread into her bowl. "Why don't you romance her now?" She bit off the stew-soaked edge.

"Because she's *your* wife and that's what *you* should be doing."

"Look, it's not like Carly doesn't know we have issues. I spend half my evenings at my old place." Jordan spooned a bit of stew into her mouth and swallowed. "Maybe she'd be happier with you."

"She probably would be, but she doesn't have a choice now, does she?" She should've been stronger, told Jordan to back off then.

"Of course she has a choice. She just has to climb down from that moral high ground she's propped herself up on and let me go." Jordan drained her glass of wine and refilled it as well as Wynn's. "I've given her the choice. Either we get divorced or we open our marriage to others."

"She'll never agree to that." She couldn't believe how callous Jordan was, putting Carly in that position, letting her think she wasn't good enough to satisfy her.

"I know. I'm hoping she'll go for the divorce."

"You know something? I hope so too." She picked up her spoon and immediately dropped it. "Are you sleeping with someone else?"

"No." Jordan shook her head. "But I've had offers." She smiled and took another bite of bread.

That wasn't news. Jordan always had someone interested. She knew Jordan would eventually sleep with other women and break Carly's heart if she didn't agree to her terms. Wynn pushed her plate away, unable to stomach the stew now. The bread and wine would have to get her through. She was so angry at Jordan right now she could strangle her. If Jordan had only left Carly alone that night last year, Wynn might very well have been the one she'd married and be planning to have a family with. She cursed herself for her part in the whole situation. She should've told Carly how she felt.

They'd shared a spectacular kiss that night last year, one that Wynn had never been able to completely erase from her mind. Then Jordan had swooped in and dazzled Carly with her charm. Once that happened, she'd never had a chance with Carly. When Jordan had told her a few days later that she'd taken Carly home that night and that they'd slept together, Wynn didn't know what to think. She guessed the kiss hadn't been special for Carly at all. Jordan had gushed about how she thought Carly was her perfect match and could be the *one*. That's when Wynn had done what any good sister would do. She'd stepped aside, let Jordan take the lead, and disappeared from Carly's life. That was the right thing to do, wasn't it? Wynn had thought so at the time, but after listening to Jordan just now, she knew she'd made the wrong decision.

Carly glanced out at the ocean as she drove across the San Francisco Bay Bridge to her in-laws' house nestled in the foothills of Orinda. She hoped one day to live in one of the many suburbs of the San Francisco Bay area, but hadn't been able to get Jordan to commit to moving out of the city. Housing was scarce and expensive in Orinda, as it was in most Northern California suburbs. When you came across a home that even remotely fit your wants and needs, you had to move with light speed to get a contract. Bidding wars skyrocketing into the millions had become common in recent years. Howard and Maryanne had bought in the area long ago, when the homes were affordable and sparse, had remodeled several times and added a pool since then. Their house had more than tripled in value.

She hit the button on her remote for the gate and waited for it to swing open before driving to the house and parking in front of the multi-car garage flanking the two-story traditional-styled home. She could hear laughing and splashing from the pool, and her heart warmed as she walked the path that weaved through the large oak trees, stopping only to smell the heirloom roses on her way.

Suzanna's kids were already here. Not wanting to wait another moment to see them, she headed directly to the backyard. Maryanne was relaxing in the padded chaise lounge under the expansive offset patio umbrella. As soon as her mother-in-law saw her, she smiled widely and waved her over.

It was unreal how much her daughters resembled her. Maryanne's hair was always perfectly colored to its natural auburn, and her light blue-gray eyes sparkled in the sunlight. Suzanna was feminine, like Maryanne, while Jordan and Wynn were more masculine in the way they dressed. Wynn, however, was the only one of the three who resembled Howard, their father, with a narrower face, darker eyebrows, and wonderfully thick lashes.

As she approached, Maryanne stood and pulled her into her arms. "Hi, honey. It's good to see you." She motioned to the pool. "The water is wonderful, and the kids have been waiting for you." She leaned closer and softly said, "They got very excited when I told them you were coming over."

The feeling was mutual. She hadn't been able to wait to finish with her last couple so she could get here to see them. The couple's decision to separate still weighed heavily on her. What bothered her even more was that they'd been afraid to tell her. Had she tried to convince them of anything? She hoped not. She was supposed to guide them to find their own feelings about each other and their marriage, not impose her own values on them.

"Aunt Carly, watch this." Her nephew Josh shouted from the diving board before he flew into the water and made a huge splash. He was six years old and about to go into first grade, definitely a mama's boy. Suzanna had told Carly she was worried about how he would adapt to a full day of school.

Carly watched Julianna swim from the deep end of the pool to the shallow end, where she and Maryanne were standing. Her strokes were getting faster. Julianna was the independent child, headed into second grade with confidence. She soaked up knowledge like a sponge with spilled milk. The conversations Carly had with her were so much more adult than her years warranted.

Julianna's head emerged from the water, and she wiped her eyes. "Are you coming in?"

She held up her bag. "Brought my suit, so I guess that means yes." Julianna smiled widely, and happiness spread through Carly. She loved these kids as though they were her own. "I guess I'd better change." She turned and walked to the back door and into the closest bedroom. All the bedrooms had their own bathrooms now, and the master was upstairs, so it really didn't matter which one she chose. This was the one she usually used. Oddly, with its moody gray walls accented by royal-blue bedding, it felt more comfortable to her than any of the others. Jordan's room was decorated in a vibrant crimson that could set off an instant migraine in anyone spending more than ten minutes there. It was totally in tune with Jordan's energized personality.

She hung her dinner clothes in the closet and set her phone on the dresser before she quickly changed into her red, one-piece suit and went back outside. She didn't want to waste another minute away from the kids. The cool pool water felt refreshing as Carly crashed through the surface in the deep end and swam underwater to the shallow end. The weather this summer was hotter than usual, averaging in the mid-eighties for the past few weeks.

"Want to race, Auntie Carly?" She heard Julianna's voice as soon as her head came above water.

"Give me a head start?"

"Then you'll win." Julianna's mouth dropped open. Her miffed expression was priceless—one that Carly loved to elicit often. Julianna always didn't catch the subtlety of her sarcasm.

"Exactly." She grabbed hold of the edge and readied herself to race. "Up and back?"

Julianna nodded. "Once or twice?"

"Just once. Are you trying to kill your old auntie?"

Julianna giggled and held the edge of the pool before she gave the cue to race. "Ready, set, go."

She waited a few seconds after Julianna took off and then swam after her. She passed her midway, but then Julianna took her at the turn. Carly never could manage a flip turn, even when she was younger. Trying to keep up with Julianna wasn't easy. She'd been on the local swim team since she was able to float and had become a champion in her age group.

"I won." Julianna stood in the shallow end holding up her arms and bragging like a champion.

"Fair and square. I didn't even give it to you this time." She picked Julianna up and tossed her toward the middle of the pool.

Julianna came up swiping the water from her eyes. "Better not've."

She laughed and then swam a few more laps before stopping in the shallow end and joining in the ring-toss target game with Josh, a much easier challenge.

Howard, Carly's father-in-law, stepped out onto the patio from the sliding kitchen door and dropped his towel onto a chair before racing toward the pool and launching into the deep end. Once the kids were completely occupied racing with Howard, Carly made her way to the steps and out of the pool. Maryanne had a towel waiting for her on the lounger under the umbrella next to her, as well as a cold bottle of water.

"So, where's Jordan? I thought she was coming with you." Marianne raised an eyebrow.

"At work, as usual. I've tried everything I can to keep her interest, but work always seems to come first."

Maryanne nodded slowly, as though choosing her words carefully. "Can I be honest with you?"

"Of course. Always."

"I can see that you're unhappy."

"What makes you say that?" She blotted her face with the towel. "I'm just a little tired."

"I know my daughter better than you think." Marianne pulled her eyebrows together. "Work is her main focus. Outside of that she has a very short interest span."

Carly couldn't help but smile at Maryanne's observations because they were spot-on. "I can't seem to find a way to keep her attention."

"Are you sure you want to keep trying?"

"I don't want to stop. I mean, I'm not sure I'm ready to just give up." She found it interesting that Maryanne seemed to cut to the core of the issue when Carly hadn't even known she was aware of it.

"I've always thought you were more suited for Wynn than Carly." Marianne spoke as though it was a fact everyone was aware of. "Suzanna agrees."

Heat rushed Carly at the thought. "What?"

Maryanne vaulted from her chair and shouted, "No running to the diving board. I'm not going to the hospital today." She sank back to the lounger and focused on Carly again. "Divorce isn't the end of the world, you know." Maryanne watched Howard as he played with their grandchildren. "Did I ever tell you I was married briefly before I met Howard?"

She snapped her gaze back to Maryanne. "No. You didn't." And neither had Jordan.

Maryanne nodded. "We were right out of college and very much in love. We had no idea where our lives were going to take us, and as time went on they just happened to take us in opposite directions."

"Wow. That must have been hard."

"Not as hard as you might think. Eventually, we were making each other more miserable than happy, and we both realized the marriage wasn't going to work. Blaming each other for giving up the things we wanted was useless, so we decided it would be best to move on. We'd rather be friends than become enemies."

"I've never thought about it that way. I've always thought Jordan and I could work it out."

"Well, it may be time for both of you to think it through again." Maryanne motioned to the pool. "She's never going to want a family as much as you do. At least not in the same timeframe, and neither of you is getting any younger."

Carly chuckled at her mother-in-law's blunt observation. She was right on all counts, as usual. She wanted kids, and she wanted them now. Thirty-two wasn't too old for having children by any means, but she wanted to be able to enjoy them while she had the energy. But divorce would mean admitting that counseling can't fix some relationships. Admitting that her own marriage was unsalvageable would be a personal and professional blow. She'd been very vocal about relationships requiring compromise in the past, and her career might not be able to withstand the contradictions of her getting a divorce.

Chapter Four

The street was bare as Wynn drove to the end of the cul-de-sac. Mr. Pritchard was sitting on the porch in his chair, as usual, next to the one his wife used to occupy. She waved at Mr. P, but he didn't acknowledge her. The unseasonably hot, rainy weather had become a glorious incubator for the weeds that had overtaken the flowerbed. Until this past year, their yard had always been pristine, the most beautiful on the block, and due to Mrs. Pritchard's help, Wynn's had been a close second. Once Mrs. P had retired from her elementary-school teaching position, she'd kept the flowers and the lawn meticulously groomed.

Not having any children of their own, Mrs. P had adopted her students and the people who lived in the neighborhood as family. Wynn missed Mrs. P's friendly face. On most days when she came home, she and her husband would be out front to greet her with a pitcher of iced tea or at least throw her a wave as she drove up. Mrs. P seemed to make a special effort to be outside just as she came home. Their conversations always brightened her day.

She'd declined a few of their invitations for dinner over the years, but the many she'd accepted had been filled with great food and plenty of laughter. She'd also had a standing dinner date with Mrs. P on Mr. P's bowling night, something she'd always looked forward to. After Mrs. P died, life was a struggle for everyone in the neighborhood, including Wynn. She'd invited Mr. P for dinner several times, and he'd accepted once or twice but eventually began declining each of her invitations and slowly slipped into the shell he kept himself isolated in now. Mr. P just wasn't the same without Mrs. P. None of them were, really.

She hit the clicker and pulled into the garage before she walked down the driveway to get the mail. Junk, junk, bills, and a letter from her neighbor next door. What the fuck was that about? Couldn't he just walk over and talk to her? What was up with people these days? She was so not in the mood for this today.

Your yard service was here at the crack of dawn again. If you don't tell them to come after ten, I'm going to call the city and complain.

Your favorite neighbor, Jack.

The service had a schedule, so she didn't decide when they came, and the city knew that about every lawn service and didn't care as long as no one complained. After folding the letter and placing it neatly back into the envelope, she glanced up to see Jack staring at her from his porch, his chocolate Labrador retriever by his side. Most days she tossed his letters into the trash without a response, but what the hell? Why not top off this mega-shitty day with an argument?

She paced back toward the house. "If you'd stop letting your seventy-pound dog use my yard as a bathroom, I'd be more likely to take care of the noise issue." She stopped halfway up the driveway, narrowed her eyes, and raised an eyebrow. "What in the world do you feed that animal?"

Jack waved a hand in front of him. "She's a big dog, and she likes to explore."

"That's why they make leashes." Buttercup ran across the lawn and nudged her head under Wynn's hand. She stared straight ahead at her jackass of a neighbor and did her best to ignore the dog. *Damn it.* She squatted down in front of the huge, lovable, chocolate Lab and rubbed her ears. Trying to avoid the numerous sloppy kisses Buttercup gave was useless. She'd have to wash her face immediately when she got in the house. The dog was sweet as could be, but her neighbor was an astronomical asshole. If the ears of her own black Lab, Shadow, didn't perk up every time she saw Buttercup, she'd have called animal control long ago. Until this point, she'd found it easier to just pay the lawn service an additional fee to clean up the mess.

"She hates leashes. I got her from the animal shelter last year. She's a puppy-mill rescue, was chained up all the time."

Her stomach clenched. She hadn't known that. She stared into the dog's beautiful brown eyes. She'd give Buttercup a pass on her bathroom habits, but Jack was getting nothing from her.

She kissed Buttercup on the nose. "I'll look into getting the schedule changed," she said as she stood. That would go on the bottom of her to-do list.

The shrill of Jack's whistle pierced her ears, and Buttercup started running to him. "Gotta go. Work is calling." He pointed to the headset around his neck.

"Right. Work," she said as she hurried to her porch. He'd already taken too much of her time. Time she could be spending with her niece and nephew.

Dressed in a T-shirt and sweatpants, with a headset hanging around his neck, the guy looked like a gamer. In his mid-thirties, bloodshot eyes, uncombed hair, rubbing the shadow of a beard on his chin, he scored high on the nerd-cred scale. Probably stayed up all night playing in game forums. She couldn't help but wonder what his gamer name was—Househoney, Eightoclock shadow, or just plain Jackass. He seemed to be home all the time, and Wynn rarely saw his wife anymore. She was probably out making the dollars to support his gaming habit. With that scenario in mind, she didn't intend to change the lawn schedule. Nine o'clock was plenty late for mowing on a weekday. He just needed to get his lazy ass out of bed and find a job.

Carly felt Maryanne gently shaking her arm. "Don't you need to get ready for dinner, dear?"

She pried open her eyes. "What?"

"I thought you and Jordan were going out tonight. Isn't it your anniversary?"

She bolted forward and rubbed her face. "Oh my gosh. Yes. It was sort of our first date. How long was I out?" She'd dozed in the lounger, letting the sun warm her like a blanket.

"Not very long." Maryanne smiled. "You were sleeping so peacefully, I didn't want to wake you. She scrunched her forehead. "Did you have a rough day?"

She moved her legs to the side of the lounger as she tried to shake the sleepy haze. "Not rough, just different than I expected. Some couples aren't meant to be together."

Maryanne smiled slightly. "Exactly my point earlier." She patted Carly's leg. "Think about what I said."

"I will." She took in a deep breath. "I've been thinking about it a lot lately." She stood, wrapped her towel around her, and walked toward the house.

Carly stopped in the kitchen to pour herself a glass of merlot before she continued through the hallway and into the bedroom to shower and get ready for dinner. She'd taken a couple sips of wine and had just set the wineglass on the bathroom counter when she heard the kids shouting outside. She glanced through the window of the bedroom and saw Wynn running to the pool and launching into the water with her dog, Shadow, soaring in after her. The kids quickly swam to her and grabbed hold, one hanging on each of her shoulders. Shadow circled them briefly before she swam to the steps and sat.

Carly smiled widely as happiness captured her. Watching Wynn with the kids stirred something deep inside her. Wynn was full of energy, just like them, and Carly immediately wanted to go outside and be part of the fun. She'd pondered more than once how things had changed between them after the fund-raiser last year. She still had no idea why Wynn had completely disappeared from her life until after she and Jordan were married. She hadn't even come to the wedding, which Jordan had found disappointing.

The alarm on her phone rang, and she hit the snooze button. She couldn't go back in the pool because she was out of time. The reservation she'd made for dinner was for seven o'clock, and she still had to shower and get ready. Any other day she'd have canceled and told Jordan to come here instead, and they'd spend the evening with her family. But she'd planned the whole night to perfection. She stood at the window and watched Wynn interact with the kids, standing in the shallow end while picking each one up and tossing them into the water like they were as light as beach balls. The strength in her arms made it look so easy. It had taken all Carly's strength to pick up Julianna earlier. The kids loved Wynn and she loved them back, seeming totally in her element with them. Did Wynn ever think about having kids of her own? She seemed to be a natural with Julianna and Josh. Why didn't Jordan have those same instincts?

Carly's life would be so different now if she'd made another choice last year. She thought about what her mother-in-law had said earlier about her and Jordan's lack of compatibility. A life with Wynn seemed so much more joyful than the one she was living now. The thought of Wynn's arms around her, her lips pressed to hers, and body contact from head to toe floated through her mind.

Her phone alarm jolted her from her thoughts. How could she remember one kiss so vividly? She shook her head and cleared the visions from her mind. Unbidden notions like that should remain only in her dreams. Sadness swept over her as she walked into the bathroom, turned on the water, and took a gulp of wine. The woman she saw in the mirror wasn't the woman she knew anymore. She was sad and unhappy with the way her life was now, not anything like she'd planned. She finished the rest of the wine before she peeled off her swimsuit and stepped into the shower.

The hot water felt good spraying across her shoulders. She turned around and let it wash her face, clearing her sad thoughts and replacing them with the excitement of the night ahead. It had been a while since she and Jordan had spent actual quality time together, and she'd been looking forward to it all week. The fact that it was a special night wasn't important. She just needed some time to feel loved by Jordan without her job getting in the way. She'd always been attracted to women who knew what they wanted. She'd never thought being with someone who was so driven would be an issue, but it had certainly created a few obstacles for them to overcome.

Carly heard Jordan's voice through the door and was happy that she'd been able to pick her up rather than meeting her at the restaurant. She stepped out of the shower, draped herself in a bath towel, and pulled open the door. She froze when her eyes locked with the electric-blue eyes staring back at her across the bedroom. The look of surprise she saw in them immediately turned to something else, and Carly fumbled with the towel beginning to come loose around her.

"Oh my God. I'm so sorry. I heard the voice through the door and thought you were Jordan."

"No, no. I'm sorry. I didn't realize you were in here. I thought you were in Jordan's room." Wynn's eyes never left Carly's as the phone slid from her ear.

"Right. This is your room." She'd always used this room to change and had forgotten it had belonged to Wynn when she and Jordan were children.

"I'll call you later," Wynn said and ended the call she'd been on. "Well, technically it's no one's room now, but it was mine for a time." Wynn smiled and let her eyes veer lower. "I'll change in Jordan's room."

The royal-blue, two-piece sport swimsuit enhanced Wynn's muscles perfectly. Heat rushed Carly as she stared at the water glistening all over Wynn's face, shoulders, legs, belly. She almost couldn't speak and had totally lost sight of the fact that she was standing in the bathroom doorway wearing only a towel. "Sure. Or I can go."

"No." Wynn swallowed hard and held up a hand as though afraid for Carly to come any closer. "You stay here." She grabbed her bag from the bed and backed out of the room.

Immediately after the door closed, Carly's phone chimed, a text from Jordan.

Looks like I'm going to be late.

What? I don't want to drive into the city alone. Then we'll have two cars to deal with.

Is Wynn there?

Yes. The uninterpretable look on Wynn's face she'd seen a few moments ago flashed through her head.

Ask her to drive you. She can join us for dinner. It's her birthday tomorrow.

She closed her eyes and let out a sigh as she dropped onto the bed. Jordan remembered Wynn's birthday but had clearly forgotten it was *their* first date.

She typed a few angry responses and immediately erased them before she typed simply, *Okay.*

Then she tossed her phone onto the bed, not knowing what to do. Without thinking any longer, she stood, crossed the room to the door, and pulled it open, surprised to find Wynn still standing in the hallway. Once their eyes met, her decision was made. "Do you want to grab some dinner tonight?"

She couldn't read the look on Wynn's face. "I think Mom's cooking."

"I have reservations at the Waterbar. Jordan was supposed to pick me up, but she's going to be late. If she makes it at all." She shook her head. "Never mind." Maybe she'd just stay and have dinner here.

Wynn stepped forward quickly. "I'd love…to have dinner with you." She seemed to stumble over her words. "I mean, it'd be nice to catch up."

"Okay." An odd sense of excitement filled her. "The reservation is at seven. I'll be ready in a half hour, give or take a few minutes."

"Same." Wynn smiled, backed up, and rushed down the hallway to Jordan's room.

It seemed Carly's evening hadn't been ruined after all.

Chapter Five

As they walked from the parking lot to the restaurant, Wynn was having a hard time erasing the vision of Carly she'd seen earlier. Having impure thoughts about her sister's wife was completely wrong and had to stop. She'd seen Carly in a towel before, but usually she wore a bathing suit underneath it. She'd never glimpsed her directly out of the shower looking so radiant. Sweet Lord, she was a sight. Cheeks flushed, hair wet, tanned legs peeking out from beneath the edge, not to mention the milky-white breasts exploding from the top of the tightly wrapped towel.

She stepped in front of Carly and opened the door for her. "Isn't this the restaurant where Suzanna holds most of her fund-raisers?" A jolt coursed through her as she placed her palm on Carly's lower back to guide her inside and felt the soft warmth of skin rather than her dress.

Carly nodded. "It's always been one of my favorites."

"Mine, too." She glanced around the room and took in the romantic ambiance of it all. "It's casual and friendly, just what I like on a warm summer evening."

The Embarcadero had plenty of restaurants, but the Waterbar had a great location on the pier, and the food was exceptional. The patio outside offered a beautiful view of the San Francisco Bay Bridge. Wynn could relax there and enjoy the view and then stroll on the harbor afterward to enjoy the fresh sea air. Considering the day she'd had, she welcomed the serenity.

She held the door open for Carly and then stepped inside after her. "Shall we wait at the bar until Jordan joins us?"

"No. Who knows what time she'll get here. Let's just go to the table." Carly followed the hostess to their spot by the window that looked out to the patio.

Wynn was glad Carly hadn't wanted to eat on the patio itself, since it was still a bit warm to sit outside. This afternoon, she'd brought along a navy sport jacket and pink button-down shirt, as well as a pair of khaki slacks and loafers just in case Jordan bailed and she ended up having dinner with Carly tonight. Carly had outdressed her with a flower-patterned, cap-sleeved, summer dress that brought out the green in her eyes more than usual. The outfit increased Wynn's struggle to not stare.

The waitress came to the table and took their drink order. With Carly's approval, Wynn ordered a bottle of chardonnay.

"We should get an appetizer too." Carly whispered the words across the table as though it were a secret item other diners weren't offered.

"Sure. "She raised her eyebrows. "A prawn cocktail? Charcuterie tray?"

"Ooh, those both sound good. I'm not sure I can choose."

Wynn looked up at the waitress. "We'll take both and share."

Carly smiled before she glanced back to the menu, and warmth spread through Wynn. She would do anything for that smile.

They were silent as they perused the dinner selections. Then the waitress arrived with the wine, opened the bottle, and poured a taste in the glass before her. Wynn pushed the glass across the table to Carly, which garnered another smile.

Carly tasted the wine and then nodded to the waitress, who poured them each a glass. "Nice choice."

As soon as the waitress left, the appetizers arrived, and they both reached for the prawn cocktail. After a bit of an awkward exchange amid soft laughter, Wynn added a few pieces of grilled ciabatta, pancetta, and salami to a plate, while Carly put a prawn on the dish in front of her. Carly handed hers across the table to Wynn, who accepted it and exchanged it for the one she'd prepared. They seemed to move in perfect sync and then enjoyed the appetizers in silence until the waitress appeared again.

"Are you ready to order?"

"Should we wait or order for Jordan?" She deferred to Carly. "Did she give you any indication when she'd be arriving?"

"Let me check to see her timeline." Carly took her phone from her purse, frowned, and then typed a message. "It doesn't look like Jordan is going to make it tonight." She dropped her phone into her bag.

"We'll go ahead and order." She glanced at Carly. "Shall we get a platter or two separates and share?"

Carly hit her again with the smile, and she melted. "Let's get two separates and share."

"We'll have the Alaskan halibut and the spiny lobster." She raised her eyebrows at Carly, waiting for approval, which she granted with an even broader smile. "And a side of roasted baby carrots."

"I'm not sure how you did it, but you picked my two favorite dishes."

"It's a gift." She chuckled. "Actually, I have to confess, I've seen you eat at Suzanna's events."

Carly's eyebrows flew up. "Seriously?"

"Yes. And I know I'll have to fight for every bite."

"Hey." Carly tossed her napkin across the table at her. "Can I help it if I like food? I'm not that bad."

"Are you sure about that?" Wynn grinned as she handed the napkin back.

"Fine." Carly snatched it from her hand. "I'll give you a five-second lead. You'd better be quick." The laughter settled, and Wynn watched as Carly looked at the door and disappeared into herself.

"I'm sorry Jordan can't make it. That's disappointing." That was a total lie. Wynn's lunch with Jordan earlier today had been a horrible insight into their marriage and had made her regret her decision to remove herself form Carly's life a year ago. She'd come to dinner only because she'd never been able to erase her feelings. She'd locked them away in a confined space of her heart and actively ignored them when they pounded on the door trying to escape. She couldn't bear the thought of Jordan standing up Carly, which she knew was her plan tonight. Wynn would make the best of it and try to keep Carly's mind off Jordan in any way she could.

"Imperfect bliss. I'm used to it. One year married to your sister has been full of disappointments like this." Carly flattened her lips. "Why should our anniversary be any different?"

"Is that today?" She checked the calendar in her head. The date had never really been cemented in her mind since she'd avoided the nuptials, skipping them for an all-inclusive tropical vacation in order to miss the wedding activities altogether. She'd gone completely alone to find enough peace within herself to move on. The distraction had worked to a certain degree, as long as she kept minimal contact, only seeing them at her parents' home for occasional Sunday dinners and the kids' birthdays.

Carly nodded as she finished the last bite of pancetta on her plate and pushed it to the side.

"Why are you here with me?" She couldn't fathom any reasonable explanation that Jordan wouldn't be here with her wife on their anniversary. Even with the baby subject prominent.

Carly shrugged. "She forgot. Scheduled a dinner meeting. Didn't want to tell me until I was already here…occupied with you, so I wouldn't cause a scene."

"Oh my gosh, I'm so sorry." Her sister was a complete idiot—had to be to leave this beautiful woman wondering whether she was important in her life.

"I've gotten used to it," Carly said with a sigh, then drew in a deep breath. "She's not at all who I thought she was when we got married." She leaned back in her chair and stared at her hands as she plucked at the stray thread unraveling from her napkin. "I lose a little more of my pride every time I ask her to come home. My unimportance has become clear." She crumpled the napkin in her hand. "How could I have been so stupid?"

How could Jordan be so cold? Carly's reality cut right through Wynn. She wanted to launch across the table and take her into her arms. "You weren't stupid. You were in love."

"Not love, lust." Carly shook her head and let out a sad laugh. "We never really had any connection other than sex. At least Jordan didn't."

Wynn's eyebrows rose, an involuntary response to the comment. She'd totally failed at hiding her surprise, which Carly seemed to notice immediately.

"Now that I'm past it, I have to call it what it was. I was so naive that I got wrapped up in a whirlwind courtship loaded with passion-filled romantic getaways and adventure." Carly rolled her eyes. "Her line was perfect: 'I'm Jordan Jamison, like the whiskey, but full bodied and smoother.' Ugh, I let Jordan's confidence distract me. I wanted an assertive partner who could take charge…take care of me and help raise a family. I could shoot myself for buying into that. I mean, who gets married two months after they start dating?"

Pain shot through Wynn as she bit down on her lip, holding her thoughts in. Jordan had always been the charming one in the family. The wedding announcement had been a total shock to Wynn. Jordan could have any woman in the world, and she'd chosen the only one Wynn was interested in. At the time, she'd pointed out to Jordan how little time she'd known Carly, practically begged her not to marry her, but Jordan always got what she wanted.

The server came with their meals and slid the plates in front of them, then put the carrots in the middle of the table, which seemed to reset Carly's mood.

Carly tilted her head and smiled. "I'm honestly having a better time tonight with you than I probably would've had with Jordan." She took a bite of the lobster and let out a soft moan.

"I'm sure that's not true." She avoided eye contact, trying not to give her feelings away.

"It's absolutely true. If she were here right now she'd be on her phone texting someone or reading email." She took another bite and moaned again before forking a chunk and placing it on Wynn's plate. "It's delicious."

Wynn ate the bite. "That's wonderful." She cut a portion of the halibut and placed it on Carly's plate. "This isn't bad either."

Carly took a bite and moaned again. "That is so much better." She pointed her fork at Wynn's plate before she set her fork on the table and picked up her plate. "Trade with me."

Wynn slipped another bite into her mouth quickly and forked another.

Carly let her mouth drop open. "Don't eat it all."

Wynn couldn't hold her laughter and covered her mouth to prevent the food from spilling out before she swallowed. "You gave me five seconds." She glanced at her Apple Watch before she picked up her plate and traded with Carly. "I had one second left."

Carly narrowed her eyes. "I think your time was up, but I'll let this one pass."

"Thank God for that, or I might starve."

Carly pushed the bowl of carrots closer to Wynn. "Veggies are better for you anyway."

She smiled as she picked up the carrots and scooped a few onto the plate. She had to admit watching Carly enjoy her food was very entertaining, if not arousing.

After finishing the halibut, Carly blotted her lips with her napkin and flopped back in her chair. "What happened to you, anyway?"

"What do you mean?" she asked, honestly confused. This conversation had gone in so many directions and wasn't at all what she'd expected tonight.

"I felt something with you back then—when we kissed, and I thought you felt it too." She took a sip of wine. "But then you seemed to become so aloof and disinterested." Carly's eyes were focused on her.

A rush of heat captured her, and she wasn't sure how to respond. A laugh escaped her throat before she could stop it. "I'm sorry. I don't mean to laugh. It's just fucking bad karma. I thought we had something going too." She hesitated. "Before you got together with Jordan."

She waited for Carly to speak, and after a moment of what looked like contemplation, she did. "Yeah, we definitely had a vibe between us. I thought you were going to ask me out, and then when your sister came into the picture, you totally backed off."

She was stunned. Why hadn't Carly said anything then? "I thought you wanted that. If you didn't, why'd you go out with her?" A rush of heat filled her. "Why'd you marry her?"

The chair rattled as Carly moved forward and planted her elbows on the table. "I just told you why I married her. Why'd you disappear?"

"I got the message loud and clear. That night, after the fund-raiser, you went home with Jordan."

Carly widened her eyes and shook her head. "I did *not* go home with Jordan. She gave me a ride. That's it."

"But she said…" She closed her eyes. "She lied." The words tumbled softly from her lips. It wouldn't be the first time Jordan had done that to get something she wanted.

"It appears so. I've found that she's very good at that."

"Jordan came to me after that night and said she thought you were the one. Her soul mate." It seemed now that everything Jordan had told her in the days following had been lies to get her away from Carly. She hadn't considered that possibility.

"That's a fucking joke." Carly arched an eyebrow.

"Then why *did you* marry her?"

"Your sister was persistent, and you were gone. About that—where the hell did you go?"

"After what she'd said, I didn't think I had a chance. You seemed interested in her as well." *I couldn't watch you fall in love with someone else.*

"I swallowed my pride—called you so many times." Carly raised her voice and kept eye contact. "More than I've ever done with anyone else in my life, and you ignored me."

"She's my sister. I didn't—"

"Think she'd lie to you? So instead of talking to me, you just stepped aside and disappeared from my life."

"I felt I should."

"Those are some weirdly archaic rules you live by, my dear."

"If you're so unhappy, why don't you ask Jordan for a divorce?"

Carly sighed. "I can't. It's done, and good or bad, I'm married for the rest of my life. I don't want to go into all the details."

"What? Now who's living by the weirdly archaic rules?"

"I'm a *marriage* counselor, one of the most prominent in San Francisco. I'd be a total failure if I couldn't save my own marriage. Everyone in my field would crucify me."

"That's ridiculous."

Carly stared across the table at her. "I don't think I would've liked being the object of a competition between you two, but I would've at least liked to have known how you felt and been given a choice."

"Would you have chosen differently?" Wynn knew she shouldn't ask, but she needed to know.

Carly raised her eyebrows. "Possibly." She looked at the ceiling and then sprang forward. "Hell, yes. It would've been different."

"Jordan can be very charming when she wants something." She'd seen her in action many times.

Carly blew out a short breath. "Not that charming."

"So she didn't try to persuade you to sleep with her that night?" She glanced up as the server appeared out of nowhere and slipped the bill onto the table.

"Oh, she tried, but my mind was still completely stuck on the kiss you and I had shared on the pier."

Her stomach dipped as she remembered the feel of Carly's body against hers that night. "Really?" She heard the insecurity seep from her voice. It had been a long time since that had happened.

Carly raised an eyebrow. "*Really.* You didn't give me much credit, did you?"

"I just thought—"

"That I had an off-the-charts kiss with you, then fucked your sister the same night?" Carly swiped at her mouth with her napkin and tossed it onto the table. "You know, Suzanna is the only one of the Jamison sisters worth marrying. Unfortunately, she's straight." The chair scraped against the floor as she got up and then practically ran across the restaurant toward the bathroom.

Wynn took her phone out of her pocket. It seemed to have buzzed a million times in the last hour with multiple texts from Jordan. She was bulleting her with questions like she was on a first date.

How are things going?

Did you order appetizers and a nice bottle of wine?

She likes that.

It's your anniversary! Wynn was so pissed right now, she could barely hit the right keys.

Oh, really? A surprised face emoji appeared at the end of Jordan's response.

REALLY! She typed back and waited impatiently as the bubbles formed on the screen.

I'll send her flowers tomorrow.

You really are an ass.

True, but I'm not standing in your way any longer.

You totally screwed me so you could screw her, and now you don't want her anymore? That's fucked up.

No need to get nasty about it. Carly made the choice. In reality, Wynn had made the choice for her.

You are such a cold bitch.

All's fair in love and war.

She wanted to hurl her phone across the room.

I really used to admire you, but now I can't think of why.

"Is everything okay?" She heard Carly before she saw her and quickly dropped her phone into her jacket pocket.

"Just checking my email for security issues at work. We had a layoff today."

"Oh. I'm sorry to hear that." Carly's anger seemed to have dissipated, and she actually looked concerned as she slid into her chair. "Did the company provide counseling resources? The loss of a job is really hard on marriages."

"Because of the lost income?" She hadn't thought about that. Human Resources was there, but they hadn't arranged any counselors. She'd see about that tomorrow.

"Loss of income, ego, self-worth—they all play a factor. A lot of couples find it to be their breaking point." Carly took a sip of wine. "Could the company have avoided it?"

She shrugged. "Possibly, but leadership wanted immediate results. Waiting six to eight months for better numbers wasn't an option." It wasn't an option, was it? They'd indicated a quick need for recovery, and that's what she'd given them. Just as she had the last time.

Carly reached across the table and touched her hand. "You know, sometimes it takes more courage not to do something than to just play along."

At this moment Wynn was sure of that truth. Her thoughts went immediately to the past, more than three hundred and sixty-five days earlier, when she was looking into confused green eyes, reliving the kiss with Carly that came next and wanting so badly to do it again. If she hadn't stepped away as Jordan had asked, tonight might have very well been Wynn's anniversary with Carly. She'd thought her feelings were gone—the whole thing was done—over—finished, but the emotions rushing her now proved she'd never truly purged Carly from her heart.

Carly stood. "Do you want to take a walk on the pier?"

"Sure." She signed the check and placed it back in the folder.

They walked out through the patio exit and ambled along the pier slowly, looking everywhere but at each other until they stopped at a lamppost, standing a few feet apart, and stared out onto the Pacific Ocean. The awkward distance between them was clear.

Wynn's neck was burning as a shiver coursed through her. She wanted to ask Carly so many things—needed to know them. "So if Jordan was out of the picture, and you were single right now, would you go out with me?" She pushed herself to journey further into this situation than she probably should. Carly would never be in her life that way. She'd clearly indicated that she wouldn't consider divorcing Jordan, and Wynn would never push her to break her vows.

Carly blew out a breath as she turned and stared into her eyes. "I honestly don't know. Back then you were different. Now you're just like Jordan—career driven. Work is your world. According to your mother, you haven't committed to anyone for more than a couple of months at a time." She shrugged. "You don't have room for anyone in your life, let alone a wife and kids. I want a family—the wife, the house in the suburbs, the picket fence, all of it. Apparently, I'm not destined for any of it."

Her heart clenched at the hopeless despair in Carly's voice. Wynn had never been able to commit to anyone because she wanted all that too—with Carly. Always had, always would. Everything had gone wrong that night after they'd kissed. She wished she could do it all over again and be the person Carly wanted and needed, the person she, herself, needed.

Thunder clapped in the sky, and huge droplets of rain cascaded upon them, but neither of them moved to gain shelter. They remained frozen, staring into each other's eyes.

"I've never been able to get that kiss out of my head either." She couldn't stop the urge and rushed toward Carly. Suddenly her hands were on her face, then in her hair, and she was kissing Carly just like she had over a year ago. She was uncertain at first, but when Carly's hands landed inside her jacket on her hips and urged her closer, she couldn't deny it. Carly wanted it just as badly.

The kiss began softly, gently, neither of them trying to conquer the other. Control was not an issue, and their tongues seemed familiar with each other. It was as if each of them knew what the other wanted—every motion, every touch set all her senses on fire. Clearly she should have been with Carly all along. How could she have ignored that fact before?

Sounds became muffled as her senses heightened, and pure joy spread throughout her as they pressed into one another. She broke away, opened her eyes briefly, found Carly's darkened emerald eyes staring back at her. Wynn's vision tunneled as the heady feeling overtook her and she immersed herself once more in the warmth, the feel, the taste of Carly. Light flashed through her head as the kiss deepened and the electricity between them surged…

Chapter Six

Wynn opened her eyes and blinked at her surroundings. She was home in bed. When had she left the pier? How had she gotten here? She pressed her palm to her forehead. The jackhammer in her head told her she'd had too much wine last night. As the evening came into focus, she found the vision of Carly's dazzling green eyes looking back at her. Then her lips, her tongue, the softness of her body pressed up against her own.

Was Carly here? Jesus, had she done something really stupid? She swept her arm across the other side of her king-size bed. No. Relief washed through her. How had she gotten home? She sprang up, squeezed her eyes closed to settle the pounding before she scanned the bedroom. She observed the lime-green University of San Francisco T-shirt she was wearing, one she'd thought she'd thrown out long ago.

"Oh my God." She launched out of bed and into the kitchen, then the living room, and to each of the other bedrooms after that. Carly wasn't here. No one here but her. "Shadow," she called, but her one-year-old, black Labrador retriever didn't come running as usual. Where the hell was she?

She scanned the living room. Everything looked different somehow. She saw the cheap art and decorations she'd taken down long ago, when she'd moved into her new position at work. Everything was fuzzy. Had someone slipped something into her drink, or was she still drunk? She needed to go back to bed. She didn't like this dream one bit. She walked to the bedroom and slipped under the covers again. No way was she going to relive that miserable time of her life.

Her phone buzzed on the nightstand, and she saw the notice of a voice-mail message on the screen. The phone was smaller. Had she broken her new one last night? The memories were fuzzy. Thankfully her code was still the same, so she hit the play button, and Jordan's voice came through the speaker. "Hey. I need your help at a fund-raiser tonight. Call me back."

She hadn't helped Jordan with events in over a year, and after the position she'd put Wynn in last night with Carly, she certainly wasn't helping her tonight. She had no idea how she'd gotten home or what she might have said to Carly. All she remembered was the life-altering kiss they'd shared. She quickly typed a message to Carly.

Thanks for taking me home last night. I'm not sure what happened after we kissed.

I think this text might be meant for someone else.

She'd thought she and Carly were on the same page last night, but it appeared she wasn't. *Sorry. Blame it all on me. I overstepped.*

She watched and waited as bubbles appeared on the phone.

Again, not me. Some other lucky girl.

Lucky girl? What was that about? The name displayed at the top said Carly Evans. Wynn had changed Carly's last name in her phone to Jamison as soon as the wedding was over—a vivid reminder that she was married to her sister—off-limits. What the hell was going on? Was someone playing a massively fucked-up practical joke? Admittedly, she'd had too much to drink, but this shit was going too far. She dropped her phone onto the nightstand, and the pillow whooshed as she flopped onto it in bed. She needed more sleep to escape from this ridiculous dream.

She'd only been asleep for what felt like a minute or two when the phone jolted her awake. She glanced at the clock on the nightstand. Seven a.m. Who the hell was calling her this early? Evelyn's name was on the screen, so she hit the answer button and said, "What now?"

"Are you sick?" Evelyn sounded angry.

"I'm fine. Yesterday was a long day." She usually didn't get into the office until after eight.

"Not as long as today's going to be if you don't get your ass in here." She couldn't tell if Evelyn was angry or being urgent now.

"What's going on?"

"I didn't want you in this position. I didn't have a choice. So, get up, get dressed, and be in my office by nine o'clock." The line went dead.

"What the fuck?" She stared at the phone screen. Considering the shift in responsibilities, Wynn had given Evelyn plenty of latitude in recent months, but just who the hell did she think she was talking to?

She dragged herself out of bed and stumbled to the bathroom. Shadow squealed as she tripped over her. She dropped to her knees and checked on her. Shadow was a puppy again. Tiny kisses and puppy breath covered her face. Joy filled her as she soaked up the love.

She looked into the puppy's eyes and wouldn't have known it wasn't Shadow. But it couldn't possibly be her. She'd tripled in size since she'd brought her home. Shadow licked her again before she stood. "Come on, honey. Let's go out first, and then you can eat."

The puppy followed her down the hallway, and before she got to the back door, she stepped in something wet. "Shit." She hopped on one foot to the kitchen, spun a paper towel from the holder, wet it, and cleaned the bottom of her foot. The puppy sprinted to the back door, where she immediately squatted and peed. "Oh my gosh." She shook her head as little black eyes stared up at her. "I thought I was done with this." She slid open the door and let her outside. April, her assistant, also known as the practical joker, was going to pay for this. She'd given her a house key only for emergencies, so it had to be her doing. Wynn would demand she return it immediately. She was always up for a good joke, but this one was ridiculously elaborate. How had she even pulled it off?

Leaving the sliding-glass door slightly open for the puppy to come in when she was done, Wynn went into the kitchen and searched for the hardwood floor cleaner under the sink before she spun a few paper towels from the holder. After cleaning up the mess, she found Shadow's bowl, filled it with puppy chow, which had replaced Shadow's food, and placed it on the floor. She hoped April was feeding Shadow the correct food. If not, that would be a whole other world of problems she'd have to deal with tomorrow when they switched the dogs again.

Once the puppy was inside, Wynn closed and locked the sliding door, then rummaged through the pantry for her usual choice of corn flakes for breakfast. Locating a box toward the back, she yawned as she took it out of the cupboard. She scrunched her brows when she saw Toucan Sam staring at her. Froot Loops? That had been her favorite sugar-coated cereal when she was younger. She hadn't eaten it in over a year. In fact, she'd recently quit eating breakfast altogether since she'd started fasting in the morning. How did it get here? She checked the expiration date, which was last year, opened the box, and found the plastic bag inside unopened. Had she stopped to buy it last night? After tearing open the top, she sniffed the contents before she tasted one piece. They seemed to still be okay, so she filled a bowl, doused it with milk, and took a huge bite.

Her cheeks puffed, and she ran to the kitchen sink and spit out the liquid that was violently attacking her taste buds. She cupped several drinks of water into her mouth and swished them around to rinse the evil taste from her tongue. It had the consistency of house paint, and she gagged a few times before she'd finally rid her mouth of the taste and swiped her face with a paper towel. She took the milk container from the refrigerator and studied the label. Soy milk. No wonder. Where the hell did that come from? She'd tried it once when that was the thing to do, but had sworn never to buy it again. She never could adjust to the chalky, bean taste. She poured it down the sink before she took a handful of cereal and shoved it into her mouth. She needed sugar in any way she could find it this morning.

She padded down the hallway to the bedroom and into the bathroom and grazed the wall with her hand, finding a gaping hole. Why was there a hole, and where the hell was the light switch? She grabbed the doorframe to steady herself before she searched the other wall and hit pay dirt. *What the hell?* She squeezed her eyes closed and then opened them again. The bathroom was incredibly small, and everything was backward. Tools were strewn on the floor, and the toilet was gone. She pressed her fingers to her head. This was no practical joke any longer. It was clearly a nightmare, set while she was having the house remodeled. She would never again live for months enduring random contractors working in and out of her house while leaving everything in constant disarray. She spun and rushed to the guest bathroom, where all her toiletries were meticulously placed on the counter. Her phone rang again, Evelyn's assigned ringtone, so she could avoid her when necessary.

The shower would have to wait until tonight. She'd had one before she took Carly to dinner last night. She wet her hands before running her fingers through her short hair to flatten the stray patches sticking out before she mussed it and added product to keep it in place. Then she washed her face, applied lotion, and spritzed herself with cologne, per her usual routine. She rushed to the closet and dressed in the first suit she found, a black, notched-collar one she'd bought from Express early in her career. Hadn't she donated it long ago? She tugged on the slacks and slipped on a white button-down before she put on the jacket. At least it still fit. In fact, it looked pretty good on her.

Carly hadn't been able to get thoughts of Wynn Jamison out of her head since she'd heard the text chime on her phone this morning and saw a message from her. She'd put Wynn's number in her phone long ago, when they'd started working Suzanna's events together. She couldn't remember the exact reason Wynn had provided the number, but it wasn't for anything more than event business. At least she'd thought so at the time.

She'd felt an odd sense of jealousy when she'd read the text, knowing it was meant for someone else. She shook her head. That was ridiculous. She'd never given Wynn any indication she had any interest in seeing her. They'd never even been on a date. Yet the sinking feeling in her stomach told her she'd thought maybe something might happen between them in the future. She read the text again, running her finger across it as she second-guessed her response.

Thanks for taking me home last night. I'm not sure what happened after we kissed.

She'd checked the name on the screen again. Although the thought of kissing Wynn had come into her thoughts before, Carly hadn't been the one Wynn kissed last night. She definitely hadn't expected the pang of disappointment she felt knowing Wynn was making out with another woman.

I think this text might be meant for someone else.

It had been a few weeks since Carly had even seen Wynn. Her dashingly handsome smile flashed through her head, and she remembered noticing her soft curves accentuated perfectly by her slim-fitting suit. She could never resist a sharply dressed, adorable butch.

Sorry. Blame it all on me. I overstepped.

What in the world was Wynn talking about? Hopefully she'd find out soon. She was helping Suzanna at the Children's Hospital fund-raiser Jordan was putting on tonight, and Wynn was usually there as well.

Again, not me. She'd moved her fingers quickly across the letters and then carefully contemplated her next words. *Some other lucky girl.* She'd hit send before she could rethink her text.

Carly had never been one to make the first move, and her response was a bolder step than she'd ever taken with a woman. She had plenty of confidence in her career, but not nearly as much in her personal life. Probably why she always ended up with the wrong women.

The phone on her desk rang, jarring her out of her thoughts, and she picked up the receiver. "Hello."

"Doctor Evans. The Baxters are here," Stephanie said.

"Send them in, please." She got up from her desk chair, crossed the room, and opened the door. They were just coming down the hallway. "Good morning. How are you two today?"

"I've been better," Mike said, and Sara gave her a thin smile. Not the response she'd hoped for. They came in and took their usual seats at opposite ends of the couch. She'd removed all but one comfortable chair and the couch from her office to prevent couples from sitting so far away they couldn't communicate.

"I'm sensing some tension today. Anything you want to discuss?" She hadn't been counseling them for long, so she hadn't picked up on all their body language yet, but they seemed frustrated today.

Sara glanced at Mike and then at Carly. "He doesn't want counseling."

"That's not what I said."

"You just sat out there in the waiting room and said it was stupid."

She closed the notebook in her lap. "Is that so?" It wasn't the first time she'd heard that sentiment from a client. "How long have you two been together?" She avoided addressing the "stupid" comment.

"A little over a year," Mike said.

"That's not very long in the grand scheme of things. Remember, every marriage evolves over time. You're doing exactly that as we speak."

He drew his brows together. "What do you mean?"

"Coming here was a huge step. You both realize you have issues that you can't resolve without help." She handed each of them a pad and pen. "I want you to write down how satisfied you are in your marriage on a scale of one to ten." She watched as they hesitated and glanced at each other. "Don't show it to each other. Fold the paper and give it to me. This is for my information only."

She collected the folded pieces of paper but didn't read them. "Now you need to explain to yourself why you chose that number."

"I chose—"

"Don't tell me." Carly put up her hand. "Write it down." This step always took longer than the couples expected. It was hard to put into words why they felt the way they did. "This is an important step, so take your time." She surreptitiously unfolded each of the pieces of paper in her hand and kept her expression blank as she read the numbers, a technique she had learned to master long ago. They were both within the five-to-seven range, which meant they would have to do some work, but they still had a good deal of hope and might be able to succeed.

"If it makes you feel any better, it takes most couples six years or more to seek counseling after they find they have issues. So, you two are way ahead of the curve."

They both smiled, which signaled that they were willing to make their marriage work.

"What's your biggest pet peeve? Other than coming here." She pulled her lips into a one-sided smirk.

"She gets upset when I talk to her about budgeting." Mike seemed to want to get right to the point.

Sara threw her hands up. "One minute we're arguing over how to load the dishwasher, and the next we're fighting about spending money on what he calls luxury foods."

"So now she won't go to the grocery store, ever."

"What about you, Sara?" The issues were sometimes the same, but usually on different ends of the spectrum.

"Your family never includes the—" she held up her fingers in air quotes "—in-laws in family photos. Do you know how expendable that makes me feel?"

That would probably irritate Carly as well. If she ever married, none of that kind of separation would happen. Family was all-inclusive, blood or not.

"My mom wants a picture of her kids. She doesn't mean anything by it."

"Why don't you ever say anything about it to her or ask if we can take a picture of all of us?"

"Honestly, I didn't think about it. It's a pain in the ass for me to get to wherever she wants us at the time she schedules a photo shoot in the first place. I didn't know it bothered you."

"Well, it does."

"Okay. I'll ask next time."

Carly held in a chuckle. If these two only knew how minimal their issues were compared to some of the other couples she counseled. She had to respect Sara for not ignoring them. Little things like that could snowball into monstrous anger and regret that overshadowed all the reasons two people became a couple in the beginning.

Chapter Seven

Wynn stopped at the specialty coffee place located not far from her house and went inside. Thank God it still looked the same. She smiled at Sally, the cute barista she'd once had a thing with, as she came to the counter holding a cup. It had been a while since Sally had done that. Wynn usually just got an evil stare from a distance. Maybe she was getting over whatever it was they'd had. Wynn had gotten past it long ago.

"Nonfat, vanilla latte, just the way you like it."

She reached for the coffee. "Thanks."

Sally moved the cup from her reach and then reared back, hurled it forward, and coffee spilled out of the cup. As if in slow motion, it hit Wynn just below her neck, splattering across her crisp white shirt.

"What the hell?" She pinched the button down between her fingers and pulled it away from her chest. It wasn't scalding hot, but it was…ick. Thankfully, she'd left her jacket in the Jeep.

"You don't get to come in here acting like everything is great when you fucking broke my heart." Nope. Not over it.

"Jesus, Sally. What was that for?"

"Seriously? You break up with me through text, and you don't know what's wrong?"

A couple of people handed her stacks of napkins. She mindlessly took them and sopped up the liquid, making her shirt cling to her chest. The coffee-shop chatter was gone now, everyone in the place watching them, eyes glued to her, waiting for her response.

"What are you talking about? We haven't gone out in months."

One of the other baristas held up a phone, and Wynn read the screen.

I'm not going to be able to make it tonight.

But I bought a new dress.

I'm sorry. I have another commitment I forgot about.

Fucking ridiculous.

Maybe we should take a break.

She still had the text? Wow, that was some attachment for casual sex. Wynn had blocked Sally's number from her phone and hadn't been back to this particular coffee shop for at least six months after the first time Sally had doused her with coffee. Had she been waiting all this time to do it again? When Wynn had sent the text, she was confused about the situation, stuck in something she didn't know how to end. Sally was awesome in bed, but she was also high-strung and hot-tempered. Wynn saw her temper often, having to tiptoe around her more than once. She just couldn't take Sally's short fuse any longer, so she'd done the cowardly thing and sent her a breakup text. It was a shitty thing to do, but her only option at that time.

She rushed out of the shop to her Jeep. She needed to find somewhere to change. The clock read eight thirty, so she was going to be late. She drove to her sister Suzanna's house and knocked on the door lightly. It was still summer vacation for the kids, and Suzanna would be pissed if she woke them this early.

The door swung open. "Hey." Suzanna smiled and then took in Wynn's appearance. "What the hell happened to you?"

"Long story." She pushed past her inside. "I need to borrow one of James's shirts."

"The barista didn't like your message, eh?" Suzanna laughed. "I told you not to do it that way." She led Wynn into the bedroom. "Why in the world did you go there for coffee this morning?"

"I wasn't thinking about it." She'd figured Sally would be over it by now. Sally must've been waiting for the perfect opportunity.

"Exactly why you shouldn't have gone out with her in the first place." Suzanna took a powder-blue shirt from the closet, held it up in front of Wynn, and then put it back. "If you were in the right relationship, you'd be thinking about her every minute of the day." She took out one that was pale pink. "This should work. I can't help you with the bra, though."

"That's fine. It's dry enough." She took off her shirt. "I'll just smell like coffee all day."

"An ingenious new scent." Suzanna smiled as she slipped the shirt from the hanger and handed it to Wynn. "You're coming tonight, right?"

"Where?"

"Jordan's fund-raiser? You and Carly always help, remember?"

Her mind was right there with Carly again after dinner last night, looking into confused green eyes, feeling the kiss that came next. She shook the thought from her head. "Right. I must've mixed up the dates." She wouldn't pass up an opportunity to see Carly again, that was for sure. Even if it meant tolerating Jordan. She finished buttoning her shirt and rushed to the door. "I gotta go. I'm already late for work. Big changes happening there."

Suzanna followed her. "I hope you're looking at the big picture and not just the near future." Suzanna had always been good at offering advice and words of wisdom to Wynn when she was confused. "Remember, one step forward and two steps back is hard to overcome."

"I got it." She raced to her Jeep and stopped before getting in. "And no birthday cake tonight."

Suzanna scrunched her eyebrows together. "Duh. Your birthday's not until tomorrow."

That was weird. Suzanna had actually forgotten her birthday, or was it just a guise to throw Wynn off? They would have cake tonight, and Suzanna would embarrass her as usual, but she would enjoy every minute of it because the whole event was created out of love.

❖

When Wynn pulled into the parking lot of Sexton Technologies, Evelyn's shiny black BMW took up Carly's usual space. This was getting ridiculous. She had to take care of this situation before it exploded into a huge mess. Leaving Evelyn to deal with yesterday's aftermath from the laid-off employees didn't give her any more power than before.

She swung the leather valise her father had given her long ago in front of the badge reader by the door, and the light changed from red to green. She waited patiently for the doors to swing open. As she rushed inside and headed past the security guard at the entrance, she heard a loud, deep voice say, "Miss. I need to see your badge." His eyes crinkled as he smiled. Large, coffee-stained teeth emerged from beneath a bushy white mustache as he waited. He looked familiar, but Wynn couldn't place him. He must be new to the front-entrance security.

She glanced around the lobby to locate Jake, the usual thirty-something guard who manned the desk. "Isn't Jake here?"

"No Jake. Just George today," he said and raised his hand.

Irritated, she slapped the leather valise onto the counter, unzipped all the pockets, searched until she found her security badge tucked into one of the side slats, and flashed it at him.

"You should wear your badge around your neck." He reached for the badge and inspected it thoroughly. "Company policy, ya know."

"Right," she said as he moved closer and draped the lanyard over her head. He probably thought this was some kind of security test. "You must be new."

"Nope, not new." He flipped the badge, making the picture face forward. "Getting ready to retire soon. Been with the company close to forty years. Just one more year until my pension kicks in." He lowered his voice. "I hear some may not have that opportunity soon."

She raised her eyebrows. "What have you heard?" It was hard keeping reorganization plans hush-hush. She should've known someone would leak something.

He pulled his eyebrows together. "Big reorg planned by that weaselly looking guy Davis."

"Steve Davis?"

George nodded. "Never liked him." He shook his head and flattened his lips. "Always in a hurry. Doesn't hold doors for people."

Davis had been gone since the workforce reduction last year. "You shouldn't spread rumors like that." She narrowed her eyes and quirked her lip into a half-smile. "I never liked him either."

George grinned. "Lovely photo." He pointed to the badge hanging from the lanyard around her neck. "Have a nice day."

"You too," she said as she glanced at him once more and still couldn't recall ever seeing him before.

After she exited the elevator, everything seemed askew as she headed straight to her office. The wall colors were a ghastly blue and orange, something she'd changed as soon as she'd received her promotion to chief operating officer last year. Some expert who'd said blue was soothing and orange prevented people from milling in the hallway too long had specifically chosen the previous color. It was all a bunch of baloney, if you asked her. Neither color had ever prevented anyone from spreading gossip in the hallways. Probably how George heard the news about the big event coming soon.

She stopped short when she saw Katie, Evelyn's assistant, sitting behind April's desk. She checked her phone. April hadn't messaged her saying she'd be out today.

"Where's April?"

Katie pulled her eyebrows together as she glanced up. "I don't know."

Fuck. "Are you kidding me?" It wasn't like April to disappear when things got tough, and April knew today was a big day. Besides, she'd never skip out on Carly's reaction to the practical joke she'd pulled this morning with Shadow. Something bad must have happened overnight, or she must be really sick

"No. I'm not." Katie stared at her over her glasses. "It's not my day to watch her. Why don't you call her?" Katie's tone was low and smooth, as usual, and the permanent frown on her face clearly signaled that she didn't give a shit. She never got flustered during any crisis.

What the hell was up her ass today? "I guess I'll do that." Wynn had learned long ago that Katie was much better as an ally than an enemy.

She trudged forward, pushed open the door to her office, and stepped into the room. Everything stilled around her, and she blinked. She glanced over her shoulder at the name plate on the door, which read EVELYN CANTOR, INTERIM COO. What the hell was going on? She hadn't seen that sign since the previous COO left last year. April was continuing to play a magnificently cruel joke on her this morning. She had to give her credit for her originality, but today was not the day for it. She'd pay dearly for this.

Evelyn spun around in her chair. "It's about time. We have a meeting with leadership in twenty minutes."

She let out a laugh. "Right. This is a spectacular gag you and April have put on here." She crossed the room and dropped her valise onto the desk. "You can get out of my chair now."

Evelyn pulled her eyebrows together. "Are you crazy? I've put a lot of effort into acquiring this chair, and I'm not getting out of it for anyone. Especially not an opportunistic bottom-feeder like you."

Oh my God. Cutthroat Evelyn is back. She moved her valise into one of the chairs in front of the desk and said, "Okay, that's enough. I'm always up for a good gag, but now you're just being hurtful."

Evelyn narrowed her eyes. "If you want this job, you're going to have to rip it from my bloody hands. I've worked too hard to get here, and I guarantee I won't let go of it easily." She tucked her hair on one side behind her ear, which was longer, blond, and all one length again—one heck of a wig that looked absolutely natural. Once Wynn had gotten promoted over her, it seemed as though Evelyn didn't give a fuck anymore. She'd stopped hiding her age—had chopped her hair off into a short cut and let the natural salt-and-pepper color take over. The look fit her so much better than this brassy blond one.

Wynn's pulse raced as anger boiled inside. She was just about to fire off another response when she noticed the calendar on the desk. August nineteenth of the previous year. An anxiety attack on the way, Wynn's vision blurred as she became more confused. "I think I need a drink," she said softly as she slid into one of the chairs.

"That's a daily need around here, so get used to it." Evelyn gathered some documents from her desk and stood. "Did you familiarize yourself with the information I gave you yesterday?" She planted a hand on her hip. Wynn took in Evelyn's clothes. She hadn't seen her in that navy, career-centered, Anne Klein suit in…forever.

Somehow she'd been catapulted back in time. Was she dreaming? She pinched her leg. *Ouch.* Not dreaming. What the hell had happened on this day last year? Jesus—it was the day *she'd* become chief operating officer—the day she'd thrown Evelyn under the bus to get ahead. She nodded as she scoured her memory. She couldn't remember everything about the meeting with leadership they'd had that day, but at least she had an idea.

"Where's the presentation?" Evelyn's voice blew through her thoughts.

"Oh, it's on my laptop," she said, still bewildered. "Which is in my office?" She wasn't sure of anything and everything right now.

"Well, go get it."

"Right." She stood, grabbed her valise, spun around, and rushed down the hallway to her old office. Holy hell, she hoped it was there, or this pivotal scene in her life would end badly this time. She pushed the door open to the much-smaller, windowless office and sped to her desk. She blew out a breath in relief. Thankfully, her old laptop was here.

She opened the top and logged in. The presentation she'd collaborated with Evelyn was on the computer desktop screen right next to the folder labeled MISCELLANEOUS FILES, which contained the alternate presentation Wynn had created alone. She slapped the laptop closed and rushed back to Evelyn, who was waiting for her at the elevator.

"Ready?" Evelyn fidgeted as the elevator doors opened.

"Ready as I'll ever be." She stepped into the elevator behind Evelyn.

"Just take a breath and follow my lead. It'll all be fine." Evelyn spoke so calmly, Wynn remembered wondering at the time if Evelyn had two personalities: the raging bitch-of-a-boss one that she'd seen a few minutes ago in her office and this calm, collected one she was experiencing right now. She remembered finding out that afternoon that Evelyn had more than two personalities to deal with. Definitely a day to remember.

At the time, other companies had poached several of their top IT developers whom they had educated and groomed once they'd gained the knowledge and experience they needed. Evelyn planned to increase developer salaries once they were through the training phase and then incentivize employees to remain with the company by providing profit sharing as well as substantial merit raises each year for those employees who excelled at their jobs and had gone above and beyond. Outsourcing their IT support desk had been one of the solutions Wynn had proposed, but Evelyn had nixed that idea right away and opted to go with the process-improvement plan she'd received from the IT support manager.

The content looked familiar to Wynn as Evelyn started to click through her presentation to reorganize the company, implement increased employee education, and promote process improvement to leadership. She had to admit these were actually some very good ideas, and if the company had implemented them the previous year at that time, revenue would've increased. With that in mind, Wynn most likely wouldn't have faced the layoff she'd had to perform yesterday.

Still confused about reality, she ran through the day in her head. *This must be some kind of a lessons-learned dream.*

Evelyn's presentation received the same underwhelming response it had the last time. From the moment she started talking, the executives' flattened lips and minimal smiles made it clear they had concerns. Spending money to save money would take time, and leadership wasn't on board with that. They wanted savings now, and they made that fact perfectly clear.

She followed Evelyn out of the office. "Well, that went over like a flat, warm beer."

"You didn't give me much support in there." Evelyn sounded angry.

"What could I say? Just give her the money and everything will be all right?"

"Yes. You could've said exactly that." Evelyn's voice rose as she paced faster down the hallway to her office.

She shook her head as she followed Evelyn, trying to keep up. "But it's not true." She stopped at the doorway. "We don't have time to recoup any money we spend. Not with your plan, anyway, and they know that."

"I suppose you have a better one?"

"No." She shook her head. "Only the one you rejected." She turned and went a few doors down the hallway to her own office. She didn't tell Evelyn, but she was going to present her ideas whether Evelyn approved or not. Her methods were very different, and Evelyn would oppose her with all her power.

Wynn sat down in the chair behind the desk and studied her surroundings. The same picture of her niece and nephew was propped up facing her on the corner. Their innocence shone through as they smiled brilliantly in front of the tall, long-legged giraffe in the background. It was one of many trips to the zoo she'd taken them on, a beautiful yet painful reminder of how much love a family could hold. Her heart contained much more love to give, and she'd always planned to have children of her own someday. Lately she'd been unsure of that capability.

It couldn't happen without the right partner, and no one she'd dated seemed to fit into the *perfect* category. Visions of her sister-in-law, Carly, floated through her mind. Maybe her standards were too high. Clearing the thoughts from her head, she took in a huge breath, relaxed into her chair, and let her mind fill in the gaps of today's events as they had happened before. Her next move had been pivotal in her career. Her fingers whizzed across the keyboard as she searched the files and pulled up the presentation she'd created. She made a few changes—tweaks to the numbers from knowledge she'd gained since then. Other than that, she was going to let this dream, or whatever it was, play out exactly as it had in the past.

She glanced at her watch and closed the laptop. It was time. Adrenaline surged through her veins as she pushed through the chief executive officer's door and found him and the chief financial officer waiting to listen to her ideas. Once inside, she reminded herself that she'd presented to leadership dozens of times over the past year and met with the CEO on a regular basis, and her anxiety calmed. She'd anticipated the types of questions they would pose and had prepared responses for each of them. Her confidence level at a high, she was fully prepared to field any other questions they had.

They'd received her presentation with trust and confidence. Leadership respected numbers, and she'd supported her idea with both real-time savings and future increased revenue. She'd suggested that an immediate reduction in workforce would guarantee a quicker, more discernible way to recoup the losses they'd experienced over the past ten years under the skewed direction of the previous COO. Plus, she'd added a few new slides addressing the direction the company should take within the next year, something she'd learned from her experience living the following year. Weren't dreams supposed to give us a chance to change the future and our destinies?

Wynn had just relaxed behind her desk when Evelyn barreled through the door, just as she had the last time. "What the hell did you do?" Evelyn's face was turning redder by the second.

"I proposed another solution."

Evelyn scowled. "The one I rejected."

"Leadership liked it." A warm feeling of satisfaction coursed through her.

"Do you know how many people are going to lose their jobs now?"

That must mean they're going to go with it. She tried to conceal her smile. "It had to be done. Otherwise there's no money."

"Oh my God, you are so naive. You've just suggested we lay off most of our workforce. Who do you think that's going to fall to now?"

"My plan doesn't suggest we cut everyone."

"You just shot loyalty out of the water. Those employees that *are* staying will leave soon enough if we pile all the work on them. Deadlines will be impossible to meet with minimal resources."

She honestly hadn't thought that part through. "Then we'll hire new people or outsource."

"Who's going to train them?" Evelyn paced the room. "And just wait for the lawsuits to roll in." She stopped, stared, and pinched the bridge of her nose. "Well, you're in charge now. So you'd better make a plan."

"What do you mean?"

"You're officially the new chief operating officer."

"So you work for me now." She'd forgotten how quickly the decision had been made.

"For the time being." Evelyn floated a piece of paper across the desk.

"What's this?"

"These are the people who have to go." Evelyn spun to the door. "I'll have my things moved into another office tomorrow."

She glanced at the list Evelyn had left. The first name that caught her eye was George, the security guard. Her heart tugged as she remembered him saying he had one more year until he retired. She opened the desk drawer and jammed the list inside. She refused to think about that now. Just as before, the fallout would be massive.

She pulled up the calendar on her laptop. Tonight was Jordan's fund-raiser. The text she'd received from her this morning made sense now. She glanced at her watch—close to four o'clock. She needed to rush home and get ready before this dream ended.

Chapter Eight

Carly whizzed through traffic, cars blurring as she passed. The built-in GPS on her car was talking like it never had before. It took her around all the accidents and construction to get her home as quickly as possible. Most days she ignored the directions, but today she let them lead her. It was only two miles, but congestion in the city made it seem so much farther. Yesterday Carly had been regretting volunteering to help Suzanna with her event tonight, but after she'd received the odd text from Wynn this morning, she couldn't wait to speed through her day to get there. Something about Wynn intrigued her. She was super-sweet and a little reserved, probably the reason Carly hadn't gotten to know her all that well. Whenever they interacted, every conversation went smoothly. They both had opinions, but most times they ended up educating each other just a little, while also finding a middle ground.

Wynn seemed compassionate, empathetic, and altruistically loyal, traits you didn't often see in women nowadays, especially not the single ones. Wynn attended every event Suzanna planned and did everything she'd been asked without complaint, even the crappy tasks. Wynn was also ridiculously sexy. Carly's body lit up like a circuit board at full capacity as she thought about Wynn's long legs, sexy strut, and soft-sophisticated manner. That hadn't happened in a very long time. Maybe she was the one she should be spending her time and energy getting to know.

She waved at her neighbor, Rosi, as she waited for the garage door to open fully and then pulled inside. Normally, she'd have closed the door immediately, but she felt bad about ignoring her. Carly had been depressed about her lack of a love life lately, and Rosi seemed to have a fairy-tale life with her partner. Carly knew avoiding her was a shitty thing to do, but she just couldn't stand to hear how wonderful her life was all the time and have such a dismal one herself.

"Hey, hey. I was just getting ready to have a glass of wine. Want to join?" Rosi stood at the back of Carly's car, waiting for her to come out of the garage.

No avoiding her now, but she didn't stop as she walked up the stairs to the mailbox by the front door to retrieve the newspaper and mail. "I wish I could, but I promised to help out at a fund-raiser tonight and need to change."

"Oh yeah? What's it for?" Rosi followed her.

"Children's Hospital."

"I guess I can't complain about that. It being kids and all." Rosi anchored her hand on her hip. "But what's going on with you?"

She pulled her eyebrows together and shook her head, trying to put on a good show. "Nothing's going on. Why?"

"You've been hibernating for weeks." Rosi frowned. "I half-expected you to go inside without talking to me."

"I know. I almost did." She blew out a breath. "I'm sorry. I've just been super busy at work."

"Jesus, girl. You need to stop listening to everyone else's troubles and find someone to create your own with." Rosi chuckled.

"Total truth." She laughed along with Rosi.

"Why don't you come out with me and Meg this weekend? I bet we can find you some good candidates."

"Let me get through the rest of the week, and I'll let you know." No way was she going out with Rosi and Meg again. The last time had been a colossal disaster. They'd taken her to a party with their circle of friends, after which she'd woken with a massive hangover. Apparently she was really entertaining after a few or five drinks and had given her number to three clingy women she couldn't shake. They'd called her for weeks afterward for reasons ranging anywhere from counseling advice to detached sex.

That was the first and last time she'd had sex on the first date, and she had sworn to herself she would never let it happen again, no matter how long she'd been without it. The sex hadn't been bad, but it lacked the passion and emotion she craved. Even though she'd been a willing participant, the regret hit her immediately—and hard. She'd finally blocked their numbers from her cell phone and stopped answering the door without knowing who was on the other side.

Carly was also successful, self-sufficient, and had a good career. That combination never failed to attract the needy ones. Just once she'd like to have a successful, confident woman show some interest in her. She knew she was unapproachable and had been working on being the one to make the first move, but after growing up as the smallest and nerdiest among all her sisters, she still found it hard to initiate conversation when it came to dating.

After entering the house, Carly dropped her bag by the door and went to her closet, immediately pulling out a few of her sexiest dresses and slinging them on the bed. Normally, she wouldn't even bother to change for the event, but the usual business-casual wardrobe wouldn't work tonight. She intended to make herself irresistible, if that was even possible. Then she would know if she had any shot with the dashing Wynn Jamison. She flopped onto the bottom of the bed and shook her head as a tingle washed through her. The whole possibility of a romance with Wynn was probably all in her head. She'd seen Wynn many times before and had never thought she had even a remote chance of Wynn being interested in her.

She tried on multiple dresses, skirts, and blouses and finally settled on a black, sleeveless lace dress that hugged her curves perfectly. Well, as perfectly as her curves could be hugged. She'd added a few pounds over the past few months due to her nonstop work schedule and much too much take-out food. Ever since she'd been featured in the health section of the *San Francisco Chronicle*, business had been steadily climbing. Soon she'd need to add more counselors to her practice, but it would take time to research doctors with the right credentials and personalities. Perhaps tonight would be the beginning of a life that involved more play than work.

❖

Mrs. Pritchard was in her yard, as usual pruning her rose bushes, as Wynn drove up. She immediately stopped and waved. Wynn returned her wave and found Mrs. P crossing the lawn to greet her, a daily event in the past. It was good to see Mrs. P, even if it was in her dreams.

"You're home early. Are we having dinner tonight?"

"I'm so sorry. I won't be able to have dinner." She closed her eyes briefly and took in a breath. She'd forgotten all about their routine. "I should've called you earlier. I have a thing to be at tonight." Tonight was their usual dinner night. While Mr. P went bowling, Mrs. P and Wynn went out to eat, then spent the evening together. Wynn had adapted to this arrangement within a month of moving into the neighborhood. She hated to cancel, because spending time with Mrs. P was always a pleasure. Mrs. P was fairly persistent, and Wynn fully admitted she enjoyed spending time with her. Mrs. P's dinner-choice variety included a range of Chinese or Mexican food, and Wynn was lucky to get Thai food on the schedule once a month.

Mrs. P raised an eyebrow. "Oh, a date? You haven't been on one of those in ages."

She chuckled. "Nope. Just a fund-raiser."

"You really should have more fun, dear." Mrs. P leaned closer. "You know, find a good woman to roll around in the sheets with on a regular basis."

She'd forgotten how delightful and forward Mrs. P could be. "I think I'm okay in that area."

"I mean the same woman—someone to settle down with. You know, a hot number to push all your buttons all the time." Mrs. P tilted her head and winked. "Like Mr. P does for me."

"Oh my gosh, Mrs. P. Even my mother isn't this honest with me."

"Then it's a good thing you have me." Mrs. P swayed, and Wynn reached out to steady her.

"Are you okay?"

"Yes. I'm fine. It's just getting a little warm outside." It had been an exceptionally hot August, with temps averaging in the upper eighties to lower nineties.

She walked Mrs. P over to her porch, where she had a tray with a pitcher of iced tea and two glasses set on the table as usual. Wynn filled them both and handed Mrs. P a glass before she set the pitcher back in its spot atop the fine doily Mrs. P had crocheted. She'd made it specifically to keep the sweat from the pitcher from pooling on the tray.

"Where's Mr. P gone this early? Bowling doesn't start until seven, does it?" She was guessing, but the time sounded about right.

"This week is his team's monthly dinner before bowling. Beer and burgers." Mrs. P sipped her tea. "It's too bad you have that fund-raiser. A longer girl's night would be fun."

"I'm sorry. Jordan would kill me if I bailed. Would you like to come with me? I can't guarantee you'd have fun, but I know the food will be good." Wynn took a drink of tea and wondered how Mrs. P managed to sweeten it perfectly every time.

"That would be nice, but I'll have to take a rain check. I'm afraid I'm not up to it tonight. The heat has gotten to me." Mrs. P sipped her tea. "Jordan. She's the older one, right?"

She nodded. "You met her at my housewarming party."

"Right. Attractive, stiff, and kind of bossy, as I recall. I bet she goes through women like a five-year-old with a bag of Tootsie Rolls."

Wynn almost spit out the sip of tea she'd just taken. Mrs. P was spot-on about Jordan and the women in her life. "She's definitely bossy."

"You're not like her at all." Mrs. P gave her a soft smile.

"Well, I hope I'm like her in some ways. She's very successful."

Mrs. P patted Wynn's hand. "Success doesn't outweigh happiness. What good is it if you have no one to share it with?"

A lesson Wynn had learned over the past year. A random thought of George, the security guard, flew through her mind. Did George have someone like Mrs. P at home waiting for him? Someone to retire with and enjoy life. Only his retirement would be cancelled because he was being laid off soon. She could change that, right? It was *her* dream, after all.

She sipped the last of her tea, squeezed Mrs. P's hand, and stood. "I need to finish some work before I get ready to go. You should head inside and get out of this heat. We'll talk tomorrow. Have dinner then, okay?"

Mrs. P smiled widely. "I'll look forward to hearing all about the party."

Sadness filled Wynn's heart as she left Mrs. P and walked across the lawn to her own front porch. She really did miss these heart-to-hearts with Mrs. P. She'd always been a ray of sunshine in Wynn's life, and she honestly missed that light.

Wynn glanced at her reflection in the darkened window before she entered the building. The streetlight behind her made her silhouette glow. She'd gone through several outfits before she'd settled on khaki pants with a long sleeved, cream-colored, button-down shirt and a tan, cotton blazer. Penny loafers were her go-to when it came to casual shoes. She'd waffled on the jacket. It had been hot when she'd left the house but was always cooler on the pier. Again, satisfied she was presentable, she went inside.

She could hardly contain herself, knowing she would see Carly tonight. She was Suzanna's best friend and always helped out at her events. Dinner with Carly the night before flew through her head, and she tried to make sense of it all. It was last night, but it wasn't. She now seemed to be reliving a day that had happened one year in the past. She had no idea which was reality and which was a dream. If it was a dream, she couldn't seem to wake herself from it.

She made her way to the private room Suzanna always used for her events. It was the perfect venue, with a room and patio that looked out onto the bay, where you could slip out onto the pier and enjoy the ocean air. The crowd was thinner than she'd expected, but she'd also arrived later than planned. Today she'd had to return multiple emails from the CEO and adjust the list of employees to be cut before leaving the house. She'd removed George. At least, that was one thing she could fix in this crazy alternate reality. The pressure she'd been slammed with when she'd first moved into the COO position was overwhelming. It demanded much more of her time than her previous position had. The energy required to remain on and available twenty-four seven for the first few months had sent her crashing after the first quarter. She'd lost fifteen pounds living on coffee and Red Bull. She'd also come down with bronchitis, but couldn't afford to take any time off and had continued in a zombie-like state—on autopilot until she'd gotten her rhythm down. The back of her neck heated and her breathing shallowed. She was surprised at how real everything felt in this dream.

Carly's anxiety was going through the roof. Since she'd arrived, she'd been casually watching the entrance looking for Wynn. The text she'd received from her this morning had sparked all kinds of crazy fantasies throughout the day, most of which would remain locked away in her mind. If nothing else, the text exchange gave her something to work with tonight—something to start a conversation, even if it fell flat. Who had Wynn been kissing last night, and why had she felt the need to apologize?

She'd watched the door open for what seemed like the gazillionth time, only this time her breath caught in her chest as Wynn entered. Jesus, she looked hotter than hot. The courage Carly had gained since this morning quickly went out the window. She turned and hurried in the other direction and right into Suzanna.

Suzanna put her arms out and took her by the shoulders. "Where are you going in such a hurry?"

"Nowhere." That was true. She had no idea where she was going to hide.

Suzanna glanced over her shoulder and smiled. "Ah. I see. Wynn is here." She made eye contact. "You've been watching for her."

"What? Why would you say that?"

"Either that or you've developed a pretty ridiculous twitch that flips your head back and forth multiple times per minute."

"Oh, shit. Was I that obvious?"

Suzanna grinned as she nodded. "Why don't you just say hello? I know my sister. She'll be fine if you make the first move. In fact, you'll probably have to."

"I can't. That's just not me." Even Carly thought it was weird that she was the perfect image of confidence in her job but couldn't manage to make eye contact with a woman who interested her.

"Then it'll never get done." Suzanna shook her head. "Do I have to do everything for you two?"

"Yes. Please. Find me a woman, do the painful part of dating and getting to know her, and then let me slip in when it's all cozy and comfortable."

"Painful?" Suzanna raised her eyebrows. "Are you kidding me? Getting to know someone is the absolute best part of falling in love." She took her hand. "Come on. Let's get this over with."

Falling in love? She let her hand slip from Suzanna's. "No. I can't. Not yet." She needed a minute to calm herself—to get herself together—or she'd be babbling like an idiot.

Suzanna tilted her head and smiled. "Okay, but if you don't make a move, I'm going to make it for you."

She nodded. "Got it." She watched Suzanna weave through several people until she met Wynn halfway across the room. They exchanged a few words, and Wynn smiled broadly. Such a beautiful smile. She'd be an idiot to let this opportunity go. She kept her eyes glued to them as they conversed, and then Wynn glanced her way and smiled again. A tingle shot through her, and she sucked in a deep breath. It was now or never.

Wynn glanced at the bar. A drink would calm her anxiety—help her loosen up. She'd just taken a few steps in that direction when Suzanna came toward her from across the room. "Wow." She stood back and surveyed her. "Dapper at its finest, as always."

"I learned from the best." She motioned to Jordan, who stood across the room at the bar dressed in a blue pinstripe suit with a powder-blue button-down. She seemed to be organizing something.

"Are you kidding me? She's got nothing on you." Suzanna grazed her fingers across the collar of Wynn's jacket. "That's business, but you've got a natural soft butch style going on here." She moved closer and whispered, "Women love that." She smiled and smoothed the lapel.

"It's not like I have a choice." She pointed to her boobs, which were fairly ample. Even a good sports bra couldn't keep them confined.

Suzanna laughed and bounced her eyebrows. "I bet they love those too."

Confidence shot through her. Suzanna always knew the right thing to say when Wynn was feeling insecure. Wynn wasn't sure if it was true. Growing up in Jordan's shadow was a challenge, and Wynn strived to be just as successful, but Jordan never made her feel like she could do anything as good as she could.

"I'll be right back." Suzanna glanced over her shoulder at one of the guests. "Why don't you go talk to Carly for a bit?"

She caught a glimpse of Carly across the room, who wore a black, form-fitting, sleeveless lace dress that captured Wynn's attention immediately. The contrasting, creamy skin of her shoulders made her want to trail her fingers along them—feel their graceful power under her lips. No matter what day it was, and apparently even in her dreams, Carly still managed to take her breath away. Carly glanced her way and smiled. Butterflies swarmed in Wynn's stomach when Carly headed in her direction, and she took in a breath to settle her nerves. Carly was the only woman who could do that to her. She'd dated plenty of women and enjoyed them all, but Carly made her feel all sorts of crazy inside.

"Don't you look dashing tonight." The smile on Carly's face was magnetic.

The heat rose in her cheeks. Her sister hadn't been lying after all. "Thanks. You look pretty magnificent yourself." And she did. Carly could be wearing a whiskey barrel, and that wouldn't change.

Suzanna reappeared between them. "If I didn't know better, I would've thought the two of you got dressed in the same house." Their colors complemented each other perfectly. "I've got an idea. Why don't you take a walk together on the pier?" She ushered them toward the door. "Hurry, before Jordan starts barking out orders."

Wynn's moment of hesitation was just a smidge too long, because Jordan spotted her and came rushing over. "Hey. You're late."

"Sorry. Long day at work."

"I was just sending Wynn and Carly out on the pier for a walk." Suzanna continued to nudge them toward the door. "Carly has been working so hard, I think she needs a break."

"Oh. I could use a break." Jordan held out her hand. "Hi. Remember me? Jordan Jamison, like the whiskey, but full-bodied and smoother." She finished her quip with a wink.

Ugh. The ridiculous line.

"How could I forget?" The sexy lilt in Carly's voice let Wynn know she didn't stand a chance against her sister. She should've used the line but couldn't bring herself to be so cheesy.

Jordan glanced at Wynn and shoved a handful of envelopes into her hands. "Can you take care of collecting the rest of the pledge cards for me?"

"Sure." She took the envelopes and watched Jordan whisk Carly outside to the patio and then to the gate that led to the pier.

Suzanna widened her eyes. "Why the hell did you let her do that?"

"I think Jordan likes her, and Carly seemed okay with it. Besides, you saw what happened. I didn't *let* her do anything." Was she really allowing this to take place again? Even in her dreams? She watched the two of them walk from the patio to the pier, catching a shrug from Carly as she glanced over her shoulder at her.

"God, you are so blind. I talked you up to Carly all night, and you totally blew it."

"I guess I did." She'd lost her chance with Carly as soon as Jordan approached, just like she had in reality. Tonight she was supposed to receive the kiss they'd shared—the one Carly remembered, the one Jordan was going to enjoy instead of her. This dream was rapidly turning into a miserable nightmare she couldn't wait to wake up from. She shoved the envelopes into her jacket pocket and headed to the bar. This night wasn't going to turn out any better than it had the last time.

❖

Carly checked her phone for text messages as she sat in the backseat of the Uber taking her home. She had a message from Suzanna thanking her for showing up and helping as usual, but nothing else.

"Can you turn on the radio?" The Toyota Prius was abnormally quiet tonight, and she needed some music or something to keep her mind busy.

Her phone chimed, and she saw a text from Jordan. She hadn't given Jordan her number, so Suzanna must have provided it. Always the matchmaker. Only Carly wasn't sure she was okay with it this time.

I'm so glad we got to spend some time together tonight.

Me too. It was nice.

Can I see you again? I mean, just you and I, alone, on a real date?

I think I'd like that. She didn't want to sound too eager. She was still working through her feelings about the whole evening… and Wynn.

Tomorrow night, perhaps?

Jordan certainly moved quickly. Carly took in a deep breath and contemplated her answer.

Can I check my schedule and get back to you tomorrow?

Absolutely. I'll be waiting.

Carly let the exchange end there. The walk on the pier with Jordan had lasted longer than she'd expected. The conversation was excellent and unexpectedly engaging. Spending time with Jordan this evening hadn't been on her radar. She'd helped out at many of the previous events she'd held because Suzanna was always short-handed. Jordan never gave her the impression she was interested in anything more than her assistance at any of them.

But on their walk tonight Jordan had made it perfectly clear that she wanted to see her again, yet technically she hadn't asked, and Carly had been noncommittal. When she'd arrived back at the restaurant from their walk, Carly had fully intended to spend more time with Wynn and continue their conversation from earlier, but Wynn had left without a word. Not even Suzanna knew where she'd gone. She felt bad about being pulled away from Wynn so quickly—without having the opportunity to tell her how much she'd enjoyed their conversation.

Jordan had offered to take her home, but she was confused enough about the events of the evening and needed time to figure out her feelings. Wynn had her interest, but Jordan had taken the first step and made her intentions known. It was as though the decision had been made for her.

Chapter Nine

Wynn opened her eyes. The glaring light from the window made her head thump harder. She cleared the glue from her eyes, sat up, and then sank back into her pillow. Her head was in no way ready for such quick moves this morning. Wynn had no idea how she'd gotten home the night before. Last she remembered she was talking to the bartender, but that was in the dream. Wasn't it? It had to be. A crazy fucking dream. She had a huge blank spot in her memory from last night.

She ran her hand across the sheet covering the other side of the bed. Alone again. She totally deserved it after losing her nerve with Carly last night. Wait, was it last night or was it last year? She didn't know—she was so confused right now. Either way, she'd chickened out. It didn't really matter which time. The alcohol had just made everything worse, and her thoughts were all blurred together. Everything that had happened a year ago had happened again last night. Was it a dream—could it have been? It was so real, she couldn't imagine it was, but it had to be. She opened her eyes and peered through the small slits at the T-shirt she was wearing, lime-green again.

"Shadow?" Her voice was low and gravelly. What had she drunk last night? Better question would be what hadn't she drunk? Once Carly had gone out on the pier with Jordan, Wynn had hit the bar and taken a shot of whatever the bartender offered. When they hadn't come back right away, she'd left the restaurant and stopped at the first bar she came across. The bartender was cute, with dark hair and eyes, and she poured a generous drink. Under normal circumstances, that would be the perfect combination, but not last night. Her thoughts were stuck on Carly.

She felt soft licks on her foot and then heard whimpers from the side of the bed. She bolted up and sat clutching the sheet on each side of her, trying to steady herself as the room spun. Puppy Shadow climbed onto her leg. She was so sweet and tiny again. Not that she wasn't adorable at a year old, but puppies always had the cutest ears and noses. She gathered Shadow in her hands and held her in her lap. There had never been any doubt that this little one loved her.

Her phone buzzed on the nightstand, and she saw the notice of a voice-mail message from Jordan on the screen. Same shitty phone. She typed in her code and listened to the message. "Hey. I need your help at a fund-raiser tonight. Call me back." No. Absolutely not. She was even pissed at Jordan in her dreams.

She quickly typed in a message to Carly. She was the only one Wynn cared about hearing from right now.

Thanks for taking me home last night. I'm a little foggy about what happened.

I think this text might be meant for someone else.

Carly had definitely kissed her back. Was she regretting it? *Sorry, I thought it was something you wanted. I overstepped.*

She watched and waited as the bubbles appeared on the phone. Then they disappeared and reappeared. The words *some other lucky girl* flew through her head. Where did that come from?

Again, not me. Some other lucky girl. The words had finally appeared on the screen.

How did she know that was what Carly was going to say? She rubbed her head. What the fuck was going on? She checked her contacts, and Carly was listed in her phone as Carly Evans again.

This was some freaky sort of déjà vu. Shadow jumped to the floor as Wynn rushed through the house just as she had before, then dropped onto the couch and examined her surroundings. Things were the same, except they weren't exactly. She closed her eyes and willed the freakish dream to end, but an incredibly loud bark startled her. She opened her eyes to find the puppy version of Shadow attempting to climb onto the couch, a habit she'd never been able to break her of. She rubbed Shadow's ears before she helped her onto her lap. She'd forgotten just how little she'd been when she'd rescued her from the shelter. No way was she going back to sleep now.

"Come on, Shadow. You need to go outside." They raced across the room together, and just as before, she stepped in something wet. "Shit." She hopped on one foot to the kitchen, spun a paper towel from the holder, wet it, and cleaned the bottom of her foot. Shadow sprinted to the back door and squatted and peed again. "Oh my gosh." Why was this all happening again? She slid open the door and let her outside before she went through the same floor-cleaning routine she had yesterday.

After filling Shadow's bowl with food, she took the box of Froot Loops from the pantry, grabbed a handful and stuffed it into her mouth, chewed, swallowed, and repeated. She needed coffee. She opened the refrigerator—nothing there *but* coffee and soy milk. She wasn't going to fall for that again.

Her phone rang, and Evelyn's name appeared on the screen, so she hit the ignore button. She wasn't up for enduring the whole ordeal at work again today. She just wanted to go back to sleep and wake from this crazy dream.

The next time she woke it was past three o'clock in the afternoon. She checked her phone and found multiple texts from Jordan about the fund-raiser as well as multiple missed calls and one voice-mail message from Evelyn. She hit the play button and listened to the message. "I hope you're happy. I'm out of a job, and you've got an ass for a boss now." Evelyn's voice was loud and angry.

She immediately hit the call-back button, and Evelyn answered on the first ring. "I guess you got my message." Her voice was full of surrender now as her words whooshed softly through the phone.

"What happened?"

"Leadership wanted an immediate fix—a work-force cut. I didn't offer them that. I wouldn't."

"Who undercut you?" Someone else had done exactly what Wynn had done that day.

"Davis," Evelyn said, and Wynn could hear the ice hit against a glass as she paused. "He's cutting staff immediately, starting with me. They gave me a month's severance and escorted me to the door to make sure I don't leak the news to the rest of the employees." The sound of her swallowing came through the phone. "Made me sign a non-disclosure agreement, or they wouldn't give me severance."

"I'm sorry, Evelyn. I didn't know Davis had a proposal. I've never heard a viable idea come out of his mouth." And she *was* sorry. Her plan hadn't included firing Evelyn. She had great ideas and was well worth her salary. She was just a little too soft-hearted sometimes.

"I'll be fine." Ice clinked in the background again. "But you're going to have to deal with the fallout from the shit show Davis will create."

She wasn't worried about Davis. She'd briefly discussed her plan with him, so he must've stolen it, somehow. He was an opportunist and wouldn't have the slightest idea how to make the company profitable after the layoff. "What now?"

"Not sure what you're going to do, but I intend to find another job." The line went dead, and she stared at the blank screen. What the fuck had just happened? This certainly didn't feel like a dream anymore.

She typed in a quick message to Jordan, letting her know she'd be at the fund-raiser tonight, and then headed to the guest bathroom, took a shower, dressed in the same clothes she had in the previous dream, and headed out. She only hoped it would go better than it had the night before.

As Wynn walked out the door, she saw Mrs. P sitting on the porch drinking a glass of iced tea. What a shit she was, even in her dreams. She'd totally forgotten again to let Mrs. P know she had other plans tonight. She crossed the yard to her porch.

"I didn't see you come home."

She sat in the chair next to her. "Well, actually, I didn't go to work."

"Oh." Mrs. P pulled her eyebrows together. "Are you sick?" She poured Wynn a glass of tea.

"No. Just needed a day off. Kind of a mental-health day." She took a sip of tea and smiled as the sweet taste crossed her lips. Perfect as always.

"It's good to do that once in a while to recharge your batteries." Mrs. P sipped her tea. "I'm feeling a little weary myself."

"I hope it's nothing serious." Mrs. P looked a little flushed.

"No. Just a little dizzy from being out in the sun too long."

"Do I need to call Mr. P and have him come home?"

"No." Mrs. P shook her head. "I don't want to interrupt his night out. I'll be fine."

"Maybe you need a nap. I usually feel much better after some rest."

"Maybe so." Mrs. P took another sip of tea.

She held up her glass. "How do you make this tea so perfect every time?" She drank down the remaining tea in her glass.

"I use simple syrup instead of plain sugar." Mrs. P held her glass up in the sunlight. "Mixes better and prevents cloudiness too."

"Can you show me how to make it sometime? Maybe tomorrow night? You could come for dinner at my place."

"I'd love to."

"You can always come with me tonight." She stood. "They'll have plenty of food, and it's always the best." Jordan didn't spare any expense at her fund-raisers.

"Thank you, but I don't want to get in the middle of your fun."

"Are you kidding? You'd be better company than anyone else there."

That got a smile out of Mrs. P. "You go ahead and have a good time tonight. Maybe you'll find a pretty lady there to spend the evening with."

"I already have a pretty lady to spend time with." She took Mrs. P's hand. "She's sitting right here."

Mrs. P grinned, and her thin lips spread perfectly. "That's very sweet of you, dear, but I don't think I'm up for a party tonight." She squeezed Wynn's hand. "We'll have dinner tomorrow."

"Sounds like a plan." As Wynn stood, she heard loud voices behind her and looked over her shoulder to see her neighbor, Jack, following his wife Maria out of the house. They seemed to be having a heated argument. "I wonder what that's about?" She watched as Maria rushed to her car and got inside. "I've never seen them fight like that. Do you think I should go see if Maria's all right?"

Mrs. P nodded. "Yes. I think you should."

She crossed her driveway and was halfway across the lawn between their houses when Maria looked up. She glanced at Jack on the porch but kept moving as the window of the car whizzed down. "Are you okay?" She'd caught sight of them fighting yesterday but hadn't really paid attention.

Maria threw up her middle finger. "Fuck you. Haven't you done enough?" She threw the car into gear, backed up, and sped down the street.

"What the hell?" she said as Jack came toward her. Wynn didn't notice the logo on Jack's shirt until they were almost face-to-face. Sexton Technologies was embroidered on the left side of it, and it sunk in. He must have been one of the casualties from today's layoff. "Oh my God. You lost your job today." She hadn't looked through the list of names when she'd prepared her plan. She couldn't. That would make it personal, and it had to remain business.

"If you'd looked at my reorg proposal, nobody would've lost their job," Jack said.

"I'm so sorry. I wasn't even there today." An invalid excuse. The workforce would've been cut even if she *had* been there, just by not as many.

"Then I wouldn't go in tomorrow because you may be out of job too," he said as he walked up his driveway.

"Hey, Jack. Where's Buttercup?" He stopped, turned, and gave her a strange look. "Your chocolate lab?"

"I don't have a dog," he said, and went into his house.

She shook her head. That made sense. Shadow was still a puppy. But he did get a dog at some point, and she remembered him saying he got her at the shelter. Wynn also remembered seeing the dog there when she got Shadow. She'd chosen Shadow because she was small and trainable. Buttercup was sweet, but she was much larger, close to three years old, and hadn't been trained at all. If this crazy dream happened again tomorrow, she would make a point of going to the shelter to get Buttercup.

As Wynn sat in traffic trying to make it across the San Francisco Bay Bridge to the restaurant, she couldn't get the sadness in Jack's eyes out of her head. He was crushed at having lost his job. Once she'd seen his shirt with the Sexton Technologies logo, she'd remembered that he ran the support desk—had started around the same time she had. The team was in horrible shape when he took over, and he'd morphed it into a knowledgeable, self-sufficient, premier service desk. His reward for that was being let go. He'd improved the team so much that he'd worked himself out of a job.

She couldn't blame Maria for lashing out at her the way she did. In an instant, nothing more than calculated numbers on paper had demolished all the stability in their lives. The red and black—the tidiness of it all had a tsunami brewing in her stomach. Even though Wynn hadn't been the one to actually make it happen this time, they were still her numbers. It would've all been on her if she'd gone to work today. Before the party, she'd looked over Jack's reorganization plan, and it seemed to be sound. She didn't wonder why Evelyn hadn't presented it instead of her own. Evelyn wasn't a team player. She wanted the COO position, the salary, and all the accolades that went along with saving the company.

Now she was out of a job. Funny, Wynn had wanted it all too, but after seeing the devastation on Jack's face, none of it seemed important anymore. She would call them both tomorrow to see if she could help them in any way. Hopefully Evelyn will have calmed down, and Maria will have returned home to Jack. What a fucking mess.

Wynn pulled up to the valet, and he directed her to her usual spot in the lot. She couldn't believe he remembered her. She hadn't been to one of these things in forever—since Carly had married Jordan. But then again, it was a dream, wasn't it? She'd arrived late, but, thankfully, Jordan always held the events at the same place, or she wouldn't have made it at all.

She didn't check her reflection in the windows as she walked to the restaurant, not caring if she looked good tonight. Knowing she still had a job when others didn't was weighing heavy on her. Was this dream her conscience's way of venting? Maybe she'd been in an accident and wasn't conscious. She reached inside her sport jacket, pinched the soft area under her arm, and winced at the pain as she walked. Nope. That was definitely going to bruise.

When she went inside, Suzanna greeted her with a compliment just as she had the night before. Wynn had to admit that Suzanna was the best of them all. She never seemed to have a bad thing to say about anyone, and her patience was saintly. Growing up, she'd always been the peacemaker of the three sisters, probably why she was so good with her kids.

She glimpsed Carly across the room, dressed in a black, form-fitting, sleeveless lace dress. Carly never failed to make her heart race, but tonight Wynn was so disappointed in herself that she couldn't enjoy the feeling of exhilaration. She couldn't be happy when she knew that a plan she'd devised had shattered Jack and Maria's happiness, as well as that of hundreds of others. Carly glanced her way and smiled, and the usual swarm of butterflies danced in Wynn's stomach when Carly headed in her direction. She immediately slipped through the guests and out onto the patio for some air. She refused to subject Carly to her foul mood.

"What's going on with you tonight?" Carly's voice broke through her thoughts, and her stomach dipped.

"I had a bad day. Some things happened at work that I couldn't control." More like didn't.

"Oh? Want to tell me about it?"

"I proposed something horrible, and someone else ran with it." She shook her head. "You're going to think I'm an ass."

"Why do you say that?"

"Because *I* think I'm an ass."

"Well, then. Can you fix this horrible thing you did?" The compassion in Carly's eyes was clear.

She shook her head and sighed. "I don't know. I'm going to try, though."

"I think that's the important part, right?" The simple smile on Carly's face was magnetic.

"I guess so."

Suzanna appeared between them. "You two make quite a good-looking couple. You complement each other perfectly." She touched each of their shoulders. "The party's winding down. Why don't you take a walk on the pier together?" She looked over her shoulder. "I've got this for a bit."

Just as they walked onto the pier, she heard Jordan behind her. "Not so fast, little sister. You don't get to come in late and take off with the most beautiful woman at the party." There it was again, the charm and charisma of her older sister snatching Carly away from her once more.

Carly's cheeks reddened, and she focused her attention on Jordan. It was just as well. Wynn wasn't good company tonight. Her mind was far from romance. She had to figure out a compromise at work—how she could improve revenue without letting people go.

CHAPTER TEN

Wynn bolted up in bed and scanned the room. She looked at her chest and saw the same lime-green T-shirt as she saw the previous days. *Oh my God. Not again.*

Her phone buzzed on the nightstand, and she saw the notice for a voice-mail message from Jordan on the screen. Same shitty phone. She typed in her code and immediately began typing a message to Carly.

I feel like something weird happened between us last night.

The same answer from yesterday appeared on the screen. *I think this text might be meant for someone else.*

Carly was probably pissed, and rightly so. *Sorry about the kiss. I shouldn't have left without saying goodbye.*

She watched and waited as the bubbles appeared on the phone. *Again, not me. Some other lucky girl.* The bubbles appeared again, and then, *Maybe we can talk tonight* popped up.

What the hell? The name Carly *Evans* stared at her from the top of the screen. What had happened last night? What was happening tonight? Where was *tonight* happening?

Definitely tonight. Where is that again?

The Waterbar @ 7:00. See you there.

She listened to the message from Jordan. “Hey. I need your help at a fund-raiser tonight. Call me back.” Holy fuck, she was going crazy. Her phone rang, and Evelyn’s name appeared on the screen. It was the same day *again*. “This can’t be happening.” She threw the phone across the room, flopped back onto the bed, and squeezed her eyes shut. When she opened her eyes, nothing had changed. “What the fuck is going on?” She was in a *Groundhog Day* time loop.

She retrieved the pieces of her phone from across the room. Totally dead. She’d have to pick up another on the way to work. By that time Evelyn would be completely pissed that she hadn’t responded. Shadow met her on the floor with a piece of the phone in her mouth. “At least you know what’s going on.” Shadow climbed into her lap. “You probably need to go outside.” She stood with Shadow in her arms and started down the hallway but turned around and slipped on her flip-flops. She wasn’t taking any chances with stepping in accidents this morning.

She let Shadow outside, then made the coffee before she filled her food dish. She took the box of Froot Loops from the pantry and poured some into a bowl. That and coffee would be her only savior today. The day was destined to go downhill from here. She let Shadow back inside and then found her laptop and searched for the notes she’d written last night. Gone—everything was completely gone. She opened a new document and retyped as much as she could from memory, which was most of it, since she hadn’t gotten drunk and purged it all from her head this time. Once she finished her notes, she headed to the bathroom to shower. She felt for the light switch but caught her finger on a wire instead. She yanked her hand back when a zap of electricity shot through her. *Fuck!* She’d forgotten about the bathroom remodel. She shook her hand to relieve the pain. It was clear this crazy phenomenon wasn’t a dream.

Even though the guest shower was smaller, the warm water felt good as it washed over her. It had been forever since she’d actually enjoyed a bath. It seemed like she was always in a hurry to be somewhere. Not today. She knew precisely how the day was going to play out, and even though she couldn’t find her exact notes, she remembered how she had intended to change her plan.

After she got out of the shower, she dried off and then assessed herself in the mirror. She was thinner again. The extra weight she'd put on in the past year was another side effect of working too much. As she spread the hair product through her hair, she also noted that she didn't have even one strand of gray hair on her head. Was the job really worth it? She spritzed herself with cologne and then went to the closet and took out the black, notched-collar Express suit she'd worn the day before. If this day moved forward, she'd remember to keep this one. She tugged on the slacks and slipped on a white button-down to go under the matching jacket.

Before leaving the house, she typed the coffee order into the app on her phone and hoped she could make it in and out of the shop without Sally coffee-bombing her. She erased her name and typed in a fake one on the order just to make sure.

When she arrived at the coffee shop, she watched through the window and waited until Sally was out of sight to slip inside. It looked like she'd gone into the back room, which would give Wynn enough time to retrieve her order from the pre-order area at the counter.

"Don't think I can't see you." Sally ran from the other end of the counter as Wynn grabbed the tray of coffees and bolted to the door. "Coward," she shouted. Sally was probably right about that, but Wynn wasn't up for trying to make a bad situation with her work any longer than necessary. Having to watch what you did and said every moment was exhausting.

Wynn zipped out and to the parking lot faster than she'd run in her life. She stopped and sucked in a deep breath before she got into her Jeep. She was seriously going to have to find a new coffee shop.

The stop at the cell-phone store had gone quicker than she'd anticipated. She'd paid whatever the asking price was, even though it seemed extremely exorbitant for an older model iPhone. As soon as she got into the Jeep, she punched in April's number at Sexton Technologies and waited for her to answer.

"Miss Jamison's office."

"Hi, April. It's Wynn. Can you transfer me to Jack Spencer, please."

"Let me look him up." She heard a few clicks of a keyboard. "Hang on. I'll transfer you."

She heard a few clicks as the call transferred. The phone rang a couple of times before he answered. "Sexton Tech, Jack speaking. How can I help you?"

"Jack, this is Wynn Jamison. Evelyn Cantor wants you in her office in thirty minutes."

"Okay. Did she say why?"

"Nope. She'll explain when you get there." She didn't wait for a response and hung up. She was going to have to haul ass to get there before he did.

After seeing the Baxters to the door, Carly went to her desk and dropped into the leather chair. If only half of the couples she counseled were as proactive as Mike and Sara, she would be out of a job. She felt confident they were on the right path and would most likely have a successful marriage, as long as neither of them discounted the other's needs.

Carly pressed her fingers to her head. She'd woken suddenly this morning from a dream she couldn't recall. Something was off this morning, and she couldn't quite figure out what. Maybe it was a migraine coming on, but it didn't feel like it. She grabbed a bottle of medicine from her desk and took a pill anyway. She had a big night tonight and couldn't let a headache get in the way.

Instead of checking her schedule herself, Carly picked up the phone and dialed Stephanie's extension. "Is that it for today?"

"Yep. You had me clear your schedule this afternoon because of Suzanna's event."

"Great. My head is splitting, so I'm going to head home and lie down for a while."

"I have something for that if you need it."

"Already took something, but thanks." She hung up the phone and gathered her things. Maybe a nap would help her recall the dream. She'd been on the edge of remembering a couple of times this morning, but just couldn't bring it into focus. If nothing else, a little sleep should help relieve the headache.

It was weird. She'd been fine until she received the text message from Wynn. She hadn't seen Wynn last night and had no idea what she was talking about, but she felt like she'd lost a conversation with her somewhere. Wynn's text led her to believe she was confused as well. Her dreams had been vivid, as usual, but her memory of them was gone—completely erased. In recent years, she didn't remember as much of them as she had when she was younger, but she usually retained bits and pieces to ponder.

Today she recalled nothing except a familiar feeling about Wynn, a warmth she couldn't explain. Was it possible for them to have had the same dream? No. That was ridiculous unless she was playing a starring role in a supernatural film. She'd see Wynn tonight. Hopefully she'd elaborate on her text this morning. Odd how her stomach clenched at the thought of Wynn kissing another woman. They'd never dated or even flirted, not that she hadn't thought about it more than once. Wynn was everything she'd dreamed of in a woman but always seemed just out of reach. She'd find out tonight if Wynn's involvement with another woman had completely eliminated the possibility of having something with her.

Chapter Eleven

Wynn was prepared for George, the security guard, this morning, her badge hanging around her neck and visible. She held the badge up to the card reader by the door, the light changed from red to green, and the doors swung open. "Good morning, George."

He glanced at her badge. "Good morning, Miss Jamison." His eyesight must be perfect to read the tiny writing. "I hear it's going to be a stormy day in the office today."

"Not if I can help it."

He grinned. "That's good to hear." He sounded perky. "It'd be a shame to break up the family." He seemed sincere. "Have a nice day," he said in the exact same chipper tone he had yesterday.

She took the stairs and went straight to Evelyn's office, where she found Jack already there. He was early, of course, and both of them were confused as to why she'd asked him to meet her there.

"Where the hell have you been?" Evelyn rounded her desk and whispered, "And why the hell is Jack in my office?" She plucked one of the cups from the drink carrier.

"We have work to do before today's presentation." She offered the last cup of coffee to Jack. "Black, right?" She had no idea.

"Sweet and light," he said, looking thoroughly confused.

Evelyn reached into her drawer, took out a handful of sugar packets along with a couple of containers of creamer, and dropped them on the desk.

Wynn motioned them to the conference table in the corner of the office as she took out her laptop and several stapled bundles of paper. "Leadership is not going to go for your plan." She tossed a printed copy of Evelyn's presentation in front of each one of them. "They're going with mine." She tossed a copy of hers in front of them.

Evelyn narrowed her eyes. "You have a proposal?"

"Of course I have one. You don't listen to anyone else's ideas." Wynn hadn't been doing that herself in recent months.

"I do too. I just think mine is better." Evelyn was a total narcissist, so getting her to recognize that her plan would never happen wouldn't be easy.

"What the hell?" Jack thumbed through Wynn's presentation. "You want to cut my entire team and outsource support."

She nodded and blew out a breath. "That *was* part of my proposal." She tossed copies of Jack's improvement plan on the table. "I want to change it, and I need you both to help me fix it before we meet with leadership."

"What's this?" Evelyn picked up the stapled papers.

"It's Jack's plan. I never passed it on."

"Seriously? You arrogant—"

"I know, and I'm sorry." She turned to Evelyn. "Jack is my neighbor, and I didn't even realize it until a couple of days ago." The sight of him in the future, standing on his porch with the headphones around his neck, flashed through her head. "I'd hate for him to turn out to be a divorced, unemployed gamer in the future." She glanced back to Jack. "By the way, there's a sweet chocolate Lab at the animal shelter you need to adopt."

"Probably not. My wife's not a fan of dogs."

Buttercup's sweet face came to mind, and sadness filled her. "We'll convince her." She cleared it quickly. She'd have to deal with that detail later.

She retrieved the easel from the corner, balanced the oversized drawing pad on it, and picked up a marker. "We need to work together as a team to combine all of these ideas for a solution that leadership will accept so no one loses their job."

❖

Wynn went over the proposal in her head as they stood in the elevator waiting for the doors to open on the executive floor. It was a good plan, and no one was going to be let go, not even George, the security guard.

"Ready?" Evelyn fidgeted as the elevator doors opened.

"Ready as I'll ever be." She stepped into the hallway, and Evelyn and Jack stepped out of the elevator behind her. Evelyn had reluctantly agreed to let her run the presentation, with each of them joining to present in different areas.

"Just take a breath and follow my lead. It'll all be fine." She said the words but wasn't sure what the outcome would be. This plan was totally different from the one she'd presented last year.

After entering and exchanging niceties, Jack connected Wynn's laptop to the large HDMI TV mounted on the wall of the CEO's office.

As soon as they finished presenting, she knew upper management's reaction wouldn't be good. Straight-faced frowns had remained on their faces throughout, and she'd heard several grumbles as well.

The CEO cleared his throat. "I asked for immediate money-saving actions. You haven't given me anything I can use."

"I'm aware we've made no staffing cuts, but I think we can turn this place around within the next year without taking such drastic measures."

"I don't agree. We should have a workforce reduction." His voice was firm.

"You can't just let people go." Her stomach clenched, and the desperation in her voice escaped involuntarily. "You'll lose too much internal knowledge."

"I can and I will." He pulled his brows together. "I thought we were on the same page here." He tossed the paper packet to the desk. "Apparently you misunderstood me."

"No. I didn't. I just realized the people that work here aren't machines. They have families and responsibilities. I guess that's where we're different." She surprised herself. She'd been just like him the last time this happened.

His eyebrows flew up. "Sounds like we're moving in different directions. I'm sure you can find employment elsewhere." He pointed at Evelyn and Jack. "As can the two of you."

"Are you serious? We're all you've got to make this work."

He raised an eyebrow before narrowing his eyes. "I want you out by close of business today. Do I need to call security?"

"No. I'll go, but please don't penalize Evelyn and Jack for my bad judgement."

Evelyn put her hand up. "I'll be out in an hour." She turned and walked to the door, and she and Jack followed.

When she reached the door, she spun back around. "Short-sighted…" She shook her head, disgusted with leadership as well as herself. She'd just gotten a glimpse of what a heartless bitch she'd turned into over the past year.

They were silent until the elevator doors closed.

"I'm sorry, Jack. If they're looking to cut, your team is getting outsourced first. Service-desk contracts are the easiest to engage and the most available. PC support will be next, and developers after that." She leaned against the elevator wall. "It'll take them a few months to find the right company to handle it, but it *will* happen." She remembered the process well.

"I need this job." Jack raked his fingers through his hair.

"I know. I'll do everything I can to help you find another one."

They stepped off the elevator and went to Evelyn's office, where she immediately took her purse from the desk drawer, rummaged through its contents, and slid a cigarette package out.

Jack eyed her. "You can't smoke in here."

"The hell I can't. I can do anything I want now. I don't work here anymore and don't really give a shit." The tip of the cigarette brightened as she lit it, took a drag, and blew the smoke from her lungs slowly.

"That's going to kill you, you know."

"I suppose you've seen that in my future as well?" Evelyn held her elbow in the palm of her other hand as she let her arm rest across her waist.

"Maybe." Wynn took the pack of cigarettes and dropped them into the trash can. Evelyn hadn't seen it, but her action might urge Evelyn to stop if she thought she had.

Evelyn held the cigarette in front of her eyes and then pulled a small, round, trinket dish from her desk drawer and snubbed it out. She appeared to smoke in her office often.

"I'm sorry, but I have to go. I need to figure this out." Davis was up next and would present her original plan, and everything that happened the year before would happen again, with the addition of herself, Evelyn, and eventually Jack losing their jobs. Now she just wanted to start this day over again, but she still had a party to attend tonight. The woman of her dreams would be there.

Wynn got home, went to the mailbox to get her mail, and just as she turned to go inside, here came Mrs. P right on cue. Just like yesterday and every Thursday since they'd started their weekly ritual. "You're home early."

She really *was* living the day over again. She shook her head, still trying to make sense of it all. "I got fired today." Losing her job was new, though.

Mrs. P motioned her over. "Come have some tea with me, and tell me what happened." She took her hand and tugged her toward her porch. Her frail hand felt like butter in her own.

She trudged behind her like a child being punished at recess and dropped into the chair. "I don't know exactly how it happened. I didn't do anything differently." She sighed. "That's not completely true. I presented a good plan, but I argued with someone when I should've kept my mouth shut." She had also changed the proposal, but apparently not enough to get buy-in from leadership.

"Some people aren't good at receiving feedback." Mrs. P pointed to the withering lemon tree in the yard. "Mr. P loves that tree, but he has his own method of fertilizing."

"It looks sick."

"It's not going to survive the summer."

"Is that number three?"

Mrs. P nodded as she poured her a glass of tea. "He'll plant number four and do the same thing next year."

They both laughed.

"But you're not kicking him out for that."

She shook her head. "If they didn't know what a treasure you are, they don't deserve you anyway." Mrs. P patted her hand. "Maybe instead of you going out, I should fix you dinner tonight. Maybe some pasta. I know how you love it." Mrs. P was awesome. She knew just how to make her feel better.

Her stomach sank. "I'm so sorry. I'm afraid I have a fund-raiser tonight."

The rest of the conversation went exactly as it had the previous day. She laughed at Mrs. P's comments about her love life, but Wynn didn't pour herself a second glass of tea this time because she didn't have as much time to chat. She needed to get inside, feed Shadow, dress, and arrive at the fund-raiser earlier tonight. Speeding through the conversation was difficult. Each time she tried to end the exchange, Mrs. P would ask another question.

Shouting from Jack and Maria's porch caught her attention. She watched as Maria rushed to her car, but Wynn didn't approach her this time. Having Maria curse at her would only make her day worse. After Maria sped off, she glanced at Jack on the porch, and he shrugged. Her stomach dropped. She couldn't help but feel bad for the guy. She'd hoped the plan they'd devised today would prevent that, but it had only gotten them all fired. If this crazy loop didn't end, she'd get up early tomorrow and figure out something new to save all their jobs, or at least Jack's. This situation had become so much more personal than business had ever been to her before.

Chapter Twelve

Earlier, when Carly woke from her nap, she'd glanced at the clock and found she'd slept longer than she'd anticipated. The throbbing in her head had stopped, but she'd had to race to change and make herself presentable for tonight. Her drive home had been filled with thoughts of Wynn, and she'd crawled into bed fully clothed.

She hoped but wasn't sure whether Wynn would be here to help tonight. The text she'd received from her this morning had been odd, and whatever had possessed Carly to respond so boldly was even odder. It wasn't as though they'd dated or even seen each other outside of Suzanna's events. *Lucky* would be the word she'd use to describe any woman Wynn chose to escort to the fund-raiser, or any other event for that matter. Carly was crossing her fingers that Wynn would come alone. She could definitely envision worse things in life than being romanced by Wynn Jamison.

Her stomach fluttered as she saw her enter the restaurant. She seemed to scan the crowd to locate Suzanna before she moved around several people to get to her. She was dressed impeccably, as always, and Carly couldn't stop the tingling heat that rose on the back of her neck. What was she thinking? Wynn was so far out of her league, she'd never be interested in her, but she wouldn't know that for a fact until she put herself out there. She took in a deep breath, calmed her nerves, and walked toward them.

"Hey. I'm so glad you made it." She touched Wynn's arm as she spoke over her shoulder.

Wynn turned slowly and met her gaze. "I wouldn't have missed seeing you for the world."

The flutter in her stomach paled in comparison to the rapid beat of her heart pounding in her chest. Wynn's electric-blue eyes seemed to become bluer, and every word Carly had planned to say stuck in her throat.

Suzanna snapped her fingers between the two of them. "It's about time this happened, but can you two put a hold on it until later? We need to get back to the checklist."

Carly smiled shyly. "Of course." She focused on the checklist in Suzanna's hands as Wynn stood by and helped her go through it item by item. Her mind flipped to autopilot as her system went into overdrive, and she tried to downshift it into neutral. Suddenly everything about Wynn was different. Super-sensual vibrations seemed to be bouncing back and forth between them. Maybe it was just her. She glanced at Wynn and could see by the darkness in her eyes that it wasn't. Why had this never happened before?

"Tables set, check. Food ready, check. Bar stocked…" Suzanna glanced up at Wynn. "Do we have a bottle of Louis XIII?" Suzanna swiped her hand in the air between them. "Let's just get through this, and then you two can make eyes at each other for the rest of the night."

"I'm sorry. What?" Wynn blinked and veered her gaze to Suzanna.

"Louis XIII? Do we have a bottle?"

"I don't know. Let's find out." They all went to the bar. "Is there a bottle of Louis XIII cognac back there?"

The bartender shook her head. "That's not something we usually carry."

"It should've been special-ordered for this event." Suzanna flipped through her checklist.

The bartender opened a few locked cabinets under the bar, then shook her head again. "I don't see one."

Suzanna flattened her lips. "Jordan is not going to be happy. She has a large donor who drinks only that particular kind of cognac."

"It must be a huge donation. That stuff is high-dollar." She'd only had a taste once before. They'd be lucky to find it with such short notice.

"Trust me, it is, and happy donors give more money."

"Let me see what I can do." Wynn took out her phone, chose one of her contacts, and hit the speaker button. "Hey, Jean. Do you have a bottle of Louis XIII you can give me at a good price?"

"Is that all you call me for now? A good deal?" The voice that came through the speaker was low and sexy.

Wynn glanced at Suzanna and Carly before she took the call off speaker. "I'm sorry. I've been busy. This is important." She shifted uneasily and lowered her voice. "I'll be happy to pay whatever you want. You know I'm good for it."

Carly wondered if they were talking about money or another more personal type of payment as she watched Wynn quirk her lip into a half-smile. When Wynn caught her staring, she turned to the bar and collected a few stray glasses onto a tray.

"Deal." Wynn ended the call and turned to Suzanna. "It'll be here in ten minutes."

Carly was impressed. "Seems you have connections."

"I know a few people here and there."

"Someone you see frequently?" She had to ask.

"I'd say more occasionally." She reached for the tray of dirty glasses Carly had gathered. "Let me get those." She spun around, ran into someone, and the trays fell to the floor. "Fuck," Wynn said as she picked them up and placed them back on the bar.

"What's the matter with you?" Suzanna asked.

Carly waited for her response, curious to know if her questions had sent her into a tizzy or if she'd done something besides the steamy eye contact to make it happen.

"Nothing." Wynn shook her head. "I just had a tough day at work."

"Anything you want to talk about? I'm good at listening, you know." She could say that without any doubt.

Immediately, Suzanna had a hand on each of them and was urging them toward the patio doors. "Why don't you two go out on the pier and take a break? As long as the booze is on its way, I've got this for now."

Neither of them protested, and they walked through the doors to the patio. Wynn held the decorative, half-gate open and let Carly lead her to the edge of the pier, where they stopped at the railing and stared at the ocean. The sun was just beginning to set, creating a fantastic color show filled with reds, purples, and oranges as the light bounced off the water. She took in the subtle scent of Wynn's cologne wafting toward her, carried by the slightest of breezes. It was the perfect night, and if Carly didn't know better, she'd have thought it was created just for the two of them.

"Tell me about your day." Wynn seemed caught up in her own thoughts as Carly moved closer and waited for her to talk.

"I made a move at work today, and I'm not sure it was the right one."

"It can't be that bad."

"It is, and I'm afraid you might not like me if you knew the damage I've done." Silence fell upon them as Wynn hesitated, seeming to find her words. "I made a decision today that negatively affected a lot of lives, including my own."

"Was that the only option?"

"I thought so, but now I'm not so sure."

"I guess there's no way to undo it, huh?"

Wynn shook her head. "No. I don't think so."

"So how about moving forward? Can you take this as a lesson learned?" The anguish in Wynn's eyes was clear, and Carly wasn't sure how to make this better for her, but she wanted to make whatever pain Wynn was feeling go away.

"Definitely a hard lesson learned." Wynn shook her head and let it hang as she stared at her fingers wrapped around the railing.

She couldn't stand seeing Wynn this way. She reached over, put her fingers under her chin, and lifted her face to gain eye contact. "This right here tells me you have a good heart." She brushed Wynn's cheek with her thumb before she took her face into her hands and kissed her softly, sweetly, then pulled back, looked into her eyes, and went back for more. The irresistible urge to hold Wynn closer had come out of nowhere. Carly couldn't have stopped herself if she'd been tethered to the pier by both hands, and honestly, she didn't want to try. Immersing herself in Wynn's warmth felt wonderful as her temperature soared. She slid her hands from Wynn's face to her shoulders, then to her waist, where she curled her fingers into the shirt inside her jacket and urged Wynn closer.

Every nerve ending fired as Carly deepened the kiss, her tongue sliding effortlessly into Wynn's mouth, being accepted, joined with Wynn's in a slow, sweet dance. She broke away and stared into Wynn's eyes. She hadn't planned that, hadn't even expected it. Yet kissing Wynn felt like the most natural thing in the world right now, like something she'd been searching for since the day she hit adolescence. Warm, sweet, and soft, their kiss held an underlying passion that promised so much more. If they hadn't been standing on the pier, she'd have her hands inside that dapper button-down shirt, touching a whole lot more.

A voice came through the hazy fog into which Carly had been transported. They both glanced at the patio to see Jordan rushing their way, shouting for help inside. More guests were arriving. She swallowed hard, looked up at Wynn, and took a deep breath before she rushed past Jordan and inside the restaurant. That kiss was a game-changer.

Jordan smiled widely at Carly as she rushed by her into the restaurant. "What's going on with her?" Jordan asked.

"Just taking a break."

Jordan raised an eyebrow. "Is that all?"

"That's all." She wasn't one to kiss and tell. In Wynn's younger days, Jordan had embarrassed her more than once when she'd found out she was interested in someone. As she'd grown older, she hadn't changed in that regard. Even though Jordan was pushing forty she'd held onto quite a bit of immaturity. Her phone chimed, and she saw Jean's name on the screen.

I'm at the bar with your booze. Buy me a drink?

I'll be right there.

"Your bottle of Louis XIII is here."

"You're amazing, sis. You know that?" Jordan grinned and put her arm around her shoulder. "Not as amazing as me, of course, but a close second."

She paced ahead quickly. "Right." Always a close second. What would it be like to have that kind of confidence and not let it hurt when rejection crushed her ego? She'd never been able to overcome that, which was why she didn't go out of her comfort zone much.

Jean was sitting at the end of the bar sipping on an old-fashioned when Wynn got there. "So how about we start that payback now." She threaded the lapel of Wynn's jacket between her fingers and let them slide along it before she motioned to the bar stool next to her. "Sit with me."

She took a half-seat on the stool, keeping one foot on the floor. "I can't tonight, but you know I'm good for it." She hadn't expected Jean to bring the bottle herself, but it made sense, considering the four-digit cost. She glanced over her shoulder and saw Carly watching them. Not the way she'd planned for this night to play out. She seemed to have created a huge pile of awkward for herself.

Jean took in a deep breath. "You'd better be extra good for this deal, love."

She quirked her lip into a partial smile. "Have I ever disappointed?" Sex with Jean was always good, but there was nothing more between them…until that night—the night that kept repeating. Wynn had lost her chance with Carly, and Jean had been there. The rebound romance hadn't lasted long. It was a short-lived affair that consisted of late-night sex without emotion or communication. She'd handled the whole situation badly, and Jean had deserved none of the fallout from Carly's rejection of Wynn.

"I can't say that you have." She gave her a soft smile. "Pity we can't do something tonight."

"Sometime next week?" She took a gulp of Jean's drink, trying to drain the glass faster and get her out of there. If her life started from this point on again, whether things turned out differently with Carly or not, nothing more would ever happen between her and Jean except the friendship they'd managed to maintain over the years. She wouldn't destroy that again.

"Sure." Jean stood. "This one's on you." She kissed Wynn on the cheek before she left.

When she glanced over her shoulder again, she saw Carly deep in conversation with Jordan. She couldn't stop her eyes from drifting her way. She studied her profile. Small nose, full lips, perfect ears. Long, dark hair with a swatch pinned back out of her eyes. She drank the rest of the old-fashioned and ordered another. She'd lost Carly again.

As Carly glanced across the car at Jordan, she wondered how she'd gotten into this situation. She'd fully intended to call an Uber, as she usually did after events where she'd been drinking. She'd had the Uber app open on her phone and was in the process of ordering the ride when Jordan had snatched the phone out of her hand and said she'd take her home. At first she tried to take her phone from Jordan and continue ordering the ride, but Jordan had laughed as she handed it back and whispered in her ear that she would be much more entertaining than an Uber driver. Jordan oozed confidence, which made her so much hotter for some reason. Possibly because in all of Carly's relationships she'd been the one to manage everything.

Although her conversation with Jordan had been enjoyable, Carly had no plans to invite her into her home—or into her bed. Jordan was probably expecting an invitation, but Carly was cautious about letting women into her life. After the one experience that had left her feeling empty inside, she never let anyone into her bed on the first date, and this wasn't anything close to that. Not that she expected to be wined and dined, but getting to know someone in a crowd of people Jordan was trying to impress wasn't her idea of perfect. Besides, Jordan hadn't been the one she'd been exchanging glances with all night. That was Wynn. *Her sister.* She'd gotten herself into something much more complicated than she'd intended.

When they pulled up in front of Carly's apartment building, she clutched the door handle and tugged on it.

"Hang on. I've got it." Jordan killed the engine, jumped out, rounded the car, and opened the door for her. "I'll walk you up."

It was nice to be treated well, but not being given the choice of walking to her door alone both flattered and bothered her.

"Thank you for tonight." Jordan smiled. "You're always there to help at these events, and I can't tell you how much I appreciate that."

"You're welcome." She didn't do it for Jordan. She did it for Suzanna.

"Besides that, I feel fortunate that I've gotten to know you better tonight." Jordan reached up and brushed a stray strand of hair from Carly's face before she leaned closer. "Maybe I can come up and we can do more of that."

Jesus. After a total scattered time of maybe an hour of small talk, Jordan was going to kiss her. She wasn't *that* hot. Carly turned her head slightly and felt Jordan's soft lips on her cheek, then the chuckle from Jordan's mouth against her skin.

"Can I see you again?" Jordan asked softly as she backed up. Apparently she'd received the message but wasn't willing to admit defeat.

She stared into Jordan's ice-blue eyes and was so entranced she couldn't refuse. "Sure."

Jordan smiled. "Okay, then. I'll call you." She turned slowly, her eyes never losing contact with Carly's before she walked to her car. She'd clearly expected to stay over tonight, but Carly wasn't about to sleep with one Jamison sister when she'd kissed another the same night.

After she entered her house, Carly went straight to the bedroom, tossed her clutch onto the bed, and unzipped her dress. The night hadn't turned out at all like she'd expected. She'd fully intended to spend more time with Wynn, but her sister had whisked her away. They'd had a fun conversation as they walked along the pier, and she'd been surprised when Jordan slipped her hand into her own. Carly's mind had been in complete chaos at that moment, not knowing what to do or even what she wanted. Jordan was definitely the type of woman she'd like to date, but, then again, so was Wynn. Carly wasn't inexperienced with women. She'd dated a few, but never in her life had she been in this position. She'd never had to choose between two women, especially from the same family.

When Carly had gone back inside, she'd searched the restaurant for Wynn. She wanted to talk to her and possibly explore the kiss they'd shared, but she was gone. Suzanna had told her Wynn had left soon after she'd gone outside with Jordan. She'd also told her to think carefully about which sister she wanted to become involved with, because she wasn't above severing their friendship if she fucked them both. Carly would never do that. So many stories of messed-up relationships flashed through her head. One of the points she stressed more than once to some of her clients was that you weren't invested if you were thinking about someone else while you were kissing another. Carly was clearly thinking about Wynn. She'd had a great time with Jordan but couldn't get the kiss with Wynn out of her head. Now she was reevaluating that advice because she honestly didn't think she'd been invested in either one of these women until tonight.

Jordan was smooth and confident, the kind of woman she wanted to date—a partner who would take responsibility for her life. The sophisticated aura she exuded was hot as fuck. Wynn, on the other hand, was just as hot physically, but she seemed nervous and self-conscious, traits Carly saw all too often in herself. Her shy demeanor only drew Carly in, making her want to find a tiny crevice to slip through and learn more about her. She truly wanted to get to know Wynn better, but Wynn had left without even a good-bye. Was a slight bit of courtesy too much to ask? Maybe so, considering the circumstances. Perhaps the feelings were one-sided, and she'd read too much into the kiss.

Her stomach bounced when she heard the text message chime. She opened her clutch and took out her phone. The message was from Jordan.

I had a great time getting to know you tonight.

My thoughts exactly.

Can we continue tomorrow night, perhaps?

She contemplated a date with Jordan Jamison, tried to talk herself out of it, but totally failed. *I'd love to.*

I'll pick you up at 8.

Looking forward to it.

She tossed her phone onto the bed. *Looking forward to it.* What the hell kind of answer was that? Couldn't she be a little more personal? Sexy, even? Of course not. Jesus. She was so inexperienced at being cool.

Chapter Thirteen

Wynn had been awake for hours when her phone buzzed on the nightstand, and she saw the notice of a voicemail message from Jordan on the screen. The sunrise had been spectacular this morning. She'd watched it through her bedroom window, enjoying the beautiful burnt orange and red colors. If the same day was beginning again, she intended to enjoy the little things.

She started typing a message to Carly, then hit the back button and erased it. It was now fully apparent she wasn't moving on from this day until she fixed a few things. To do that, she needed to keep her mind clear. She dropped her phone onto the nightstand and whistled for Shadow, who didn't answer, as usual. She went into the living room and scooped her out of her bed, totally sleepy-eyed, and carried her back to bed with her.

"You and I have to make a plan." She stared into bleary black eyes. "As soon as the shelter opens we're going to get Buttercup." Shadow's ears perked up. "You remember her." Shadow licked at her nose, and she chuckled as she got out of bed. "Come on. Let's go outside, and then I'll get you some food."

Her phone chimed with a message from Evelyn, but she ignored it. She would recreate and email Evelyn the proposal from yesterday with a few tweaks. The changes probably wouldn't make a difference, though. Leadership wanted much more than she'd thought, and she wasn't up to having her confidence crushed two days in a row. Today was going to be a day about saving Buttercup from however many more months in the shelter. At least that would give her some feeling of worth. She remembered the beautiful chocolate Lab from the shelter when she picked up Shadow. Wynn had been looking for a younger dog she could train, so she'd adopted Shadow, who was still a puppy.

She also remembered Jack saying yesterday that he'd adopted Buttercup from the shelter six months ago. Wait. No. That wasn't yesterday. That was next year. Her life was getting so complicated, and it was all blurring together. Jack didn't have Buttercup yet, because he'd adopted her in the future, one where Maria had left him sometime during the year before, which would mean Buttercup had stayed in the shelter for an additional six months after Wynn had adopted Shadow.

She shook her head. It was all so confusing. She felt like she was living out someone's bad idea of a screenplay. At least she had some control of the dialogue.

❖

Wynn decided to take Shadow with her to the shelter, probably not the wisest decision, considering she didn't have a cover for the backseat of her Jeep or barrier to keep her from getting into trouble. A wire crate would be ideal, but she'd decided to let Shadow have her freedom and hadn't bought one for the house. She was seriously rethinking that decision as she heard but couldn't see Shadow exploring the floorboard behind her. It was all new to Shadow because Wynn hadn't taken her many places other than her parents' house yet.

When they arrived at the shelter and she turned off the engine, Shadow immediately launched from the backseat onto the console between the front seats. She was eager to get out, but once they neared the door to the building, she seemed frightened to go inside. Wynn picked her up, held her closely, and rubbed her ear. "It's gonna be fine. We're going to get your buddy."

She walked straight to the girl she saw working behind the counter, who seemed familiar, even if it had been a year since she'd been there.

The girl looked up at her and smiled. "Hey. It's good to see you again. Are you and Shadow doing okay?" She must have sensed Wynn's confusion. "I mean, you haven't called."

Damn it. She wished she remembered names and faces better. "Sorry. I've just been busy." She returned her smile. "I saw a dog here last week when I adopted Shadow. I think her name was Buttercup."

"Oh, yeah. She's the sweetest girl."

"Is she still here?"

She nodded. "Yep. We keep her in one of the viewable slots in the visiting area. She's had a tough life in a puppy mill and deserves a good home." The girl led her to the viewing area. "Everyone wants puppies, but no one wants the mom."

Her stomached dropped. "No one told me any of that when I was here before." It hadn't dawned on her that she was Shadow's mom. No wonder they loved each other so much. "I didn't put the two together since Buttercup is a chocolate Lab and Shadow is a black one."

"Most people don't. Chocolate is a recessive gene. You can't get black puppies from two chocolate parents. Shadow's dad must have been black."

When Buttercup came into view, Shadow immediately started squirming to get out of Wynn's arms. "Hang on." She set her on the floor, and the two dogs scratched at the glass between them. "Can you bring her out?"

"Sure. We'll need to do it in here, though." The girl led her into a visitation room. "I'll be right back."

When the door opened again, Buttercup bounded in, nails slipping and clicking on the tile floor. She immediately went to Shadow and sniffed every part of her. Thankfully all mothers didn't do that. It seemed a little—no, a lot, invasive. Wynn chuckled at the way they danced around each other and how Shadow grabbed at Buttercup's snout with her front paws. They were adorable together.

Shadow followed Buttercup as she searched the room, appearing to look for more puppies. That pulled at Wynn's heart, but Buttercup soon turned around and sniffed at Shadow again. Tails were wagging like windmills, and Buttercup let out a yip as Shadow slipped in and out of her legs. She seemed elated to see her baby. That sealed the deal. No way Wynn wasn't going home without Shadow's mom.

"I want to adopt her." She watched the girl's face change. "Is that okay? I can adopt two dogs, right?"

"Absolutely." The girl chuckled. "It's just unusual for someone who hasn't had pets before." She'd forgotten she'd told her that. "I'm still available to help out if you need advice or hands-on assistance." She nervously bit her lower lip.

Now Carly remembered why she was so familiar. She'd had pets growing up but had never really cared for one herself. She'd been ridiculously nervous about the whole thing. This girl had given Wynn her phone number, and Wynn had indeed called her for help. That had turned into a whole lot more than just puppy help but hadn't lasted more than a few months. What an ass she was for not even remembering her name. Note to self…do not call her no matter how lonely you are.

The adoption process went even faster this time, since Wynn had been vetted the week before, when she'd adopted Shadow. They even gave her a bag of Buttercup's favorite food to take home.

Wynn put the dogs in the back, and the ride home was uneventful. They'd been quiet, so she'd thought they were sleeping. But when she opened the back door of the Jeep, dog food spilled from the seat to the ground. Both Buttercup and Shadow were chowing down like they hadn't eaten in weeks.

"What the hell?" Two guilty puppy-dog faces looked up at her like they had no idea who had created this monstrous mess. It would've been the perfect Christmas-card picture if she hadn't been so pissed. "Everybody out. Right now."

Uneaten chunks of dog food spilled from Buttercup's mouth as she slinked out of the Jeep onto the driveway and sat perfectly still, cowering like Wynn was going to hit her.

She sighed and dropped to her knees. "It's okay, baby. You must've been hungry." She scratched her neck and kissed the top of her head. Buttercup's ears perked up, and she gave Wynn a sloppy kiss on the cheek. She swept what food was left in the back of the Jeep onto the driveway, deciding to leave it for the birds. "Okay. Let's go inside, girls."

After racing back and forth through the house, exploring it thoroughly, Buttercup finally circled several times on the pallet Wynn made for her and fell asleep. Shadow was propped up against her in the most adorable position. She grabbed her cell phone and snapped a photo. This *would* be her Christmas-card picture. How could she not love these two babies? She raked her fingers through her hair and got real with herself. It wasn't about loving them. It was about handling their energy and destruction without killing them both.

After taking a nap, Wynn opened the front door to see if Jack was home. She spotted him sitting on his porch drinking a beer. It was past the time for the destruction at Sexton Technologies to have occurred, and apparently Maria had already given him an earful and left.

"Come on, girls. Let's go meet Jack." Both dogs sprang up and ran to her. They followed her across the yard to Jack's porch, where each of them found a place near Jack's feet and immediately went back to sleep. So much for her being the favorite.

"Hey. I need a favor."

"Why not? I've got nothing better to do. I adopted another dog today, Shadow's mom, and I need you to watch them. I have a thing tonight, and I don't think I can leave them at home alone." She watched them sleeping at Jack's feet, amazed at how harmless they seemed now. "They've been pretty rambunctious since I brought them home." Destructive was a more accurate word.

"I don't like dogs."

"Why not?"

"Too hairy, and they slobber."

"Seriously? You're going to use that as a valid reason?" He was using his bad mood like a four-year-old, disagreeing with everything.

He pulled his eyebrows together. "You know about the plan to cut people at work, don't you?"

"I do."

"I suppose you get to keep your job."

"Nope. I'm on the list to go." She had no idea if she was or not, but if the multiple voice-mail messages from Evelyn were any indication, she had been. It didn't matter anyway. If her life started from this point on, she wouldn't stay at Sexton. "You'll find another job quickly. Your plan to restructure the service desk was really good."

He smiled slightly. "Thanks." He reached down and petted Buttercup's head. "How old is she?"

"Around three or four. They weren't really sure at the shelter. They rescued her from a puppy mill. Maria likes dogs, right?"

He shook his head. "She's afraid of them."

"Buttercup's harmless. I bet she'll like her."

"Not sure she'll like anything until I get another job." He drained the last of his beer. "I'm sorry you got caught in the layoff plan too."

"Looks like job hunting is in both our futures." She didn't want to think about that right now. If the loop ended now, she'd be unemployed tomorrow. If not, she'd have another chance to fix it all. "Maybe the dog will provide a good distraction?" She let her voice lilt up, hoping for a positive answer.

"Fine, but just tonight." He smiled slightly as he petted Buttercup on the head. "Keep me in mind when you're checking the online job sites."

"Definitely. I owe you." She patted each one of the dogs. "You be good girls for Jack." Then she turned and sped back home. She had to devise a new plan for work and get ready for the party in the next three hours.

She glanced at her custom wood blinds on the back window as she sat at the kitchen table. Buttercup had totally shredded them when she spotted a squirrel in the backyard. Between that and the trash strewn all over the kitchen, Wynn was ready for a break and definitely in the market for a covered trash can. To think all of this had occurred in the span of her two-hour nap. She kept reminding herself that dogs are pure, innocent, and everything good.

Chapter Fourteen

Carly's stomach bounced when she saw Wynn heading their way. She'd been talking to Jordan on the patio for close to an hour. Jordan was charming and seemed perfectly put together in both her work and personal life, but something about Wynn intrigued her.

"I need to talk to you for a minute." Wynn took her hand and tugged her toward the gate to the pier.

Jordan took Carly's other hand. "That's ridiculously rude. Can't you see that Carly and I are having a conversation?"

Suddenly caught in what seemed like a tug of war between the two, Carly slipped her hands out of each of theirs, crossed her arms across her chest, and watched the drama playing out in front of her.

"Listen. I had a tough day today. I just need to talk to Carly."

"It can't be so bad that you've forgotten all your manners."

"I got fired, okay?" She raised her arms and let them drop. "I was trying not to let it ruin everyone's night, but there it is. Are you happy now?"

Carly's stomach clenched. "Oh my gosh. Are you okay?" She hadn't seen that coming at all.

Jordan glanced back at her. "She'll be fine." Then at Wynn. "Buck up, little one. You'll find another job in no time."

"Thanks for the support." Wynn seemed really agitated, and rightly so.

Carly was stunned. She'd never seen Wynn upset before, and her situation tugged at her heart. "Can you excuse us?" She glanced at Jordan but didn't wait for an answer before she took Wynn's hand and led her onto the pier. She hadn't expected Jordan to talk to her own sister that way. The exchange between them had been nasty at best. Family was supposed to build each other up, not tear each other down. At least that's the way it happened in hers.

When they got a distance down the pier, Wynn stopped and gazed at the ocean. "I'm sorry. That *was* rude of me. I didn't intend to ruin anyone's evening. I just…"

"You don't have to talk about it if you don't want to." She squeezed Wynn's hand. "We can just watch the sunset." It was filled with beautiful hues of reds, purples, and oranges that all seemed to move together with perfect synchrony.

"I'm not really upset about losing my job. Like Jordan said, I can find another one." Wynn released Carly's hand and clenched the pier railing. "My boss lost her job today too, and a lot of other people are going to be let go soon. People who don't deserve it." She shook her head. "I had a plan and it didn't work."

"You can't blame yourself."

"Yeah. I can. I set the whole thing into motion. Got too greedy for my own good and couldn't dial it back."

"What do you mean?" Carly wasn't sure, because Wynn seemed to have money, and her life seemed to be well put together.

"I promised myself I would be chief operating officer somewhere by the time I turned thirty." She laughed at herself. "That's tomorrow."

"So, I guess you'll be pushing that to thirty-one." She grinned and got a smile in return from Wynn. "Sorry. I'm not trying to make light of what happened, but CIO by thirty is a huge goal. Most people haven't even found their path by that age."

Wynn shook her head. "I've been reconsidering that goal—actually reconsidering all of my goals. Time seems to be getting away from me. I think I'd rather work less and enjoy life more."

"There you go. That's the way to look at the positive side of things." The jolt that shot through her when Wynn smiled was unexplainable. "What can I do to help?"

"You're helping right now." Wynn turned to Carly and leaned against the railing. Her eyes were glassy, as though tears were about to spill out.

The urge to protect Wynn from all the bad things in the world overwhelmed her, and Carly slipped her arms around Wynn's waist and held her close. Rose, jasmine, and gardenia filled her head. Accompanied by a touch of patchouli, the scent was intoxicating, and it blended perfectly with Wynn's style.

If she didn't let Wynn go soon, she'd get wrapped up in something more and would want to forget all about the party. She took in a deep breath and reluctantly released her. "I'm sorry you've had such a rough day."

"Thanks." Wynn pressed her lips together. "At least one good thing happened today. I mean, besides you right here and now." She blushed as she continued, and Carly was even more captivated. "I adopted another dog." The smile that came across Wynn's face was gorgeous. Carly's pulse quickened. She caught herself watching Wynn's mouth move as she talked, memorizing the way her lips curved, the way her cheeks crinkled when she smiled. "Another dog? You already have one?"

Wynn nodded. "I didn't really think it through, though. They might be a little more than I can handle, but they're both so sweet." She chuckled. "Buttercup is a chocolate Lab, rescued from a puppy mill, and Shadow is one of her pups."

"That's so sweet. You adopted her because you didn't want them to be separated."

"Well, not exactly. I didn't realize they were related until I went back to get Buttercup."

"But you went back to get her?" Wynn had just captured a little more of her heart.

She nodded. "Yeah. I couldn't get her out of my head."

Carly's heart exploded with love, and she took Wynn's face in her hands and kissed her. Her mind swam as she filled with the excitement of something new but a familiarity she couldn't shake. They fit perfectly together, and she hadn't even kissed her before. Wynn's hands slipped around her waist and urged her closer. When they touched, the fire between them stoked even higher. Why had she never kissed Wynn before? She deepened the kiss, dipping her tongue inside, teasing Wynn as she responded, keeping control as she'd never done before, and desire raged through her. She was ready to take or be taken right here, right now on the pier. The feeling of surrender that overwhelmed her was almost too much to grasp, and she broke the kiss.

Cheeks pink, and eyes wide, Wynn stood staring at her. "That was—"

"Bold. I know. I'm sorry." Heat blazed within Carly as she touched her own lips, felt their swollen tenderness.

"I was going to say wonderful." Wynn tilted her head and scrunched her lips into a cockeyed smile. "Don't be sorry." She slipped her arm around Carly's waist and urged her closer to continue the mind-blistering kiss.

Carly caught sight of Jordan watching them and now coming their way. She placed a finger on Wynn's lips. "Hold that thought, please." She dipped her chin toward Jordan.

Wynn looked to the sky and shook her head. "She has the *worst* timing." She curled her fingers into Carly's back, which sent a breathtaking quiver streaming through her. "Can we continue this later?"

Carly couldn't think of anything she wanted more. "I certainly hope so." She backed up, cleared her throat, and swiped her hands across her hips to smooth her dress.

"What are you two still doing out here?" Jordan asked as she joined them.

"Wynn was just telling me about her dogs."

"Did you say *dogs*? As in more than one?"

Carly nodded.

Jordan's eyebrows rose. "You adopted another dog? When are you going to have time for them?"

"I'm unemployed. Remember?"

"Right, but that won't be for long."

"I don't know. I might take a break from work for a while." She turned to Carly. "I don't suppose you'd like to travel the world on a sailboat with me."

Her nerves were all aflutter. Traveling the world with Wynn sounded like an absolutely wonderful adventure. There were worse things than making love under the stars, waking up floating in the wide-open ocean, and looking into those dreamy blue eyes.

"Don't be stupid." Jordan scoffed. "A woman like Carly is too sophisticated to be a deckhand on your crazy adventure." She glanced at Carly. "That's exactly what you'd be because Wynn is ridiculously cheap."

"I like to do things myself, that's all. Unlike you, I don't need a crew of twenty to push away from the dock."

"You can't afford it either."

That remark seemed to silence Wynn for the moment. "I'll get you a drink." Wynn smiled at Carly as she turned to go to the bar.

Jordan watched Wynn walk away. "Wynn's a good kid, but she's got a lot to learn when it comes to business."

"Really? I wouldn't have thought that at all." There was a time and place for brutal truth, and it wasn't at an event in front of others, especially after your sister had just been fired.

"She's still pretty naive when it comes to reading people. Like you, for instance."

Heat flashed across her neck. "What about me?" What could Wynn or Jordan possibly read about her?

"That you'll be easy to conquer. She's a bit of a Casanova. Watch out for her."

"I will." The words escaped her lips slowly as she glanced at Wynn leaning on the patio bar, thinking about their discussion earlier. Had that all been an act to get her into bed? Now who was the naive one?

Wynn made eye contact as she came across the patio with their drinks.

"Get lost, little sister. Carly and I are making magic here."

Wynn looked at Carly and smiled and then back at Jordan. "Don't you think you should be mingling with your donors?" Wynn pointed to the guests who were now spilling out onto the patio. "It's your fund-raiser. Shouldn't you be using that charm to beg for money?"

Jordan pulled her eyebrows together. "Is that your third or fourth scotch?"

Wynn lifted her glass. "First. I'm sure you passed me before I even arrived."

Jordan quirked an eyebrow. "First glass, third refill, you mean?"

Wynn sucked air through her clenched teeth. "Oh, that's right. You stick to vodka at these things so it looks like you're drinking water."

Carly watched and listened as the urgency in their voices became clearer as they interrupted and talked over each other. They were fighting over her. She'd been through this before and didn't like it *at all.* Soon they would be discussing who was taking her home without even considering she was going home alone.

No matter how amazing the kiss she'd shared with Wynn was, Carly wasn't a trophy to be collected in *any* competition. Especially one that wasn't of her own making.

She held up her hands. "Stop it. Right now." She looked at Wynn, then at Jordan. "I am not a prize to be won. Tonight or any other night. You two need to grow up." That was the last straw. She was done for the night. She'd text Suzanna when she got home.

❖

Carly tossed her clutch onto the couch after she got inside. She'd never been so irritated by two women. Number one, Wynn and Jordan were acting like idiots, and number two, because she'd felt the need to leave the event early. Both of them had acted like Neanderthals. She wouldn't have been surprised if each of them had pulled out a club and started physically fighting over her. She hadn't even been able to sneak a bite to eat yet. Thankfully, she had leftover lasagna from dinner at her parents' home earlier in the week. Her mother never let her leave the house without food.

Her urge to text Wynn was overwhelming, but she wasn't about to play into whatever game she was playing. If what Jordan said about Wynn was true, Carly refused to become another notch in her belt. But, sweet Lord, the kiss they'd shared had been off the charts.

It had awakened all kinds of nerve endings she'd thought to be dead long ago.

After finishing the last bit of leftover lasagna, she crawled under the covers and found herself caught up in that kiss with Wynn again. Holy fuck, it was hot. Her phone chimed, and she hoped with everything she had that it was Wynn. She didn't seem to be finished with her yet. She picked up her phone, and a tingle ran through her.

I'm sorry for the way I acted. I never intended to make you feel anything but special.

That was all she needed. *You're forgiven.* She added a smiley face before she typed, *Are you okay?*

No. Not at all.

A sinking feeling appeared in Carly's stomach as she watched more bubbles appear on the screen.

I've never felt like this with anyone before, and I didn't want Jordan to spoil it. Seems like I did a great job of spoiling it myself.

She typed, *Felt like what?* Then she immediately erased the question because she was fully aware of the feeling. She typed, *I know what you mean.*

Then she erased that and stared at the phone for a moment before she hit the call button. She didn't understand the emotions fleeting through her and needed to hear Wynn's voice to see if she was feeling the same.

"Hey." Wynn's voice was soft and low, a sound she hadn't been able to get out of her head all night.

"Hey." She hoped one word wasn't enough to reveal her excitement.

"I was an ass, and I'm sorry."

"Yes. You were. Both of you were." Although she'd been flattered at first, the banter between Wynn and Jordan had morphed into something ugly. Carly didn't intend to remain the cause of it, but she had to address the feelings she'd had before the argument started. "About the kiss…I don't know what came over me earlier. You were just so vulnerable, and it touched me."

"Thank you for listening. Honestly, I'm not one to air my feelings so publicly."

"Can I see you again?" Carly surprised herself with her boldness again.

"Yes. Of course." Wynn chuckled. "I was afraid I'd blown it."

"You kinda did, but I'll give you a chance to make it up to me."

"Phew. That's a relief."

"I'm glad you messaged me."

"Best decision of my life."

"So far."

"Right. I'm hoping you'll be involved in the next one too." The soft contentment in Wynn's voice had crazy things happening in Carly that she'd thought might never happen again.

The line was silent for a moment. "I'm sorry if I woke you. I'll let you sleep."

"Please don't hang up. I don't want to be alone tonight." The vulnerability in Wynn's voice was clear. "I mean with all that happened today."

That was a relief. Carly really didn't want to hang up either. "How are the pups?"

"Buttercup is asleep between my legs, and Shadow is snoring on my chest." Carly's mind went immediately to the gutter, thinking how she'd love to be in either one of those positions. "I couldn't move if I tried. Shadow is dreaming. Listen." Soft whines of puppy dreams came through the phone.

"What are you going to do about them? You're not going to take Buttercup back to the shelter, are you?"

"No. I would never do that." Wynn sighed. "I'm going to have to persuade my neighbor to take her. Then she'll be right next door, where Shadow can visit her."

"You don't sound like that's going to be easy."

"His wife has an aversion to dogs."

"Can you elaborate?"

"I think she had a bad experience when she was a kid."

"Oh, that's not good and might be hard to overcome."

"I know, but I have to try."

"Maybe I can help her work through it. It's not my specialty, but I have a little experience in how the mind works."

"That's right. I can't believe I forgot." Wynn chuckled. "I hope you don't know too much about how my mind works, or I'm in trouble."

A thrill coursed through Carly, and her cheeks burned. "I think we may be on the same path." Again with the boldness.

"Tell me some things about you that I'll never forget." Wynn's voice was soft, but seemed eager.

"I love the ocean. I don't really have a favorite food, but if you feed me Italian or Chinese for the rest of my life, I'll be happy."

"Noted." Wynn let out a slight snort. "When did you learn to swim?"

"When I was five."

"Wow. That's young."

"My dad taught me, so I could join the swim team with my sisters." She chuckled. "I used to cry every day when they went to practice because I couldn't go too."

"You're the youngest in your family?"

"Yep. The baby, and my brothers and sisters never let me live that down. They complain that I got everything they didn't."

"My sisters say that too." Wynn's voice rose as her excitement came through.

She laughed. "It's probably true."

Carly soaked up the happiness in Wynn's voice as she relaxed. The only place she'd rather be than in her own bed right now was closer to Wynn, watching her facial expressions as she spoke. Such a beautiful face. "Tell me more."

"I have a scar just above my hairline from a bicycle accident when I was seven, and I…"

Wynn's voice faded as Carly's eyelids became heavy. She couldn't force them open any longer. She drifted off to sleep listening to all things Wynn and couldn't feel more content.

Chapter Fifteen

Wynn rubbed her eyes, glanced around the room, and sighed. The same day was beginning again, and she had no idea why, but she was grateful for another chance. She'd fucked up royally at the restaurant last night. When she and Jordan had started sparring, firing insults at each other like children, she saw the disapproval in Carly's eyes. It was evident that she'd said something wrong, if not crossed the line completely.

When Carly had called last night after she'd gone to bed, she'd tried so hard to stay awake. She'd had a bit of false hope during the night when she'd dozed briefly and the phone had gone silent. She'd immediately called Carly's name, and she'd responded—her soft, sleepy voice came through the line and she'd said she was still listening. She ached to see her face as she slept, wanted to bolt out of bed and go to her, so she could wake up next to her this morning.

She'd tried talking until dawn to get through this crazy day. She wasn't comfortable talking about herself, but Carly had asked, and she'd honestly give Carly anything she wanted. She'd rambled on about herself until she heard tiny little snores coming through the speaker, which made her love Carly all the more. Somehow, the universe had given her a second chance. If she could just put all the correct pieces into play, maybe—just maybe she could change her destiny with Carly.

Her phone buzzed on the nightstand, so she picked it up, hit the button, and said, "I'll call you back." She knew exactly what Jordan wanted. She now realized the opportunity it presented with Carly. She would be at the fund-raiser later, but she had to accomplish other things during the day to make this weird time loop turn out right. She immediately sent a text to Carly.

I could use your help today. Are you free for a couple of hours? That should be enough time to go to the shelter, adopt Buttercup, and hopefully convince Jack and Maria to adopt her.

Hi. I can probably make time if it's important. The smiley face at the end made Wynn's smile broaden more than it should have, but spending time with Carly made her ridiculously happy.

You're awesome! Can you meet me at my house at noon? She dropped a location pin into the message. *Wear jeans.*

Okay. I'll see you then.

She immediately called the office and talked to Jack, told him to meet her in Evelyn's office in an hour. He was curious just like the last time, but he didn't question her once she said she wanted to discuss his improvement plan. There would be no ass-hauling involved this morning. She was fully prepared for what would come this time.

Now she had to get to work and make sure no one got fired, including herself. She went to her closet and pushed through the suits until she found something different to wear today—something less "I mean business" and more "I care about my people."

She ordered coffee on her phone and zipped in and out of the shop, narrowly escaping Sally again. Once she got back to her Jeep, she sent her a text acknowledging what an ass she was and apologizing for the way she'd handled things. She received an unexpected and unwanted response letting her know that Sally was open to letting her apologize over dinner. But that wasn't going to happen, because it would put her right back in the same shitty situation.

When she arrived at work, she was, again, prepared for the security guard this morning, her badge around her neck and visible. She held the badge up to the card reader by the door, and the light changed from red to green. She smiled and said, "Good morning, George," as she passed the security desk. He smiled and waved her on. Stopping before she reached the elevator, she spun around and walked back to talk to George. "I might need your help."

"Sure. What can I do?" He glanced at another employee who was entering and waved.

"I need to play a harmless practical joke on a colleague."

He immediately grinned. "Whatcha got in mind?"

"It's Joe Davis's fortieth birthday, you see, and I'd like to decorate his office. Maybe rearrange the furniture. You know, just for fun."

George's eyes widened. "What do you need from me?"

She glanced at her watch. "Can you call him at, say, quarter to ten and tell him his car alarm is going off? That should give us enough time to get into his office and set everything up."

"Sure. I can detain him longer if you need me to."

"I might take you up on that. If he comes back in less than fifteen minutes, keep him occupied until I give you the green light. Better yet, send him to security to get a new badge." She would need George to detain him. She'd have Evelyn notify security to deactivate his badge long enough to keep him sidetracked. Davis parked in the back lot, where the mantrap was installed, so she hoped that would be enough time.

George took out his phone. "Quarter to ten." As he set an alarm, he grinned as though he'd been included in the surprise party of the century. "Got it."

"Thanks so much, George. I don't know what I'd do without you." And she didn't at this point. He'd just taken a huge task off her plate.

"Always here to help."

She turned and rushed to the elevator. Evelyn would be waiting, getting angrier by the minute that she wasn't already in her office. When the elevator doors opened, she raced across the floor and pushed open the door to Evelyn's office. Jack was there, ahead of her, like he'd been before, and Evelyn was both pissed and confused. Not a good look for her.

"Where the hell—?"

"I've been working on a presentation I think leadership will accept."

Evelyn rounded her desk and whispered, "I already have a presentation."

"But it sucks. We have to fix it." She set the coffees on the table before she pulled out her laptop and turned it on. "They're not going to go for anything that doesn't reduce cost immediately, and in a few hours Davis is going to present a proposal for a considerable staff reduction."

"How do you know that?"

"Just trust me. I know." She didn't want to disclose much more for fear Evelyn wouldn't listen at all.

Evelyn put her hand on her hip. "Have you been working with him to undermine me?"

"Not exactly, but I'm fully aware of his plans, and since you won't listen to anyone else, he's going to make his own." She couldn't tell them it had been hers to begin with, or they'd both lose all faith in her.

Evelyn took a cup and opened the top before she drank.

Wynn looked up at Jack and then pointed at the remaining cup. "That one's for you. Sweet and light, right?" She'd remembered how he liked it today.

He seemed confused as he picked it up, pulled off the top, and examined the cloudy contents.

They both stood frozen, watching her.

"Well, sit down. I need your help. I can't figure this all out on my own." She tossed printed copies of Evelyn's presentation, the modified plan they'd come up with before that leadership had rejected, and Jack's improvement plan in front of each one of them. "We have to combine these to save money." She also handed them each a list of areas she'd identified as possible money savers.

"Listen. I know you didn't want me in this position, and I know you don't trust me. I'm young and smart, and you think I want your job. That might have been true a year ago." She blew out a breath. It was absolutely true. "But now my only goal is for this company to succeed and keep everyone employed." She glanced at Evelyn, whose narrowed eyes indicated she still didn't trust her, and then to Jack. "Isn't that what we all want?" They both nodded. "Then we all win, right?"

Jack started writing on Wynn's list. "We can outsource PC purchases, change them to leases, and have a vendor distribute the new ones."

"That's a great idea. We'll be able to provide better customer service then too." She retrieved the easel from the corner, balanced the oversized pad on it, picked up a marker, and wrote down Jack's first idea. "How much savings will that give us?"

"A couple hundred thousand."

She wrote the amount in a column next to it and then glanced back at Jack. "By the way, there's a sweet chocolate Lab at the animal shelter I'm going to bring home later, and you're going to adopt her."

"Probably not. My wife's not a fan of dogs, was bitten when she was a kid."

"Buttercup is the sweetest dog, ever. I have a friend who can help Maria get past that fear."

"I'd love that, if she can. I've always wanted a dog."

"Okay, what next?" She had complete confidence that by working as a team they were going to come up with a great plan. They would need to include a few more substantial savings ideas for leadership to approve it.

Evelyn jotted something on her notepad. "Start charging for food in the canteens. To avoid handling money, we could pull a monthly fee from everyone's paychecks, like we do for benefits."

"Acceptable." That was a huge savings. "I think everyone would agree that's a minimal price to pay for keeping their job."

"Can we get enough buy-in for that?" She glanced at Jack, since he worked with a lot of the staff.

"If it was at a discounted rate for those that sign up. We'd have to give them the choice to opt out."

"Of course." Evelyn added to her notes.

"What about letting people telecommute? We'd save on operating costs and overhead."

"Awesome idea, Jack." She wrote it on the board. "Employees would save on gas and get their commute time back."

"My whole team would be on board with that."

"We seem to waste a lot of time on useless meetings. Let's cut a lot of them and bring the remaining necessary ones online. At the very least, leave out the people who aren't needed in them."

Jack wrote something on the paper in front of him. "What about moving to the cloud? That would save on onsite servers and storage."

She added the suggestion to the list. "Jack. You're on fire."

Evelyn spoke up. "We can take on more interns. They're a minimal expense and are considered an investment in the company's future." She scribbled on her notepad. "And cut back on the expensive office supplies." She held up her gel pen that had the Sexton Technology logo printed on the side. "Go back to off-the-shelf stick pens and also forced default to black-and-white copies."

They continued naming items until they had enough savings to interest leadership. Their brainstorming session had really paid off. The only thing left was to make sure Davis was detained long enough for leadership to realize it.

She exited the elevator into the lobby and sped to the security department. She'd brought Evelyn along with her because she wasn't sure they would disable a badge without her authority.

She and Evelyn laid out their plan to detain Davis by deactivating his badge. Getting him outside would be easy, since George was already on board with calling him down and telling him the alarm on his car was going off. Once out of the building, he'd have no way of reentering any of the secure areas of the building without a new badge and permission from Evelyn. George would send Davis to security badging, and they'd be conveniently down for a few hours. George was all in. Thankfully, he loved a good prank.

❖

Carly was surprised to receive a text from Wynn this morning, and after their short exchange she immediately called Suzanna. She'd just agreed to meet Wynn at her house at noon for help with something she had no clue about.

The ringing stopped, and she didn't wait for Suzanna to speak. "What's going on with your sister?"

"What? Which one?"

"Wynn? She sent me a text that said she needs my help for something."

"I don't know." A sigh came through the phone. "You didn't ask what or why?"

"No. I figured she didn't want to go over it on the phone or she would've called." She'd been so caught off guard by the message, she hadn't thought to ask why.

"She's been really focused on work lately. Maybe something's going on there."

That was disappointing. She'd hoped it was something more personal. On second thought it was probably better for it not to be personal. She didn't want to be a counselor for any relationship issues Wynn might be having. That would end any chance she'd have of developing anything more than friendship with her.

"Maybe so. I thought it might be important, so I cleared my schedule."

"I'll call her and find out."

"No—absolutely not. I don't want her thinking I called you for advice."

"But you did. Wait. You cleared your schedule for her?" Suzanna chuckled. "You like her."

"That's still up for discussion." She envisioned the goofy smile on Suzanna's face and bit her lip in an attempt not to get all giddy. "But I *would* like to get to know her better." She was sure the excitement in her voice made her sound like a ridiculous fifteen-year-old.

"Okay." Suzanna chuckled again. "So what do you want to know?" Something whirred in the background as Suzanna spoke.

"What are you doing? Tearing down the house?"

"Blender. Making a smoothie."

"Always the healthy one."

"Running after two kids all the time, I have to do something to keep up."

"So what's Wynn's relationship status?"

"Definitely single. She never lacks companionship, but she always keeps her options open."

Carly wasn't sure what to think about that. "So, she sees a lot of women?"

"I wouldn't say that. I think she's testing the waters. You know, waiting for the right one." The blender whirred again. "That might just be you."

"Don't even think about it." She was now regretting making this call.

"What? I won't do anything except maybe give you a little push. Tonight at the fund-raiser."

"That will depend on what she needs my help with today."

"I'm going to put my money on work. Wynn doesn't open up much about her personal feelings."

That isn't good either. "Just what I need—another closed-off control freak."

"Stop. I didn't say she's closed off, and she's definitely not a control freak. That's Jordan. Wynn just has to warm up to people first."

"Okay. I'm trusting you on this."

"Have I ever steered you wrong?"

"There was that one girl in college."

"Not my fault. She gave off all the vibes."

"For you, but not me."

"Can I help it if I'm irresistible? It's not like you didn't benefit from any of those crushes."

"Total rebounds."

Suzanna laughed loudly. "Are you seriously complaining?"

"Nope. I knew exactly what they were."

"Listen. I have to go. The kids are running around like maniacs, and I just heard a crash in the other room."

"Okay. I'll see you tonight. Don't call Wynn."

"I won't, but I'm going to give you that push later. This has been a long time coming."

"Plan on being my lifeguard if I start drowning."

"I'll bring the life preserver."

She heard the kids squealing in the background, and the line went dead. She took in a deep breath and blew it out.

Right after she'd received the text from Wynn, she'd called Stephanie and had her clear her schedule this afternoon. Being totally distracted throughout all her sessions wondering what she could possibly need help with wouldn't be good for anyone, especially her clients.

Normally she wouldn't have been so accommodating, but she'd been wanting to get to know Wynn better for a long time, though she'd always seemed out of reach. Suzanna had just laughed. It seemed she'd always thought the two of them would make a good couple. She shook her head. How had she never seen that? Suzanna had apparently put that scenario together long ago and was just waiting for it to happen. What had she gotten herself into? It might be less than she anticipated, but then again it might be more.

Chapter Sixteen

Wynn was satisfied with the meeting with leadership this morning. The brainstorming session with Evelyn and Jack had been draining but successful. They'd used a combination of Jack's and Evelyn's plans and added a few more cost savings to seal the deal. Leadership wasn't thrilled at first, but she'd managed to convince them that keeping experienced employees was much less expensive than hiring and training new ones. She'd also proposed a new budget and forecasted sales with regular monthly reviews to back up her plan. Last, but not least, she'd promised that if they didn't start gaining return on investment in six months, she would resign. To her surprise, both Evelyn and Jack joined her in that promise.

Leadership indicated they'd like Wynn to be the new COO, but she refused to take on the responsibility alone. Wynn had the technology business sense and Evelyn had the compassion necessary to be in the position, a perfect balance. It was agreed that together they would bring the company back into the blue. Jack would bump up to IT Director and would handle all day-to-day operations and struggles. All in all it was a good mix.

Wynn had been home for close to an hour waiting nervously for Carly to arrive and was in the driveway getting her Jeep Wrangler ready for the dogs. On her way home from work, she'd stopped by the pet store to pick up dog food and a crate that would fit in the cargo area. She wasn't making the mistake of leaving the dogs free again. The Jeep had been an impulse buy last year. She'd been hoping to take advantage of its off-road capabilities but hadn't had the opportunity to undertake any adventures since the purchase. Maybe Shadow and Carly would change that. She was getting way ahead of herself. She had to get out of this fucking time loop first.

She glanced at her watch as she finished situating the blanket she'd placed in the crate. Not long until Carly arrived. She went to the front door and let Shadow out, who immediately raced to the lawn and started sniffing. What else could she do to keep herself busy for the next fifteen minutes?

"Taking a vacation day, finally?" She heard Mrs. P's voice and glanced over to see her standing on the porch holding two cups and a decanter Wynn knew to be filled with coffee. Mrs. P loved company.

She waved and then crossed the small yard. "As a matter of fact, I am." She took one of the cups and held it while Mrs. P filled it with steaming-hot coffee. She'd probably seen Wynn out front and brewed it just for her. Mrs. P was sweet that way.

Shadow finished her business and raced toward them. "It looks like you have an adventure planned with your new puppy."

She sat and relaxed in one of the porch chairs. "Something like that." She took a sip of the coffee, hissing when it burned her tongue. "A friend of mine is coming over, and we're planning to go adopt her mother at the animal shelter." Mrs. P's brows pulled together. "Shadow's mom. Not my friend's." She picked up Shadow, who settled on Wynn's lap.

"That's a relief. I think your friend's mom would need a larger crate." Mrs. P gave her a sideways smile. She was always quick with the dry humor. "This friend. Is she a love interest? Are you dating?" Mrs. P also always stated her thoughts and got to the point quickly. No dancing around anything with her.

"Not currently, but maybe in the future." She winked. "Let's see how today goes."

"Is this some kind of test?" Mrs. P reached over and scratched Shadow's back. "Making sure she likes dogs?" Shadow immediately rolled over for her to scratch her belly.

She shook her head. "No. Not at all. At least not for her. Carly's perfect." A sporty, red, two-door Honda Accord pulled up to the curb, and Carly got out. "Thanks for the coffee. I have to go." She put Shadow on the ground.

Mrs. P put her hand on Wynn's knee. "Not so fast. I'd like to meet her. Make sure she's suitable for you."

"Trust me, she's more than suitable."

"I'll be the judge of that." She couldn't fight it. Mrs. P was going to insist on an introduction.

Wynn vaulted from her chair as Mrs. P threw up her arm and waved. "Carly, dear. Wynn is over here."

Carly turned and smiled widely before she reversed direction and headed their way. She was dressed in jeans, sneakers, and a coral, V-neck shirt. Her jet-black hair bounced slightly on her shoulders as she walked around the yard on the sidewalk and up the driveway. She was absolutely radiant in the sunlight.

Shadow met her halfway, and she dropped to a squat to pet her. "Hi there, little one. What's your name?" She gathered her in her arms and continued walking as Shadow licked her chin.

"That's Shadow, and this is Mrs. Pritchard, my neighbor. I call her Mrs. P for short." She spoke quickly, well aware that her nerves were showing.

Carly held Shadow against her chest with one hand and extended the other to Mrs. P. "It's so nice to meet you."

"She has manners. That's good."

Carly smiled, and Wynn grinned before she twisted her neck to look at Mrs. P with widened eyes and clenched lips. "Carly helps Suzanna at most of the events she plans." It dawned on her that she hadn't told Mrs. P about her plans. "That reminds me. I won't be able to make dinner tonight. Suzanna has an event scheduled, so I'll be helping out as well. We can do something tomorrow night, though."

"Okay. Perhaps Carly can join us?" Mrs. P glanced up at her.

Carly raised her eyebrows. "Sure. I'd love to."

"You would?" She couldn't contain the gleeful surprise in her voice, prompted by the tickle in her belly.

"I would," Carly said softly, and everything else in Wynn's vision disappeared as she watched her lips form the words and then break into a beautiful smile.

"You two had better get going before someone else adopts that dog." Mrs. P's voice broke through the fog.

"You're adopting another dog?"

"She's going to get Shadow's mother." Mrs. P. had answered before she could get the words out. "Do you have any pets?"

"No. My life is too busy right now, but maybe someday. My family had a cocker spaniel when I was growing up, and I've always wanted another one."

"Well, three would be too many, anyway." Mrs. P. was getting way ahead of them.

Carly smiled and glanced at Wynn. "Yes. Three probably would."

"We'll see you later." Wynn kissed Mrs. P on the cheek. "Shall we?" She swept her hand in front of her, indicating for Carly to lead the way.

Carly nodded. "It was nice to meet you," she said as she turned and allowed Wynn's hand to brush against her back as they walked across the lawn.

"I've got everything loaded already, so we're ready to roll." She followed Carly around to the passenger side and opened the door for her. "Thank you for coming. I didn't think I could handle both dogs on my own."

"Of course. I'm glad you called." She climbed into the Jeep and settled Shadow on her lap.

On the way to the shelter, Wynn told her the whole story about how she'd adopted Shadow without knowing that Buttercup was her mother. Once she'd found out, she couldn't bear the thought of her ending up in a bad home.

They managed to load both dogs into the back of the Jeep before the rain started coming down. The timing sucked, but considering the drought they'd been experiencing, she wouldn't complain. Carly wasn't nearly as wet as Wynn. Once they pulled out of the lot and onto the road home, Wynn was silent. She seemed to be somewhere else in her head.

"Are you okay? You're quiet all of a sudden."

"I need to tell you that there's a little more to this story than just adopting Buttercup." Wynn glanced from the road to Carly. "I need your counseling services."

"Okay." The word dragged across her lips like molasses spilling out of the jar. She hadn't meant for her disappointment to show so clearly, but if Wynn was going to ask her for professional advice, any kind of future relationship with her would be off-limits.

"Not for me. For my neighbor, Jack. He's a work colleague who wants a dog, but his wife had a bad experience when she was younger and hasn't gotten over it."

"Oh." Relief washed through her, and her voice rose as she smiled. "You want me to help your neighbor's wife?"

"Yeah. I saved his job today, and he promised to adopt Buttercup if he can convince his wife that she's harmless."

"You saved his job?" This woman was a saint.

"Well, we really all saved each other's. I had a plan, my boss, Evelyn, had a plan, and Jack had a plan. None of them were acceptable to leadership on their own. So I got them together, and we created a compromise." Wynn hesitated. "Honestly, I was originally going to cut staff and promote myself for the COO position."

"That sounds pretty cutthroat." Maybe not so much of a saint after all.

"I know. That's why I didn't do it." She pressed her lips together tightly. "Evelyn isn't very flexible and wouldn't listen, so at first I thought it was the only way. But I gave the discussion another shot, and she surprised me today by actually cooperating. We changed the whole plan. Evelyn's position is solid, and no one else got fired."

"What about you?"

"I still have the same job I had before, but that's okay. The company will do well, and I'll have more opportunities in the future."

"Opportunities that don't depend on hurting others?" Back to being a saint.

She nodded. "I don't want to be that person." She pulled into the driveway and killed the engine. "The one that steps on other people to get ahead."

"Look at you." Carly smiled. "You saved hundreds of jobs today and don't even realize what an awesome thing that is."

Wynn shrugged. "I was just doing my job. Only better than I was doing it before."

"Even so. What you did today was wonderful." Carly kissed her on the cheek, then crinkled her nose as she caught a whiff of the wet-dog scent filling the Jeep.

Wynn pulled the collar of her shirt to her nose and sniffed. "Is it me that smells so bad?"

Carly let out a laugh. "I think Buttercup needs a bath. She kind of smells like the shelter."

Wynn got out of the Jeep, opened the back, and let the dogs out. They immediately ran to see Mrs. P, who was still outside tending to her flower garden. "Shit. They're going to trample her marigolds." Wynn rushed after them, trying to round them up as Mrs. P shooed them away.

Carly put her hands on her hips and let out a loud whistle that pierced even her own ears. The dogs stopped immediately, as did Wynn and Mrs. P, and looked at her. "Come on, girls," she shouted, and both dogs came running like they knew who was boss.

Wynn's eyes widened. "Wow. That sound came out of you?"

"It comes in handy when you're from a big family and want to say something. My brothers and sisters can get pretty loud and rowdy sometimes." She took Wynn's hand, and warmth spread through her. "Come on. I'll help you get these girls cleaned up." Being with Wynn was fun, magical even. Nothing had ever felt this right in Carly's life before.

Bathing Shadow was the easy part, but they'd managed to get themselves completely soaked along with Buttercup. Apparently she thought bath time was playtime and seemed to love the water. Every time they soaped her up, she shook it all off and did the same when they rinsed her. Once they had the dogs semi-dry, Wynn let them out into the backyard to finish drying in the sun, which was now shining. The burst of rain hadn't lasted long, as usual.

Wynn glanced at her. "To the groomers next time."

Carly burst out laughing. "Definitely." She swiped her hands down her coral, V-neck shirt. It was completely soaked. When she glanced up at Wynn, she was watching her with vivid blue eyes, and a sizzling tingle coursed through her and settled gloriously in her belly.

"You probably want to take a shower." Wynn seemed to fumble the words, which Carly thought was ridiculously cute. "I'm sure I have something you can wear."

"What? You don't like my new scent? It's called Chanel eau de Buttercup," she said in her best French accent, which didn't even solicit a laugh.

Wynn moved down the hallway. "You can use my bathroom. There's no toilet, and the lights in there don't work, but the window gives a lot of light, and the shower's fine. Kind of in the middle of a renovation." Wynn seemed nervous and eager to get away from her. "I'll clean this up and shower in here."

"I don't mind helping."

Wynn swallowed hard. "You've already helped me so much." She took a couple of towels from the hall closet as she led her through the master bedroom to the bathroom. She set the towels on the counter. "I'll get you some clothes." She took a T-shirt and shorts from her dresser and handed them to Carly, then stood in the doorway looking absolutely gorgeous. "Take your time." She remained in the doorway for another moment before backing out of the room and closing the door.

God, she was captivating. Wynn had just the right amount of confidence and vulnerability. She had Carly completely turned on without even trying. What was she going to do about this?

Chapter Seventeen

Panic swept over Wynn as she crossed the hall to the guest room, went into the bathroom, and turned on the water. She'd never imagined having Carly in her house this close. She'd completely erased all thoughts of her last year after she became involved with Jordan. She closed the door and gripped the counter. The woman she saw in the mirror was second-guessing everything she'd done for the past year—everything that made her who she was—but she didn't care. In this moment, she was happy. Her life was changing, turning out so much differently than it had before—than she'd planned.

The smell of wet dog filled her nose as she peeled off her T-shirt and shorts, but right now it didn't bother her at all. She'd just had the most fun *ever* with Carly, and they'd been completely covered with water while washing the pups. Wynn could only imagine how much happiness she would discover while living a life with Carly.

The hot water felt exceptional spraying across her shoulders. With the whole distraction of Carly, she hadn't realized how cold she'd been. She turned around, closed her eyes, and let it wash across her face. A jolt shot through her as Carly's beautiful smile filled her head. The battle started in her head. *She's married to Jordan. No, she's not. It's last year. She hasn't even started dating Jordan yet. Carly won't even have any interest in Jordan until the party tonight.* Maybe they shouldn't go. Could she keep Carly occupied here, erase any interaction she'd had with Jordan? Make her forget about helping Suzanna? Could she, herself, forget about helping Suzanna? She ducked her head under the water again. This whole weird situation was confusing her.

She didn't realize until after she got out of the shower that she'd forgotten to take some clean clothes for herself. She tapped lightly on the bedroom door. "Carly." No answer. She was probably still in the shower. She opened the door a crack. "Carly. Are you finished showering?" Still no answer. The coast was clear. She'd sneak in, grab some clothes from the dresser, and slip out. She'd just made it to the dresser when the bathroom door opened and Carly appeared draped in only a towel. It was absolute déjà vu from the night this crazy dream had begun, only she wasn't at her parents' house just out of the pool from playing with the kids. They were completely alone.

She froze, then Carly froze. Their eyes locked, and Wynn found herself staring into deep green eyes filled with so much more than surprise.

"Sorry. I forgot to get clothes."

"No need to be sorry. This is your house…your bedroom." Carly tugged at her bottom lip with her teeth.

Suddenly the room seemed very intimate. "Right. My bedroom." Her gaze never left Carly's as she fumbled to open the top drawer. She veered it slightly, and when she locked it on Carly's again, her expression had changed. She stood frozen—she had to let Carly make the first move—Wynn needed to know she wasn't the only one feeling the connection.

Carly's eye's flitted from Wynn's lips to her eyes. "Stop." Carly came closer. "You're beyond beautiful, and you don't even realize it." She pushed her fingers through Wynn's short, wet hair. "Kiss me before I lose my nerve."

And she did. Softly, sweetly, with the newness of a first kiss but the familiarity of old lovers. Sweet and tentative and then all in—it was glorious. She immersed herself in Carly's aura, tried to hold onto time and space as she kissed her with everything she had—with a passion that exploded inside that surprised even her. This sensation was a thousand times better than any high she'd ever received from a takeover at work. Carly brought out hidden feelings locked deep inside, never released until now.

Cool air whooshed as their towels dropped to the floor, the coolness quickly replaced by Carly's warm, soft skin. As a red-hot bolt of electricity zapped her whole midsection and shot straight between her legs, it became clear that Carly had always been the one who held the key to her heart and so much more. Wynn was completely aroused, and she hadn't even begun to explore Carly's body—the best part. How this woman had such power over her was a complete mystery, but she'd had it since the day they met.

Carly's soft breasts pressed against her own as Carly nipped at her neck, the spot where it met her shoulder, and Wynn almost lost it right then. She'd been waiting for this moment for so long. She let out a moan, and Carly returned her mouth to hers. Tongues and hands battled for control as friction built between them, and they tumbled onto the bed. Carly sucked a nipple into her mouth, sending another bolt of red-hot arousal through Wynn. Carly left her nipple, quickly replacing her mouth with her fingers. Wynn squirmed beneath her as she trailed a wet, hot path to her stomach with her tongue. She watched as Carly skimmed her lips across the dark patch covering her center and then settled between her legs, pushing them farther apart.

Carly glanced up, made eye contact, and her arousal spiked. Wynn's response was staggering. She was almost embarrassed at how wet she was, but Carly didn't seem to mind. She slipped a finger inside, drew it up through her folds, circled, and took it back down and inside again. Each whimper that came out of Wynn's mouth seemed to delight her more as she continued the rhythm. Suddenly Carly was buried between her legs, her tongue sending her skyrocketing into orgasm. She'd wanted to slow it down, savor it, but Carly made that impossible. Suddenly she found herself being taken on a thousand-mile journey to ecstasy, one she wanted to experience a thousand times more and never wanted to return from.

Carly gently kissed the nerve endings she'd just set on fire and then laid her head on her thigh. Every pulse point in her was still thrumming as Carly traced her finger between her folds, and she quaked involuntarily.

"Stop. Please." She could hardly get the words out as her belly bounced, spikes of pleasure shocking her like a low-voltage zapper.

"But I kinda like watching you."

"You're going to kill me."

Carly chuckled and took one last swipe with her tongue before she crawled up Wynn and hovered above her. She tugged her lips into a half-smile. "Well, that was an unexpected pleasure."

"An absolute pleasure." She dragged her fingers lightly along Carly's sides. "I'm really glad I forgot to grab some clothes."

"If I didn't know better, I might have thought you planned it."

She smiled. "Not that much of a forward thinker."

"Well, to be honest, I'm not usually *this* forward. I can't tell you the last time I've slept with a woman I barely know." Carly's cheeks reddened. "Let alone made the first move."

Usually the one in control, Wynn had forced herself to let Carly take the reins, and she'd done so without question. "Why don't we remedy that?"

"Umm, I think we just did."

"I want to know everything about you." Even though she wanted to touch every part of Carly, she wanted more than sex from her. She wanted to soak up every bit of knowledge she could in case this moment disappeared tomorrow.

"Now?" Carly kissed her softly and then smiled.

Carly was so seductive yet so sweet. Wynn couldn't help but get caught up in the tingle Carly produced in her. "Maybe more of this first." She pressed her lips to Carly's and immersed herself in everything Carly brought out in her. Wynn would change a thousand more things in her life to spend the rest of it with her. How had she let this opportunity escape her the last time? She wasn't about to let it happen again, even if this all turned out to be a crazy dream. Jordan flitted through her head, and she felt guilty. She quickly pushed the thoughts away. Jordan was a survivor and really didn't even love Carly, did she? No. Not the way she should.

❖

Carly must have dozed mid-sentence. Wynn had held her, listening to every word Carly said about herself and also answered each question she'd posed in return. Even after Carly had told Wynn so many things about herself, she'd wanted more. With everything Carly had learned about Wynn over the past few hours, she'd found her to be intelligent, compassionate, loyal, and loving. That last facet had come into play more than once this afternoon. Wynn possessed all the qualities she'd hoped for in a significant other. She honestly thought she could spend the rest of her life with Wynn, if everything Wynn had told her proved to be true.

They'd already made love multiple times, Wynn taking her to heights of pleasure she was unaware she could achieve. She didn't want to leave the warmth of the woman who could expand her in that way. She felt safe and content curled up close to Wynn, surrounded by her strong arms. Wynn's eyes were closed, and she seemed completely relaxed now. She watched her sleep, soft breaths coming from her chest as it rose and fell. She traced a finger around Wynn's nipple and saw it come alive.

Wynn's lips pulled into a smile. "You're insatiable."

"Seems you are too." Carly couldn't get enough of the pleasure in Wynn's face, the sound of her tiny whimpers, and the growl from her throat when she climaxed. Pleasing Wynn had turned out to be more exciting than her own orgasm, which was off the charts every time.

"I should go home and change." Carly crawled across Wynn to check the time on her phone. "Oh my gosh. It's already six. I'll never make it there on time."

Wynn wrapped her arms around her, settled Carly on top of her, the complete length of their bodies against one another. "Text Suzanna. She'll be okay with us being late." Wynn watched her as she started to type in the words with only her thumb. "Jordan will be pissed, but she'll get over it."

Going to be late tonight. Sorry. I got hung up helping Wynn.

That's good news. Stay there...help her more. We'll be fine here. She punctuated the end with a heart-eyed smiley face.

You sure?

I'm sure. Have fun. This time Suzanna punctuated the end with a fire emoji.

Carly smiled and held the phone up to show Wynn the text exchange.

"I'll have to remember to thank her tomorrow." Wynn took the phone from Carly's hand and set it on the nightstand. Then her eyes darkened as she moved closer and kissed Carly softly, barely touching her lips with her own, a sweet taste of what was to come. Kissing was one of Carly's favorite activities, but kissing Wynn transported her into an erotic haze she didn't want to escape, a sensual rhythm that made her body fire in every sense. Their kisses were a simple, but sweet, a preamble of what they were about to share…again.

Chapter Eighteen

Wynn woke up alone at the same time and in the same space she had for the past five days. The promises Carly had made last night were gone, and Carly would never remember them. She rolled out of bed, let Shadow outside, then made the coffee. Once it had finished dripping, she leaned against the counter feeling sorry for herself. Felt the warm tears on her cheeks. It was real. Feelings that deep didn't come in dreams. She didn't know how many more times she could stand reliving this day. She should grab the exposed wires in the bathroom and shock herself back to reality.

Was she just going to let everything go? Could she go on with a life without Carly? Fuck no, she couldn't. Coffee spilled from her cup, burning her hand as she launched herself across the room. She shoved everything from the kitchen table to the floor and took multiple sticky notepads of different colors from her laptop bag. She was going to figure out what went wrong in the only way she knew how, by charting each event that happened throughout the day. She began writing furiously and organizing notes on the table.

She came up with three areas to look at. Work, home, and the fund-raiser. Now she had to define them further. "Okay. Work includes Evelyn and Jack." She wrote each one on a sticky note and placed it below the title. "Home is Jack again, plus Buttercup, Maria, and yesterday, Carly." She positioned the notes accordingly. "Fund-raiser includes Suzanna, Jordan, and Carly." Warmth rushed through her as she thought about the night they'd spent together instead of going to the event. "We must need to be at the fund-raiser."

She heard a soft scratch at the glass door and glanced up to see Shadow staring at her. She dropped the pen to the table, let Shadow inside, and fed her. "What next?" Could she go through a day like yesterday with Carly again, only to have it ripped away from her once more? She refilled her coffee cup and let the emotions she remembered so vividly trickle through her as she sipped. "Yes. I'll do it over and over to be with Carly. I have to until I get it right." Shadow sat in front of her, having finished her breakfast. "And you need your mom close by."

She found her phone, and the voice mail from Jordan had already arrived on schedule. She cleared it and thought about her next steps. Carly was going to think she was crazy, but she didn't care.

Can we meet for breakfast? I need some advice.

Her stomach jumped when the bubbles immediately appeared.

Sure. Where?

That little bakery by your office is good. I don't want to interrupt your morning too much.

That wasn't completely true. She wanted to burst into Carly's life in the best possible way.

No interruption. How about 9:00?

That's perfect.

Okay. See you then.

Oh, and thank you.

You're very welcome. The line was punctuated with a simple smiley face, which did crazy things to Wynn's pulse.

Could she just sit across from Carly and have small talk after seeing her naked? After having made love to every inch of her multiple times? After never wanting to leave her arms? How was she going to explain to Carly what she'd been experiencing without her thinking she was delusional?

When Carly arrived at the bakery, Wynn was already there and had taken a table by the window in the front of the restaurant. She'd caught a glimpse of her as she walked by, and Wynn had smiled and waved. Though she'd always thought keeping company with Wynn would be nice, this was the first time she'd had any contact with her alone, outside of activities that included Suzanna. They'd attempted once or twice before, but something always seemed to get in the way. She remembered Wynn being there at all Suzanna's professional events to help and also at any personal parties she threw. At personal events, such as birthday parties for Suzanna's children, Wynn always managed to spend most of her time with the kids. They seemed to love playing with her, something Carly had noticed long ago and had been a factor in her wanting to get to know Wynn better.

She walked through the door and straight to the table. Wynn immediately hopped up and pulled the chair out for her—gorgeous and sweet. "Hey. Thanks for coming."

"Of course. It's always good to see you." She tried to shake the buzz that ran through her but had to let it run its course.

"You too." Wynn's smile was beautiful. Her full, pink lips pulled into slight indiscernible dimples that became visible only when her smile stretched widely. Carly had been lucky enough to be on the receiving end of that smile more than once.

She tingled, suddenly feeling as though she'd been sprinkled with pixie dust. "Your text this morning was an unexpected surprise."

She watched as the color in Wynn's cheeks reddened and immediately wondered why they hadn't done this before. What was keeping them apart?

The waitress brought two cups to the table and slid them in front of them. Carly wasn't one to be rude, so she would drink whatever Wynn had ordered for her. She took a sip and realized it was a non-fat, vanilla latte prepared exactly as she liked it. "You knew what I usually order?" She tilted her head, trying to remember if they'd ever met for coffee before or even had the opportunity to drink it at the same time. "How?" She knew it was never in the morning. She'd seen Wynn only at Suzanna's events or at afternoon parties, and she didn't usually drink coffee later in the day.

"It's a long story."

"I have time." She was intrigued and really needed to know how Wynn knew her coffee drink of choice. Had she asked Suzanna? If she had, that was ridiculously flattering.

Wynn looked away and fiddled with the spoon on the saucer next to her cup. "Say you knew someone who told you a story you thought to be impossible, but they were adamant that it actually happened. What would you do?"

"I'd listen and try to be open to what they were telling me."

"You'd believe them?"

"That's not quite what I said. I would consider the person and the story, and try to understand what's happening." She touched Wynn's hand and tried desperately to hold her composure as a jolt of familiarity shot through her. "Are you okay?" she asked, unsure of what had just happened and if she, herself, was okay. Her heart raced as she slid her hand back across the table and held her coffee cup. She tried to concentrate on Wynn, but the cup felt cool now in comparison to the heat she'd felt when their hands touched.

"No. Not at all." Wynn took in a breath and blew it out. "I'm just going to get right to it." She pushed her hands down her thighs and gripped her knees. "I spent the most wonderful day with someone yesterday, and she doesn't remember any of it."

Carly's heart felt heavy knowing Wynn was about to confide something to her about another woman. "Tell me about it."

Wynn ran through a story about adopting the mother of her dog, Shadow, a chocolate Lab, named Buttercup, and bathing the dogs

"After all that, we became very close, which led to…" Wynn averted her eyes, hesitating when she reached what Carly thought to be the intimacy she'd shared with this other person.

"I'm not sure I'm the one you should be talking to about this." Carly was disappointed and couldn't hide her reaction. She didn't want to be invested in Wynn's love life as a spectator. Why would Wynn even think that?

"You're exactly the right person." Wynn bolted forward in her seat. "It was you—all of it. The fun, the banter, the intimacy."

Now she was concerned. She pulled her eyebrows together as she thought about what Wynn had just told her. She hadn't seen Wynn in weeks. She hadn't even gone out last night, hadn't run into her anywhere or drank too much. They certainly hadn't gotten together to adopt a dog. "I didn't see you at all yesterday. Are you sure it wasn't a dream?" Why would Wynn be having intimate dreams of her? Could Wynn be making all of this up to get her attention?

"That's entirely possible. But that doesn't make it any less real to me." Wynn reached across the table and held Carly's hand.

A red-hot sizzle of heat blazed through her, and somehow she knew it was all true. "I don't know what to say."

"Say you'll see me tonight after the fund-raiser."

"Okay." She raised her eyebrows. "Probably not naked." At least not yet. "But I'll spend time with you afterward." She watched the smile creep across Wynn's face. "Oh my God. *We had sex* in your dream." She lifted an eyebrow. "If it wasn't a dream you'd know about certain things."

"Like the butterfly tattoo on your hip, just below your panty line."

It couldn't be. How could she know that and Carly not have any memory of showing her?

"You got it when you were sixteen on a dare from your best friend. She has the same one." Wynn's face became redder as she spoke. "When your mom found out, she grounded you for a month."

She shook her head. "My little sister—"

"Carolyn told her because she was pissed at you for something you can't even remember now."

"How did you know that?" She looked around the restaurant like someone was punking her. "What the hell is going on? Did Suzanna tell you?"

"No." She rolled her lips in. "You told me, and I saw the tattoo myself."

"This is unreal. It can't be happening."

"I'm just as confused. I've been reliving the same day all week. I know it's really freaky and just as scary, but it all happened, every minute of it, and I can't get you out of my mind."

"The same day over again?" She put her hand to her mouth. "How many times have we slept together?"

"Technically only once, but we spent hours together other times."

Heat invaded her. Her neck was on fire now. "Hopefully, it was good." She had to know.

"Phenomenal—every time."

She widened her eyes. "*Every* time?"

Wynn nodded and grinned. "You really like sex."

She quirked her lip into a half-smile. "This is so puzzling and embarrassing." She didn't just randomly sleep with women she didn't know very well. She made herself live by this rule. She'd never hid the fact that she thought Wynn was attractive. She'd told Suzanna that more than once. She'd known Wynn for a while, but she didn't really *know* her. What was so special about Wynn that would make Carly break her own rule and sleep with her so quickly? Was she really going to buy into this craziness?

"You're telling me." Wynn's voice rose slightly. "I've been confused for days. I need to figure out what to do to stop the loop—to make the day stop repeating. I keep changing things, but nothing seems to work."

"Maybe we're not meant to be together." The thought was oddly crushing.

"I don't think that's the case." Wynn took in a deep breath. "If it is, then this is some sort of cruel joke the universe is playing on me. I can't imagine not having you in my life now."

She stared into Wynn's eyes, and heat rushed through her again. "I can't imagine that either." She was completely turned on. "So, what do you want to do next?"

"I'm not sure it'll work, but I have a plan." Wynn leaned forward like they were plotting some covert attack. "We have to go to the fund-raiser tonight."

"We didn't last night." She shook her head, trying to get on track with what was happening. "I mean during the last loop?"

"No. We stayed home. At my house." Wynn seemed to hesitate until Carly connected the dots.

"In bed?" The thought of how Wynn could have made her forget all her rules still baffled her.

Wynn scrunched her nose and nodded. "The time before, we talked on the phone all night." She chuckled. "I was an ass and you forgave me."

"That's good to know." She laughed along with her. "I mean, that you can admit when you're an ass. I'd hate to think you don't have some redeeming qualities."

"During these past few days I've come to realize that I'd do just about anything for you."

No one had ever said something that romantic to Carly before. She didn't know what the hell was going on but felt compelled to explore it.

"I'll pick you up at five. We'll help Suzanna with the fund-raiser and then go someplace and talk?" The uncertainty in Wynn's voice was disarming.

"Okay." She drank the rest of her latte before she got up. "I'll see you then." She gave her a subtle smile. "Don't be late."

"Nope. Never. You hate that."

And she did. Carly walked out of the bakery feeling a thousand times happier than she had when she walked in. Happier than she'd felt in a very long time. She didn't know if any of what Wynn had said was true, but her heart wanted to believe it so badly.

CHAPTER NINETEEN

Wynn's day had gone exactly as it had before. She'd picked up Buttercup, who was now safely tucked away with Shadow at home. She would take care of persuading Jack and Maria to adopt her tomorrow if she had the opportunity, or she'd just go to the shelter and adopt her all over again.

Everything was done at work, and no one had lost their job. When Wynn had entered her office, Evelyn was turned in her chair gazing out the window. She was just about to head out for the day when Evelyn summoned her. "You wanted to see me?"

Evelyn spun her chair around to her desk and reached for something in her drawer. "I think this day deserves a celebration. Don't you?" She set two Waterford highball glasses and a bottle of bourbon on her desk.

"It was a pretty good one."

"You have plans tonight?"

She glanced at her watch and calculated the time she could spare. "I do, but I have time for a drink."

"Great." Evelyn poured them each a finger of bourbon. "If you want ice, you'll have to fetch it from the canteen."

"Neat is fine." She took one of the glasses and held it up. "To saving jobs." That benefit resonated most for Wynn.

Evelyn clicked her glass against Wynn's. "To saving this company."

She sipped her drink and enjoyed the burn as it crossed her tongue and entered her throat before she pulled a chair next to Evelyn's and faced the window.

Evelyn spoke to the window as she drank. "I have to say, I didn't expect the turnaround from you today. Working *with you* rather than against you was refreshing. You and I make a good team."

"I agree. We do."

"To be honest, I knew you had a plan of your own and fully anticipated a battle. I didn't expect all those nice things you said about me to leadership." Evelyn shook her head. "Did you mean them?"

"Yes. Absolutely. Everything I said was true." She hadn't seen the benefit of Evelyn's wisdom until the past few days, and she'd developed an admiration for her. Evelyn always seemed to be looking out for the employees and the company.

Evelyn sipped her bourbon. "I've been kind of an ass to you since you started reporting to me, and I thought you'd retaliate."

"True. As I told you earlier, that was my original plan."

Evelyn laughed. "What prompted the change?"

"I guess you might say I got a glimpse of what my life would be in the future if we remained on paths working against each other. Kinda of like Scrooge in *A Christmas Carol*."

Evelyn swirled the liquid in her glass. "That's a much deeper explanation than I expected."

"What *did you* expect?"

"You knew you'd lose and wanted to keep your job." Evelyn smirked.

"Maybe that too." She smiled slightly and drank the remaining bourbon in her glass. If Evelyn only knew how much today had impacted her future, she'd be stunned. She'd keep that information to herself, for Evelyn would never believe her if she told her the truth. Obviously they both had a lot to learn about being humble, which they could both gain from watching Jack.

The voice that came from behind them was loud and angry. The clang of the door against the wall prompted them both to twist in their chairs. Davis had pushed by Evelyn's assistant and was coming at them hot.

Wynn launched out of her chair and blocked his path, taking a hard hit to her shoulder as she fell against the desk. She bounced back and gave Davis a palm strike directly to his nose, which stopped him. He immediately grabbed his face as blood dripped from his nose.

"What the fuck?" He looked at the blood in his hands. "You broke my nose."

She held her shoulder as pain shot through it. "You assaulted me."

"Call security." Evelyn shouted to her assistant. "And medical."

Wynn turned to Evelyn. "I'm sorry."

"No. Thank you for stopping him." Evelyn pulled her eyebrows together and touched her shoulder, and Wynn winced at the pain. "Are you hurt?"

"My shoulder may be dislocated." She was familiar with the feeling. It wasn't the first time.

She was going to be late picking up Carly tonight, and Carly hated it when people weren't punctual—one of the things she'd learned over the past few days. She found her phone and ordered a car to drive Carly to the event. Hopefully that would be okay. She'd instruct the driver to come here to get her after he dropped off Carly. She wouldn't have time to run by the house and change, which was disappointing. She wanted to look her best for Carly tonight. She'd have to wear the suit she'd put on for work this morning. In fact, her shoulder hurt so badly, she couldn't even change into the spare shirt in her office. She'd just started a text to Carly when the medical crew entered the office and went toward Davis, who sat in a chair holding a wad of tissues under his nose.

Evelyn pointed at Wynn. "Check her first."

One of the on-staff doctors came to her immediately. "Where are you hurt?"

"My shoulder."

Evelyn assisted the doctor in removing Wynn's coat before he examined her. "Have you ever had a dislocated shoulder before?"

"Once. In high school." She'd been on the softball team and had collided with another player while fielding a ball.

"I'm going to try to move it back into place."

"Okay." She closed her eyes and braced for the pain, which came almost immediately. She bit her lip to avoid screaming.

"Got it." The doctor ripped open a package, adjusted a sling to hold her arm semi-immobile, and placed it on her arm.

Apparently nothing was broken except Davis's nose. Thankfully the company had an on-campus clinic and she hadn't had to go to the emergency room. She sent a text to Carly telling her she was sending a car and hoped she wouldn't be angry.

Carly was confused when the driver from the car service rang her bell and said Wynn had sent him to pick her up and take her to the restaurant. He knew all the particulars of where and when the event was being held, so she believed him.

"Where is Ms. Jamison? Are we picking her up next?" She slid into the backseat of the car. Her place was closer to the venue than Wynn's, which was a clear indication they weren't.

"She's running late."

She checked her phone, and just then a text from Wynn popped up on the screen.

I'll meet you there. Running late at work. Fixing things. I sent a car.

Irritation filled her, spoiling her mood. She had never been a kept woman and didn't intend to be. She closed her eyes and calmed herself before she responded.

Already figured that out. This is not how things will work between us. I'm not a convenience and won't ever be considered one.

Definitely not my intent to make you feel that way. More bubbles appeared, went away, then reappeared before another message came through. Wynn was obviously rethinking her message. *I'm really sorry. I'll probably be explaining this whole day to you again tomorrow. Hopefully you'll still believe me.*

Carly had to laugh at that. The whole scenario *was* unbelievable.

That's entirely possible. She sent the message back. Then she hesitated before she typed, *Hurry. If that's the case, we don't have much time.*

After their conversation this morning, Carly had been thinking about Wynn all day, and she really wanted to explore whatever was happening with her. She was still on the edge of believing her, but that could change soon. If Wynn was only trying to get into her pants, she wouldn't have been late. Wynn's behavior at the party would dictate how the night would end.

She'd been at the event for close to an hour when Wynn came in the door, escorted by another woman. She blinked her eyes to make sure she was seeing things right. The woman had a bottle of something in one hand, and her arm was laced through Wynn's arm. *What the fuck?* Now she was really angry. Everything Wynn had told her this morning appeared to be a fabrication.

She rushed across the room. "Is she why you didn't pick me up?"

"Not exactly." Wynn looked from Carly to the woman and then back again.

The woman interrupted them. "Let me explain. I'm Jean. A friend of Wynn's." She held up the bottle. "She came by to get the Louis XIII. I thought I should bring it myself since she has some drugs in her."

She'd been so upset, Carly hadn't even noticed the jacket draped over the sling holding her arm. "Oh my God. What happened?"

"Dislocated shoulder. Things got a little out of hand at work today."

Now she felt absolutely awful. She'd reached all the wrong conclusions about Wynn without even giving her the benefit of the doubt.

Jean laughed. "Apparently saving jobs can be dangerous." She handed the bottle to the bartender. "Keep that under lock and key."

Jean leaned Wynn against the bar as she glanced around the room. "So, where's this sister of yours?"

"I'm going to introduce Jean to Jordan. I think they'll hit it off."

"Oh. Let me find her."

"No." Wynn's voice was urgent. "I sent her a text before we came in. She's going to meet us here." Wynn reached into her pocket but quickly put her hand on the wood rim of the bar for balance.

She took the phone from Wynn's pocket and held it up for her.

"The code's Julianna's birthday."

Carly typed in Suzanna's oldest child's birthday and read the text from Jordan to Wynn. "She's on her way over now." She slid the phone back into Wynn's pocket before she slipped under her shoulder to help steady her.

"Sorry. The muscle relaxers the doc gave me are really strong."

"You're fine. I'm just glad you're all right." Someone else would have to take care of what was left to be done tonight. She needed to get Wynn home to rest. After she caught Suzanna's eye from across the room, Suzanna did a double take before she weaved through several groups of people to the bar.

"What the hell happened?"

"Just a small accident at work."

"I don't think that's completely true." She glanced at Wynn. "Somehow she got a dislocated shoulder. I'm not sure why she even came tonight."

"I came because of you." Wynn smiled widely. "That's why I'm always here."

Suzanna grinned. "Apparently she's been given some super-powerful truth serum."

She quirked her lip up to one side. "Seems that way. She needs to go home and rest."

"I'm good here." Suzanna glanced around the room. "Why don't you take her and explore more of that free-flowing truth?" She pulled her eyebrows together. "How did she get here?"

"Car service, I assume." She hadn't told Suzanna that Wynn had sent a car for her earlier. She fished Wynn's phone from her jacket pocket and handed it to Suzanna.

"She's got the car for the night. It should still be around here, somewhere. I'll send a message that she's leaving, and you can take her out front." Suzanna handed the phone back. "Just tell him to wait while you get her inside her house. Then he can take you home." She glanced around the room again. Suzanna was always watching to make sure everything ran smoothly. "Oh, and you'll probably need to let Shadow, her puppy, outside to go to the bathroom."

She has a puppy. Her heart melted at the adoption story Wynn had told her earlier. Could this woman be any more perfect?

While she'd been talking to Suzanna, Jordan had made it to the bar and had now captured Jean's complete attention. They didn't need to stay any longer.

❖

Wynn had woken when the car pulled to the curb due to an emergency vehicle passing them going the other way. Once they arrived at her house, Carly walked with her to the porch. She seemed steadier now, the pain medication probably wearing off. Wynn struggled to take her keys from her coat pocket, so Carly found them and opened the door. Immediately a black puppy and a larger chocolate Labrador greeted them.

Wynn scooped up the puppy. "Hey, Shadow. How's my sweet girl?" She nuzzled her against her neck before she handed her off to Carly and reached down to pet the other dog. "And how're you, Buttercup?" She crossed the room to the back door, let them outside, and stepped onto the patio.

She followed her out. "Suzanna doesn't know you adopted another dog yet?"

"Nope. She's Shadow's mom. I just got her today. Couldn't leave her at the shelter." Wynn grinned. "I already told you that, didn't I?" Wynn still seemed a little high from the pain medication.

She nodded. "It's a beautiful night." The yard was lined with accent lights that brought attention to the multiple flower-filled pots surrounding the grass. "You have a gorgeous yard."

"Thanks. I don't get to spend as much time here as I'd like."

"Oh? Why's that?"

"Work is busy." Wynn rubbed her forehead. "I've been trying to make it to chief operating officer before my thirtieth birthday." She shook her head. "Not going to do that."

"Because?" Her education had taught her how to ask open-ended questions to get to the heart of any subject.

"Tomorrow's my birthday, and today I changed my whole plan." Wynn stared into the yard. "It was completely necessary. What I had planned for today was going to ruin a lot of people's lives."

"Then I'm glad you changed it."

"Me too." Shadow appeared at Wynn's feet, and Wynn scooped her up again and held her against her chest. "All done, baby?" She kissed Shadow's nose before she turned around, went back inside, and waited for Carly and Buttercup to follow her. "I'm sorry. I totally ruined your night."

"Don't worry about me. I'm fine. I should be thanking you. I got out of cleanup, which is always a plus."

"You're so sweet." Wynn sighed. "Why can't we ever make this work?"

"We can discuss that tomorrow."

"You won't remember any of it. We should use our time wisely." Wynn grinned and bounced her eyebrows at her.

She was so cute, so relaxed, so happy. Carly hated to reject her, but whatever future foundation they built together would not start this way. "Why aren't we together in the future?"

"You married Jordan."

She was stunned. "What?" Jordan had never had any interaction with her even at her fund-raising events. How could she go from being so intrigued by Wynn to being married to Jordan? Wynn must have done something to put some distance between them, or Jordan must have done something really spectacular.

"My sister sucks, and you fell in love with her anyway."

That response didn't give her much to go on. "Why would I marry your sister when you and I clearly have so much more in common?"

"She's very charming. But she can also be a complete ass. You're not happy." Wynn took a bottle of pills from her pocket and fumbled with it.

"I'm not?" She took the bottle from Wynn, popped the top off, and let one spill out into her palm.

Wynn shook her head. "And that sucks because I'm in love with you." Wynn popped the pill into her mouth and washed it down with a drink of water from the sink.

"You are? In the future or now?" She stared into Wynn's eyes and could see her feelings clearly. The thought of marriage had always worried her. Finding someone to spend the rest of your life with was enormously important. Second chances in life were scarce. Actually connecting with the woman she would be with forever was much scarier than anything else in the world. How did Wynn know her so well without really knowing her at all? "Are we involved in the future?" This whole story Wynn was telling seemed crazy. She refused to believe she would cheat on her wife. Why was she even buying into it?

Wynn shook her head. "Nope. We're not going down that path. Can't." She went to the bedroom, took off her jacket, then stepped out of her loafers before she unbuttoned her pants and let them fall to the floor. "You refuse to get a divorce." She yanked the blanket back and slipped under the sheet. "You think your reputation won't withstand the scandal, and I would never hurt you."

That's exactly what Wynn was doing now. She was breaking her heart without having even held it. "You need to rest."

"Yes. Rest." Wynn patted the spot on the bed next to her and then curled on her side facing her. "Please stay. I want to wake up next to you and watch the sunrise. I'll be good. Promise." She let out a heavy sigh. "Say you'll remember me tomorrow, lying here with you, staring into each other's eyes, even if it's only in your dreams."

"Of course I will, silly. I'll never be able to forget you."

She lay down next to Wynn and scrunched the pillow beneath her head. She wasn't ready to leave yet, and she'd sent the driver on his way after he'd dropped them off. "Have you ever watched the sunrise on the beach?" It had been one of the things Carly had imagined in her future—stepping out from her home onto the beach each morning. "Sitting in the sand, wrapped in a blanket to keep the chill from filling you?"

Wynn nodded. "You wrapped in my arms within that blanket. My heat keeping you warm."

The vision rushed through her head, and she warmed at the thought. "Yes. Exactly that." She stroked Wynn's cheek. "You seem to be my match in every way."

"I've been waiting for the day I can see the sunrise on your face—in your eyes." Wynn's eyes drifted closed. "Destiny."

She remained silent as she imagined waking up next to this beautiful, compassionate woman until she heard long heavy breaths of sleep coming from Wynn, which happened quickly due to the pain medication. "I could easily fall in love with you." Carly covered Wynn with the blanket, careful not to move her arm, and covered herself with the throw from the bottom of the bed. The whole scenario, lying here with Wynn, listening to her breathe, was oddly comforting. Familiar even.

Chapter Twenty

Fuck. Fuck. Fuck." Wynn pulled the pillow from behind her neck and threw it across the room. Shadow squealed, and she launched out of bed to find her. "I'm so sorry, honey." She held her against her chest and soothed her before she held her up and looked into her little black eyes. "What am I doing wrong?" Shadow licked her nose. "Right. You think I'm wonderful." She padded to the living room, avoiding the puddle in her path, and opened the back door. "Go potty, and I'll get breakfast." She dropped a wad of paper towels onto the wet spot and walked into the kitchen.

After she filled Shadow's bowl with kibble, she checked her phone and saw the voice mail from Jordan. Today she wasn't going to text Carly. She was just going to wing it. She took the sticky notes from her laptop bag and recreated the list she'd written yesterday with all the events of the day and what had happened within each repetition. What more could there be besides the three areas she'd focused on?

"Think, Wynn. What else happened on this day last year?" She went to the coffeemaker, spooned several scoops of coffee into the basket, filled it with water, and flipped the switch.

Work. She'd fixed everything there. No one had lost their job, not even that snake, Davis, until after he'd assaulted her. Home. Jack and Maria were good, and she'd adopted Buttercup, which made Shadow happy. The fund-raiser. She'd done that several ways—gone early, gone late, hadn't even gone at all. It didn't seem to make a difference. What was she missing?

She slipped on a flannel shirt, went out on the deck, and sat. Maybe a little meditation would help her figure it out. Maybe she wasn't meant to be with Carly. She shook the thought from her head. No. Everything between them had been perfect each time. She stretched her arms above her head and felt no pain in her shoulder, but she wished it hurt like a motherfucker right now. At least then the day would be new.

Carly's last words to her the night before echoed in her head. *I could easily fall in love with you.* She'd really said that. She'd wanted to turn over, gather her in her arms, and hold her for the rest of the night. Carly had curled up behind her, draped her arm across her waist, and pressed herself into Wynn's back. It was the most comforting feeling in the world. If only she had found her there this morning, life would be perfect, but the day had reset again.

Carly wants kids. Maybe she needs reassurance that I want them too. What about Jordan? She hadn't considered where she would end up in this whole thing. What if she needed someone other than Carly? Jesus. Who would she set Jordan up with? Last night it was Jean, but maybe she needed a challenge like Evelyn. Was Evelyn even gay? If anyone could make that happen, it would be Jordan. Maybe something totally different hadn't even entered her mind. Talk about a never-ending list of possibilities.

Her cheeks burned with the heat from her tears. Shadow stared up at her from her usual spot near her feet. "I'm okay, baby." She wiped the moisture from her face, then slapped her legs, summoning Shadow onto her lap. "We'll be okay." Shadow licked her chin. "We're going to get your momma today." She would do everything all over again until she got it right.

The door flew open, and Wynn burst into Carly's office with Stephanie, her assistant, right behind her. "I'm sorry, Doctor Evans. I couldn't stop her."

"Wynn?" She was confused. Why was she here, and what was so urgent? "I'm in the middle of a session." Terror rushed her. "Is Suzanna okay? The kids?"

"They're fine, but I need to talk to you."

"Can it wait?" She glanced at her patient.

It didn't seem to faze Wynn that other people were around. "Two days ago we had the most spectacular day together adopting a chocolate Lab named Buttercup. The next night we spent the whole night making love, and you still looked gorgeous. Last night I injured my shoulder, and you took care of me." When she tried to interrupt, Wynn put her hand up. "Wait. I'm not done. Tonight, I'm going to take you home from the fund-raiser…" She hesitated when her voice cracked. "And I'm going to hold you close and never let you go." The tenderness in her voice was palpable.

"Oh my God, that's insanely romantic." Her client looked from Carly to Wynn and then back again. "Is this your girlfriend?"

"Yes," Wynn said immediately and dropped to her knees in front of Carly's chair.

Her client covered her mouth with her hands. "Oh my God. She's going to propose."

"No," Carly said firmly. "She's not." She pulled her eyebrows together as she felt Wynn's forehead. "Are you okay?"

Wynn nodded and stared into her eyes. "It wasn't just a dream, was it?" she whispered.

She could see that Wynn was distraught but didn't know what to say. She'd always hoped there would be something between them, and lately Wynn had been in her thoughts constantly. But nothing that Wynn just said had ever happened.

"Can we talk about this after my session is over?"

Her client stood. "I think you should take care of this now. I'll reschedule." She headed across the office. "Wow. Nice play." She gave Wynn a thumbs-up.

Carly launched out of her seat. "I'm so sorry about this." She followed her client to the door.

"Don't be. This has given me hope. Romance still exists in the world. I might have a chance for happiness in life." She glanced at Carly before she went out the door. "Hold on to her."

She smiled and waited for the door to completely close before crossing the room to Wynn. "Explain this to me. Now." She couldn't calm the anger in her voice.

Wynn took the chair across from her and leaned forward, her elbows on her knees. "It's all true. Every word of it. I swear. We've made love many times. I know every part of you by memory. The curve of your hip, the swell of your breasts, the way you spoon perfectly into me when you sleep." She swallowed hard. "And the small tattoo just below your panty line, the way you jolt when I press my lips to it."

What Wynn said completely aroused Carly, but she hadn't experienced any of this. "Wynn." She blew her name out slowly and shook her head. "Maybe this is all real in your mind, but none of what you're saying happened with *me*. Three days ago I was here all day, and the last two nights I was in bed *completely alone*."

"Completely?" Wynn tilted her head and gave her a half-smile.

"Just me." She raised her hands. "All by myself."

Wynn grinned. "You're not seeing anyone because most women are too clingy. They want more from you than you can give." Wynn scooted forward in her seat. "You want a woman who can support herself and has the confidence to support you in your career without getting jealous of your time or attention."

Warmth shot through Carly as the back of her neck began to burn. "How do you know that?"

"You told me."

She searched her mind. "I don't recall ever telling you anything like that. In fact, I don't recall us ever having a conversation with you that extended past the weather or the kung pao chicken at Suzanna's events."

"I've been living today over again. I guess it's going to happen until I get it right, which I can't seem to do."

"Where is she?" She bolted up, went to the door, and pulled it open.

"Who?" Wynn looked confused.

"Suzanna. She put you up to this, didn't she?" She went to her desk, picked up her phone, and hit Suzanna's number.

Wynn raced to her and took it. "It's no joke. It really happened." She pleaded with her. "You love sunrises on the beach. We're going to buy a house there and watch them every day together."

"Oh my God." It was like she'd read her every thought. "Tell me more."

"And you want kids. Lots of them." Wynn's face lit up like she'd just made a new discovery. "You're going to be such a wonderful mother to our kids."

"You want kids?" She tilted her head.

"Absolutely. I love kids." She smiled widely. "Have ever since Suzanna brought those sweet little munchkins of hers into the world."

Warmth captured her. Wynn was her perfect match. "I didn't know that about you." She'd heard Suzanna talk about how much her kids loved Wynn, but they'd never discussed Wynn's thoughts on having children of her own.

Wynn continued to explain the events of the past few days, and Carly didn't know what to say. Wynn knew details of her life that she hadn't shared with even Suzanna, and she was her closest friend.

"I know you think I'm crazy, but it all happened."

"Something must've happened." She put her fingers to her forehead.

"Do you believe me?"

"I don't know. I'm not sure what to believe or what you want from me."

"I want what we've had the past few days."

She scratched her head and blew out a breath. "Uh. I don't know what we had, but I'm not even close to the intimacy you're describing."

"I know. I'm not asking you to jump into bed with me, just to trust me and give us a chance. See where it leads." Wynn looked sincere. She didn't see any sign of deception, but none of this could be true. Could it? What was she going to do? She should call Suzanna. But how could she tell her that her sister was delusional? Panic raced through her. Maybe she was the one who was delusional.

She went against every professional thing she knew and said, "Okay. I'll give us a chance."

The expression on Wynn's face went from distress to pure joy. "Thank you." She took her hand and held it between hers. "I'll pick you up tonight at six."

"You don't have to do that."

"I want to. A beautiful woman like you should never go anywhere unescorted."

In that moment, with that one small gesture, somehow amid all the craziness, Carly knew everything was going to be all right.

❖

As soon as Wynn left Carly's office, Stephanie rushed in. "What was that about?"

"She's apparently had some epiphany about life that includes me."

"Have you two ever dated?"

She shook her head. "No. Not really. I mean, we've spent time together at events, but not alone."

"Are you going to in the future? It sure sounds like she wants to."

"I agreed to see her tonight. Yes." She closed her eyes and second-guessed her decision. "I'm not sure that was the right choice." What if everything she'd said wasn't a dream? What if it was some alternate reality created in Wynn's mind?

"I think it's a great decision." Stephanie grinned. "You never go out. It'll do you good to loosen up. I can think of worse things than indulging in some pleasurable satisfaction with someone as hot as her." She fanned her hand in front of her face. "Even if it turns out to be only short-term."

"I don't think it would be all about sex with her."

"Even better." Stephanie strode to the door. "Your next appointment isn't for another hour, so you have time to think about it." She glanced over her shoulder and grinned as she closed the door behind her.

Carly paced her office and then flopped onto the couch and curled up on her side. What had she gotten herself in to? Everything Wynn had said spoke to her deepest desires. That had to mean something. Didn't it?

❖

Wynn knew she'd sounded desperate this morning. She'd seen that probability in Carly's eyes as she explained the past few days to her. But the way Carly's shocked expression had changed to one of curiosity as she provided all the details of what they'd shared over the past few days gave her hope. The intimate details of Carly's hopes and dreams had seemed to make her more willing to listen and to give Wynn another chance tonight.

After they'd successfully united and presented their solution to leadership, Wynn, Evelyn, and Jack had entered each floor together and walked the halls reassuring the employees they would have no workforce reduction, that their jobs were safe. The relief among the different teams was evident, and the news seemed to precede them on each floor they entered until the last floor full of employees actually stood and applauded as they exited the elevator. A lot of fear, uncertainty, and doubt had been circling through the masses for close to a month now.

On each floor of the building, they'd also let all the employees know what they expected of them in the future. Anyone who wasn't up to the task of bringing this company back into the black was free to find employment elsewhere. Not a threat by any means, only a subtle way of bringing everyone on board with their future success. They would all receive bonuses and salary increases when the company made money, but they needed to earn them. Their new positions in the company would ensure the plan was followed.

Once they were done spreading the good news, they all headed back into the elevator. When it stopped at the floor where Wynn and Evelyn's offices were located, Evelyn stepped out while Wynn held the door and turned back to Jack.

"Can you meet me at my house in an hour? I have a favor to ask." She didn't go into the details of Buttercup's adoption. That would take more time than she needed to waste this morning. She would find a way to make sure his wife, Maria, fell in love with her immediately today.

He glanced at his watch. "I guess I can go home for lunch."

"Great. Can you get Maria to meet us there as well?"

"I'll check." He scrunched his eyebrows together. "What—"

"Thanks. I'll see you both then." She let the elevator doors close and then went into Evelyn's office. Now to get her to come to the fund-raiser tonight.

"So. Hey. I'm going to a fund-raiser my sister, Jordan, is putting on for Children's Hospital tonight. You want to come along?" She tried not to be too obvious.

Evelyn raised an eyebrow. "Where is it?"

"The Waterbar, her usual venue. The food is always fabulous."

"Your sister works for a non-profit?"

"Yep. Has for years. Some influential people should be there." She knew that would get her. Evelyn was all about schmoozing to get ahead.

"She must be very different from you."

"Somewhat." She saw the scrutiny in Evelyn's eyes and didn't dare tell her she'd learned all her business tactics from Jordan. She wanted her to see Jordan's charming side first. "She does a lot of good for the community." Which she did, but she just handled things in a different manner than Wynn.

"Open bar?"

"Always."

"See you there."

She gave herself a silent fist-pump. Now she had two matches for Jordan. Hopefully, she was one step closer to ending this crazy day.

Chapter Twenty-one

Wynn hadn't been able to find a spot anywhere near Carly's townhouse, so she'd called her and let her know she was double-parked in front of the building. Nob Hill was a beautiful area of San Francisco, but Wynn would never be able to stand the traffic or the noise. She enjoyed the serenity of the suburbs as well as the space. When she saw Carly come out the front door, she had to catch her breath. Dressed in the same black, form-fitting, sleeveless lace dress she'd worn every night before, Carly was stunning. The contrasting, creamy skin of her shoulders made memories of kissing them fill her mind. She shook the thought from her head and tried to calm herself as she got out of the Jeep and raced around to open the door for her.

"You look positively gorgeous tonight."

"You look pretty dashing yourself." Carly's eyes roamed her from head to toe.

"Well, thank you." She smiled as she held out her hand for Carly to hold as she got into the Jeep. She'd worn the same khaki pants with a long-sleeved cream-colored, button-down shirt and a tan cotton blazer just to match Carly.

The ride to the event wasn't long, but it had been quiet. Did Carly's silence indicate that she'd had second thoughts about everything they'd discussed this morning? She reached across the console and took her hand. Carly seemed to startle and then took in a deep breath.

"You're not afraid of me, are you?"

"No. Not at all." Carly glanced at her. "I'm just puzzled. It's a lot to comprehend."

"I can work with that." She smiled, relieved Carly still *wanted* to understand.

"Everything in my nature—*and my education*—tells me this isn't possible." She glanced at their hands, clasped together perfectly. "Yet the lightest of touches from you does something to me that I can't explain."

She attempted to release Carly's hand, and Carly held it tighter. "Do you want me to stop?"

"No. Please don't. It's a wonderful feeling. I want to follow my…" Carly veered her eyes to the road. "Instincts."

She sighed as the familiar warmth rushed through her. Wynn knew exactly what Carly meant. She'd felt it since the day they'd met. "How was your day?"

Carly grinned. "You mean besides the distraught woman who broke into my office this morning."

"Yeah, besides her." She instinctively lifted Carly's hand and pressed the back of it to her lips, holding it there briefly, indulging in the softness of her skin.

"It was interesting. I'll tell you about it later." Carly watched her as Wynn kept her hand in hers and rested them on her thigh.

The sexy, sideways glance Carly gave her sent a jolt directly between her legs and practically knocked her out of her seat. This was going to be the longest event ever. She returned her eyes to the road. All in good time. "That'll be the highlight of my night."

"Tell me about your day."

"I did a few good things, I think." She smiled as she weaved in and out of traffic. "I saved a few jobs at work."

"Really? What happened?"

"There was a plan to cut the workforce, and three of us—me, my boss, and another manager—brainstormed a plan to save money without cutting jobs."

"Hmm." Carly pulled her eyebrows together. "What exactly do you do for a living?"

"Technically, I'm a corporate suit. In reality I manage day-to-day IT operations."

"That sounds quite fulfilling."

"It can be on days like today. Others not so much." She glanced at Carly, who seemed to be scrutinizing every inch of her.

When their eyes met, Carly blushed. "Anything else?"

"I also adopted the mother of my Labrador-retriever puppy, Shadow."

"That's a cute name. How did you come up with it?"

"She has a habit of blending into the darkness during the night. I've tripped over her several times. Plus, it's the only name she'll answer to. Apparently, she didn't like Raisin, Eggroll, or Rhubarb." She grinned.

"Eggroll?" Carly raised an eyebrow. "Really?" She blew out a breath as though thoroughly disgusted. "I'm with Shadow on those. Who wants to be named after food?"

"Okay, Miss Smartypants. What would your choice have been?"

"If you were going to stick with food, Taco would be the best."

"Why's that?"

"No one would ever question when you brought her along because there's always room for tacos." Carly winked, and the familiar tingle in Wynn's stomach appeared. "Shadow is good, though. I like it."

"Okay. So, Taco is for our next dog." She smiled as she pulled up in front of the restaurant.

"Deal." Carly hadn't hesitated. Maybe this would work out after all. The valet opened Carly's door, and she slid out of the SUV.

Wynn usually parked herself because she could get out quicker at the end of the night. The valet always kept a spot for her, but she refused to make Carly walk even a block to the restaurant in heels.

She rounded the Jeep and took Carly's hand before she opened the door for her. Suzanna raced across to meet them as soon as they entered the restaurant. "Wow. Aren't you two prompt this evening." Suzanna glanced behind them. "Did you come together?"

"Yes." They responded at once.

Wynn bit her bottom lip and grinned as so many other meanings for that question flew through her head. Her cheeks were definitely on fire now. Carly seemed to notice and turned a beautiful shade of pink. Embarrassment had never looked so good.

"Wow. Now you have me wondering what happened in the car. You're both glowing like you just ran a three-minute mile."

She cleared her throat. "Carly's place is on my way."

"She offered to pick me up." Carly finished the sentence.

Suzanna observed them suspiciously. "Um, I gathered that." She moved her finger through the air in front of them. "You look good together."

She smiled widely. She'd made the right decision by wearing the same clothes as before. They complemented Carly's dress perfectly. Just one more thing to seal the deal.

Wynn glanced around the room, trying to get the spotlight off them. "Looks like everything is already done. What can we do?"

"We still need to bring a few things out from the kitchen. Napkins and silverware, but the restaurant staff has everything else under control. They hired extra staff tonight to help. Apparently, they like us." She glanced at Jordan across the room, who was now greeting early guests. "If I can just manage to keep Jordan away from them, we'll be in good shape."

Jordan wasn't very forgiving when it came to slow responses or dillydallying. If you were working an event, you should always be doing something.

Wynn smiled when she saw Jean enter with the bottle of cognac. She was dressed in a royal-blue slip dress that Wynn knew would enhance her eyes as much as all her other lovely body parts. She'd called her earlier and asked her to bring it by, told her she'd introduce her to her sister, who was much more interesting than her.

Evelyn always showed up late, so if Jean and Jordan didn't hit it off and Jean left early, she'd be none the wiser. Hopefully her plan of finding someone to spark Jordan's interest wouldn't blow up in her face.

Wynn helped Carly and Suzanna with the mechanics of the event, and everything was running smoothly. Carly had stepped out of the kitchen to use the restroom. She just hoped nothing went wrong in the kitchen. Thoughts scrambled through her head—wrong food, not enough food, dwindling liquor. Fire. She took a sip of her drink. She had to stop panicking, or the night would go to shit anyway just because of her anxiety. She leaned back against the counter and heard a crash behind her. *Fuck*. She spun around to see that a huge bowl of lettuce had spilled to the ground. She immediately grabbed the metal bowl and began shoveling it back into the container.

"Wow. You sure know how to impress a woman, don't you?" The amusement in Suzanna's voice was ridiculous. "Don't worry. She's not back yet."

She grabbed the back of her neck, which was on fire. "Unfuckingbelievable." She glanced around, looking for any sign of Carly. "Do I need to go get more?" This was the third accident she'd had in the kitchen tonight. They weren't huge, but her mojo was definitely off.

"Nope. We have plenty." Suzanna stared at her for a moment. "I was just teasing earlier, but you really like her." She found a broom and dustpan and started sweeping the lettuce into a pile.

She nodded as she took the dustpan from Suzanna. "You have no idea."

"Wow. I've never seen you like this. Are you okay?" Suzanna seemed concerned.

She knelt and held the dustpan while Suzanna swept even more lettuce into it. "Let's just say the past few days have been a little freaky."

Suzanna clenched the broomstick and squatted next to her. "What do you mean?" She plucked up a few outlying pieces of lettuce that had landed under the metal platform.

"I feel like some supernatural power is happening around me. It's not like things are moving on their own around me, but it kinda is."

Suzanna stopped as she knelt, lettuce in her hands, and drew her eyebrows together. "You're scaring me a little."

"I'm fine. Some things have happened with Carly, and I don't know how to make them permanent."

Suzanna laughed as she grinned. “Just be you, silly. You’re a fucking awesome woman.”

“I don’t know about that, but I’m trying to be a better person.”

Carly came through the door. “Oh, my. What happened?”

Suzanna sprang up and swept the remaining mess into the dustpan. “I caught the bowl with my arm.” Suzanna rubbed her elbow. “You know how clumsy I am.”

Wynn couldn’t love her sister any more than she did right then. She always had her back.

After the spectacle Wynn had made of herself this morning at Carly’s office, she’d told herself to stay cool and keep the conversation light, and to let Carly talk about herself more. Most people liked that, but Carly wasn’t having any part of it. So far this evening she’d managed to do the opposite on all counts.

“Let me have that.” Carly took the broom from Suzanna and continued to sweep the remnants of scattered lettuce into the pan Wynn was holding on the floor. “What else needs to be done?”

“Roll these napkins.” Suzanna went to an unfolded pile on another counter.

“We can handle that.” Carly glanced at Wynn, who was dumping the remaining salad into the trash can. “Right, Ms. Butterfingers?” She winked.

“How’d you know it was me?”

“You’ve been a walking disaster area since we arrived.” Carly smiled softly. “You don’t need to be nervous around me. I’m just your average, everyday girl.”

But Carly was mistaken. She was so much more than average to Wynn. Carly was way out of her league, and Wynn couldn’t stop the butterflies from fluttering in her stomach every time Carly looked at her.

“Come on.” Carly reached for her hand and then pulled back, seeming to second-guess her actions. “You grab that basket, I’ll get the napkins, and let’s find a table in a corner somewhere and knock these out.”

They had just about finished folding napkins. The restaurant staff had already provided plenty, but Suzanna was always prepared.

Everything was going smoothly since they'd moved out of the danger zone of the kitchen and into the restaurant area.

"So, you didn't tell me earlier. Do you have any pets?"

Carly pursed her lips. "Not another word about me until you share-more about yourself."

"Okay." She set the last bunch of perfectly rolled napkins into the basket and relaxed into her chair. "What do you want to know?"

"Family? Work? Or both?" Carly's face was intense. She was on her second glass of wine and still hadn't seemed to relax.

"Does it have to be one or the other?"

Carly raised an eyebrow. "If you know anything about me, you know which one is the most important."

"Family," she said softly. "Your love and devotion for them astounds me."

A smile crept across Carly's face. "Spot-on."

"My family is different. We're close but don't spend as much time together as I'd like." She leaned forward and settled her forearms on the table. "Tell me this. If you had family plans and got a call from a client who needed you right now, would you answer? Let it pull you away from your family?"

"That's different."

"Is it?"

"Hell, yes, it's different. Sometimes it's life or death for my clients."

The passion she saw in Carly made her love her even more. "Okay. I understand that, but what if it wasn't? Say it was just a simple question? Would you still answer?"

Carly flattened her lips. "I wouldn't know it was simple until I answered."

"So let's compromise. Work *only* comes first if it's a dire emergency." When Carly raised an eyebrow, Wynn lifted a finger. "I stipulate that we will determine the definition of dire at a later date."

"Agreed." Carly observed Wynn over her glass at her as she took a drink of wine. "And kids? What about kids?"

"You want lots of them."

"I know that." Carly reached over and tugged at her pinky finger. "What about you?"

She rolled her lips in and took a deep breath. Carly's smile faded, and she couldn't make her think she didn't want the same. "I want just as many of those heart-twisting little rug rats as you." She laughed and Carly smiled her beautiful smile.

Wynn's pulse quickened as they stared into each other's eyes. All sounds of the party happening around them quickly disappeared to a low muffle compared to the rapid beat of her heart thumping in her ears. Was it possible for Carly to hear it as well? The smoldering darkness in her eyes made her think she could. It seemed Carly knew everything going on in her heart.

Carly stared into Wynn's eyes, and she tingled as the dream she'd had this morning after Wynn left her office filled her thoughts. Them pressed into each other, soft breasts in her hands, sweet nipples in her mouth. Legs tangled together and sheets tossed to the floor. Everything Wynn had told her came vividly to life in high definition, and she was completely aroused again.

"Are you okay?" Wynn's voice broke through her thoughts. "Your cheeks look a little flushed."

"Do they?" They were on fire. She slapped her hands to them, trying to cool the inferno radiating from them, and launched out of her chair. "I have to go." She didn't know how she was going to process the electrifying, erotic dream she'd had, but no way could she remain in the same room with Wynn without acting on it.

"Carly, wait," Wynn said as she shot up and took her by the hand.

The bolt of electricity zapped up her arm, down through her midsection, and then settled between her legs. She froze as Wynn's full, red lips opened slightly and vibrant blue eyes stared at her in confusion. Why had they never impacted her before today?

She pulled her arm free. "No, really. I have to go. Now." The warmth in her arm remained like she'd been branded by Aphrodite, the goddess of desire herself, and she would never have free will again when it came to Wynn Jamison. How could she fix this? Panic shot through her. How could she sit across the table from Wynn tonight and act like everything was the same, when clearly it wasn't? Every shred of interest she'd had in anyone else remained only clutter in her head, wiped clean by a dream she'd had about Wynn—with Wynn, which had penetrated her very core.

"Can we still talk later?" Wynn asked, her voice so soft, pleading.

"I don't know," she said into the air in front of her, not daring to turn around again. If any more talking happened, it had to be someplace very public, in the middle of the crowd.

She'd barely moved three feet away from Wynn when Suzanna caught her, draped her arm around her waist, and moved her back into Wynn's space. "Don't you two look awesome tonight. If I didn't know better, I'd have thought you dressed at the same house." Suzanna grinned.

Carly knew Suzanna was only trying to help, but she wasn't. Carly didn't like not being in control of her emotions, and the constant zaps hitting her system whenever her eyes met Wynn's made it clear she wasn't maintaining any constraints at this moment.

She took a breath. "Thanks. You're looking pretty gorgeous tonight yourself."

"Hey. I've got an idea. Why don't you two take a walk on the pier?" She ushered them toward the door. "Hurry, before Jordan starts barking out orders."

Wynn held out her hand. "It's only a walk." She gave her a soft, pleading smile.

Carly reluctantly took it and swallowed hard as the familiar jolts coursed through her. How could Wynn do that to her with just one touch?

They strolled silently until they reached a lovely spot where they could take in the view of the Pacific Ocean as it floated effortlessly under the Bay Bridge. The sun was just beginning to lower, and the purples and reds of the sky created a beautiful backdrop to the perfect evening. She glanced at Wynn, enjoying the colors of the sky reflecting on her face, and decided, as hard as it was for her, she should enjoy this beauty and serenity.

Wynn glanced her way and caught her staring. "What?"

"Nothing. I just had a dream this morning after you left my office, and you were…" She shook her head. "Never mind." She looked at the sunset.

"Please don't do that." Wynn guided her chin back to see her eyes before she rolled her lips in, then chewed on the bottom one. "Not after I said all those things to you this morning."

She moved closer and put her hand on Wynn's cheek. "It started like this." She stopped fighting and let it happen—took Wynn's face in her hands and kissed her. Their tongues danced in a slow waltz, each pushing against the other, swirling perfectly in motion together. Every one of her nerve endings exploded like a sparkler on the Fourth of July. Heat spread throughout her and settled between her legs. The strongest of winds from the bay wouldn't be able to douse the fire Wynn stoked within her. She broke the kiss and stared breathlessly into Wynn's eyes.

"That was a pretty good beginning." Wynn quirked her lip up. "How did it end?"

Another jolt zapped through her cheeks. "At your place. I think." She looked away. "In bed."

Wynn grinned, her cheeks producing the tiniest of dimples, which made her even more gorgeous than before. "We don't have to go there tonight, or anywhere else for that matter. I would love nothing more than to just walk the pier and be in your company. To learn more about you." Wynn touched Carly's lips lightly with her own, and heat spread through her again. Much more than talking would happen if she went anywhere with Wynn tonight. Even an innocent stroll on the pier would wind up with them in a dark corner somewhere making out until she had to find a room to finish what they would start.

She broke the kiss and pushed out of Wynn's arms. "I'm sorry. I can't." She spun around, rushed back to the restaurant and through the patio gate.

Wynn caught up with her on the patio before she made it inside. "Can we just go somewhere and talk?" The pleading look in her eyes was heartbreaking.

She knew she shouldn't. Staying within fifty feet of Wynn right now was dangerous, but her desire was overwhelming. "Okay." She wanted so badly to finish what they'd started—what she'd dreamed about.

Wynn took her hand and led her back out the patio gate and around the side of the building. In a flash, Carly had Wynn pushed up against the building kissing her again. Why was this pull to Wynn so powerful?

"I want to get out of here. Go somewhere private." Wynn's voice was soft and breathless.

"I need to let Suzanna know I'm leaving."

"I'll text her from the car."

"No. I can't just leave. I need to tell her."

"Okay." Wynn backed up and threaded her fingers through her hair. I'll get the car and meet you out front?"

"Okay." She walked back where they'd come from, past the restaurant, and farther down the pier to another restaurant, where she grabbed hold of a railing to steady herself. The emotions coursing through her were paralyzing; she couldn't catch her breath, walk, or even think straight. She didn't intend to go anywhere with Wynn—she couldn't until she got herself under control. She pushed her way through faceless obstacles inside to the front door and rushed out to get as far away as she could as fast as her feet would move her.

She was close to the point of no return as it was, and she had rules about moving too quickly, no matter how right it felt. The dream she'd had this morning was so real, she was about to combust and couldn't imagine how spending more time this evening with Wynn would end in anything less than a marathon night of lovemaking.

Chapter Twenty-two

Wynn lay in bed staring at the ceiling. What had gone wrong tonight? Everything seemed to have been progressing well, and it seemed like the connection she'd shared with Carly was solid until something spooked her.

After they'd worked so well together to help Suzanna, the night had been filled with fun optimism. Of all things, they'd bonded over spilled salad, and she'd been looking forward to being alone with Carly outside of the fund-raising event. You could discuss only so much with fifty or more people milling around.

Carly had wanted to know more about Wynn and hadn't stopped bulleting her with questions after they'd arrived. That was fair, since Wynn had spent the entire conversation this morning talking about herself and her needs. Thankfully, it hadn't scared her off immediately, but it seemed to have confused her. The disbelief she'd seen creep across her face had slowly turned to confusion when Wynn told her everything she'd learned about her over the past few days. She'd either thought she was a stalker or truly believed her.

Carly had appeared unsure at one moment, but then they'd talked more, and everything between them seemed to be good. She hadn't pressured Carly, had she? She recalled their conversation.

"Can we just go somewhere and talk?"
"Okay." Carly seemed hesitant.

She glanced toward the restaurant, saw a flash of Jordan through the doors. She would be upon them soon. "Come this way." She took Carly's hand and quickly led her through the gateway and onto the pier. They rushed around the side of the building, where they stopped for breath. "I think we escaped." She braced herself against the building and laughed. Then before she knew it, Carly's hands were on her cheeks and she was kissing her with intent.

"I want to get out of here. Go somewhere private."

She'd said she needed to let Susanna know. Carly was adorably polite, another thing Wynn loved about her, a trait she was sure Carly had gained from her profession. So, she'd agreed to get the car and meet her in front of the restaurant.

Wynn couldn't believe this was happening. She had a chance to change her destiny and have a life with Carly. All she could think about were the promises they'd made each other the night before to see this thing through—whatever it was—whatever the outcome. They both knew with absolute certainty they were meant to be together.

But Carly had vanished, left without her, and hadn't answered any of her calls. She'd wanted to accomplish so much tonight and had so little time for it to happen. She wanted to learn more about Carly and share everything going on in her head with her. They hadn't even touched the top layer of their lives. The intimacy they'd shared over the past few days had brought them exceedingly closer, at least in Wynn's eyes. Carly's abrupt exit made it clear she wasn't feeling the same. How could she? Wynn had only been a blip on the radar of Carly's life. Tonight had been another disaster to add to the growing pile of confusion.

The doorbell rang, and she checked the Ring app on her phone. Her heart raced when she saw Carly standing at her door. As she launched out of bed and pulled on a pair of sweatpants, the bell rang two more times, and a text notification appeared on her phone.

She ran through the house and yanked open the door. "Are you okay?"

"I'm sorry. I know I shouldn't have left you like that at the restaurant, but I'm still trying to wrap my head around how you know all that about me."

She moved aside to let Carly enter, watched her walk into the living room. She'd changed and was now wearing skinny jeans and a button-down plaid blouse tucked in loosely at the waist.

"I have no other explanation for it other than the one I've given you." She watched as Carly paced across the room. "I know you think I'm crazy, but it's all true. I'm in love with you, and you can't even remember what happened between us yesterday." She moved closer to the front door. "You should just go. It must not be meant to be." The tears rained down her cheeks. She couldn't believe this was the last time she would see Carly, but it had to be. For her own sanity, she had to get over this woman, get out of this loop.

Carly moved swiftly across the room, and instead of leaving she kicked the door closed and took Wynn into her arms and kissed her. Soon she was pressed up against the wall being kissed with such urgency she almost couldn't breathe. Her mind scattered, and she immersed herself in the heat of Carly's body, the softness of her breasts, the strength of her arms, her skillful tongue swirling inside her mouth. Carly's hands worked her way under Wynn's shirt and up to her breasts, which were completely free of any restraint. Carly pinched a nipple, and liquid gushed to Wynn's boyshorts.

"I don't know how to explain it either. I've never felt this close to anyone," Carly said as she broke free for air. "Bedroom?"

Wynn quickly led her through the house and through the door into her bedroom, stopping just short of the bed. "Is this what you want?"

"More than I've ever wanted anything." Carly kissed her again, slipped her hands beneath her T-shirt again, let them drift up her sides, and Wynn shuddered. She would never get over the pleasure of Carly's touch. Loving Carly and letting her do the same in return had been everything she'd imagined it would be. She would live this day over forever if Carly ended up in her arms every night. Only tonight Wynn would take control.

She moved Carly to the bed and watched her fall back before she tugged her T-shirt over her head. Carly watched, her eyes raking over her without scrutiny. She slipped her thumbs under her sweatpants, and Carly sat up and pushed her hands out of the way, then slid the pants slowly from her hips to the floor. Wynn shuddered as Carly grazed her fingers up her calves, creating tiny circles as she moved to her thighs. She jolted when Carly's lips touched her belly just below her navel.

Carly held her tightly as she laughed against her skin, then looked up at her with dark eyes. "Take me there. To the place you told me about this morning." She dropped another kiss on Wynn's belly and pulled off her shirt before she leaned back on her arms, waiting.

The wetness between Wynn's legs multiplied as she dropped to her knees, unbuttoned Carly's pants, and slid them from her soft, smooth legs. Everything she'd ever wanted was right here, and she was going to do just as Carly asked in the slowest, most methodical method her desires would allow.

She memorized the soft moans escaping Carly's lips as she trailed her tongue down her belly, settled in, and kissed each thigh. Then she stared at the glorious sight in front of her. Slowly snaking her arms under her legs, she moved her to the edge of the bed, placed a leg over each shoulder, and buried herself between them. She took in all of her and felt Carly press against her mouth, wanting more as her back arched from the bed. She did just that, gave her so much more—licking, sucking, tasting without hesitation. She'd wanted to savor the familiar taste, enjoy every moment to its fullest, but she would give this first one to Carly quickly and then do it all over

Carly enjoyed pushing her body to the limit in more ways than one. She'd done just that tonight and felt extraordinary with Wynn. Every touch, every kiss made her react. That had never happened this perfectly with any other woman. When couples told her about their connections and mind-blowing sex, she'd always wondered what they meant. Now she knew. She'd had good sex—even great sex—but what she'd just experienced with Wynn was on a level all its own. She couldn't comprehend the electricity coursing through her when Wynn's fingers grazed her skin, nor how she read each reaction and took her higher, to a level she'd never thought possible. A level she craved. She'd tumbled into orgasm more than once, quickly and thoroughly without any effort or concentration. All outside thoughts of work and the world around her had completely dissipated when Wynn kissed her. The whole evening had been spectacular, but the intimacy between them now was the pièce de résistance. The woman she'd dreamed of was right here in her arms. All she had to do was love her.

She grazed Wynn's nipple with her palm before she let her hand travel down her side, across her hip, and then slipped it in between her legs, feeling the warmth that awaited. The wetness she felt only intensified her arousal. She slid her fingers inside Wynn, then out again, with a circular rhythm that took them around up through her folds and back inside. Wynn grabbed Carly's ass and pulled her closer, trapping her hand between them, creating more friction. Silent moans exchanged mouths as Wynn reacted, and Carly tugged on her lip with her teeth as she cried out.

She'd just settled in on Wynn's shoulder when she felt the warm heat on her forehead. "Are you crying?"

"I'm sorry. You just...and I'm afraid—"

"I know. Stop worrying. I'm not going anywhere." She held Wynn tighter. "I'll never let you go." She kissed her gently. "I promise."

"I just want to hold you through the night, wake up to the sunrise with you in my arms, and do it all over again. Every day for the rest of my life." Wynn wiped the tears from her cheeks. "What if this day starts over again?"

"You're going to fix it for us. Tell me everything again—kiss me every day until we get it right."

"We?"

"Yes, we. You can't quit. What we have here is too perfect. It has to be meant to be." A wave of helplessness took her, and she couldn't stop her own tears.

Her heart hurt thinking that if everything Wynn had told her was true, she wouldn't remember a thing about what they'd shared. How could she feel so deeply for someone she hardly knew? She ached to hold her in her arms, make love to her again, and share her innermost secrets. Yet she literally knew nothing about this woman except what she'd told her today. Wynn filled her with joy without even knowing how. There had been no preamble to what she'd experienced tonight. No five-date warning. She was completely in love with Wynn and couldn't explain why. There had to be a chance for them.

Chapter Twenty-three

Wynn opened her eyes and found herself in the same space and time as she had the past seven days. Her life as she saw it in the future was over. She'd fallen for a dream that would never come true. She wasn't going to get through this day, at least not the way she wanted to—with the outcome she hoped for. Chances of a happy ending with Carly were dwindling. Not knowing whether she would ever see a future with Carly, or anyone else for that matter, frightened her. How many more times could the day repeat? Would they all be frozen in time for eternity? Would she be able to accept that fate? Could she? She shook her head. No. Then she remembered what Carly had said to her last night as she was drifting off to sleep: *Kiss me every day until we get it right.* So, she would do just that, live the day over again until she got it right.

She rolled out of bed, went through her usual morning routine, and loved on Shadow for a bit before she sent Carly a text.

Good morning, beautiful. She kept it short and sweet today.

Carly's usual response appeared. *I think this was meant for someone else.*

Nope. You're gorgeous, Carly. Always have been.

I don't know what to say. Thank you? The text ended with a smiley face.

Say you'll have breakfast with me. I have things to tell you, plans to make with you. Her stomach rumbled as she waited for a response. *Please?* She'd never begged for a woman's attention, but she would do anything for Carly's, until the end of time if necessary.

Okay popped up on the screen, and her stomach settled.

I'll pick you up at your office at 9:00.

I can meet you somewhere. The bakery near my office?

I'll come to your office first. We'll walk over from there.

Okay. I'll see you then.

Now to look at the past few days to figure out what was making her life repeat, what was wrong, and make plans to do it differently *again*. She had to be missing something.

After she'd placed all the sticky notes in their appropriate headings on the kitchen table, she picked up Shadow, nuzzled her close, and studied all the events that had occurred throughout each repetition. The table looked like a horrible abstract piece of art. She'd thought Jordan was the last piece of the puzzle, but evidently not. Maybe Carly could help her figure it out, or maybe not.

She held Shadow in front of her and looked into her small, black eyes. "Maybe I'm not supposed to tell Carly any of it. Just let her fall in love all on her own." She kissed Shadow's nose. "Do you think that could happen?" Shadow pawed at her face. "You think so? You have a lot of faith in destiny. Much more than I do."

She'd never just let things happen. She'd always controlled everything around her. Otherwise she would've never gotten to where she was today at Sexton Technologies, which was still up in the air, depending on how her day went. On the other hand, she might be happily married to Carly by now if she'd just let go of that stupid goal. Wynn took a deep breath. She had to have faith in destiny—to embrace the fact that whatever would or wouldn't be wasn't her choice.

❖

For some reason, Carly had thought about Wynn more than once during the past few days. She wasn't sure why, but she'd been excited when she received the text from her this morning and still was. She'd bypassed her usual conservative slacks and jacket for a skirt and blouse.

The door opened, jolting her out of her thoughts.

Stephanie led Wynn through the door. "She said you knew she was coming?"

"Yes. Thanks, Steph." She'd had Stephanie clear her schedule this morning, but had gotten distracted thinking about Wynn, wondering what she needed to discuss.

As soon as Stephanie was gone and the door closed, Wynn seemed nervous. "I'm sorry to bother you this morning, but I need to resolve something." She paced for a moment before she crossed the office quickly toward her.

Carly was surprised when Wynn took her into her arms and kissed her. She relaxed into Wynn, kissed her back, and immersed herself in the tingle coursing through her body as it settled deep in her belly. When the kiss ended and Wynn put some distance between them, she felt like a heated blanket had been snatched away.

Wynn jerked her lip up to one side. "Well, now that we've done that."

Still in a daze, Carly swallowed hard and tried to regain her composure. No one had ever kissed her so thoroughly, and she wanted Wynn to do it again. "I don't think I'm done yet." She hooked her hand behind Wynn's neck and guided her back. When their lips touched again, all her nerve endings exploded. She'd been waiting for something like this all her life and wasn't about to let it end so quickly.

She trailed her lips across Wynn's jaw. Wynn leaned her head back, giving her a clear path to the beautiful neck she wanted to taste. She could feel Wynn's pulse throb against her lips as she made her way to the sweet spot that joined with her shoulder. Knowing Wynn was aroused made her want Wynn even more.

She put her hand on Wynn's chest and felt the same rhythm pounding in her chest. "You're nervous."

Wynn nodded. "You do that to me."

She captured Wynn's mouth and kissed her thoroughly again. When the kiss broke this time, they were both breathing hard.

"You are so beautiful." Wynn shook her head. "I never thought you'd kiss me like that."

She wanted to do a whole lot more than kiss Wynn right now. She turned, walked to the door, and locked it. As she caught Wynn's gaze, she could hardly contain herself as she strolled across the office to her and returned her mouth to her neck.

"You don't sleep with women you haven't dated at least five times," Wynn choked out with a gasp.

She had no idea how Wynn knew that, but she didn't care. "I know." She licked a path to the open area of her button-down shirt. "We've been through at least ten or more events together. I'm counting those." She unbuttoned the first button and moved to the next.

Wynn moaned. "I'm not going to argue with that logic."

Somehow they made it to the couch, and she pushed Wynn onto it, then sat on her lap, straddling her. Wynn slid her hands slowly up her sides underneath her shirt. A tremor filled her as she grazed the side of her breasts. Jesus. She was about to explode. Buttons seemed to unfasten themselves, and her shirt was pushed to her arms. The clasp of her bra released, leaving it loose on her shoulders. She hadn't realized Wynn had even touched the clasp. The moan that escaped her as Wynn slipped her hands up her sides and brushed her thumbs across her nipples was loud and erotic. She'd always been super-sensitive and never held back. She grabbed Wynn's hair and held on as pleasure sizzled through her. She slid closer on Wynn's lap, attempting more friction against her waist.

Wynn stopped her, swallowed hard, and took a deep breath. "We need to stop."

"What? Why?" She'd just gotten half-naked on Wynn's lap, and now she didn't want her?

Wynn began buttoning Carly's blouse. "I don't—"

"You don't want me?" She pushed Wynn's hands away. "Well, this is embarrassing." She tried to move from her lap. "Talk about mixed messages."

Wynn grabbed her hips and stopped her. "Of course I want you. There is *nothing* in this world I want more than to make love with you. I just don't want our first time to be rushed, here on the couch in your office." Wynn took her face in her hands and kissed her.

The world disappeared again, and Carly wanted nothing more at this moment than this woman. She broke the kiss and growled. "Let's get out of here." Then she stood, straightened her clothes, and kissed Wynn again before heading behind her desk to grab her bag from the drawer. "My place is close."

Someone knocked on the door, and Wynn glanced her way, she assumed to make sure she was settled enough to see whomever it was. She nodded, and Wynn opened the door.

Stephanie stepped into the office and assessed them both. Carly didn't make a habit of locking her office door, ever.

"The Baxters are here."

She'd thought all her morning appointments had been rescheduled. She raised her eyebrows, and Stephanie seemed to notice her confusion.

"I wasn't able to reach them, and they didn't receive my message."

"I…" She glanced at Wynn.

"It's okay. We can talk later."

"Give me a minute, Steph."

"Sure." Stephanie backed out of the room, still assessing them as she closed the door behind her.

Wynn walked to her where she stood behind her desk and brushed a strand of hair from her face, letting her thumb graze Carly's cheek as she tucked it behind her ear. "Are you okay?"

"I don't know." What the hell had just happened to her? Magical things *were* sparking between them. "You touched me and something happened." She glanced around the room, trying to make sense of the mix between excitement and calm coursing through her. "I feel we've experienced something together, but I don't know why." Wynn touched her arm, let her hand slide down to Carly's. Heat radiated through it, and she almost couldn't speak. "I can't explain any of this—not the kiss, not the familiarity, not the...burning desire to make love to you. I just don't know how it's possible." She was on fire and couldn't explain that either. She wiped the moisture from her forehead. "I'm thoroughly confused. And completely turned on."

Wynn smiled. "That makes two of us." She kissed her softly, and electricity zapped through Carly.

"I'm not going to be able to concentrate on my patients with you lingering in my mind."

"I'm sorry about that, but then again, I'm not." Wynn grinned. "Can I escort you to the fund-raiser tonight?"

"Absolutely. In fact, I'd be pretty upset if you didn't."

"Okay, then." Wynn backed away and went to the door. "I'll pick you up at six."

"You need my address." She picked up a pen and began to write, then dropped it to the desk. "You know it already, don't you?"

"I do." Wynn smiled broadly. "I'll see you tonight."

As soon as Wynn left, Stephanie came through the door. "What was that about?"

"You have no idea."

"I think I do." Stephanie came across the office and began unbuttoning and rebuttoning her blouse. "You missed one." She pulled the hem to straighten it. "Did you have sex?"

She shook her head. "But we were close." She plucked a hair tie from her desk drawer, then pulled her hair into a ponytail and fastened it.

"I interrupted you." Stephanie flattened her lips.

"No. She stopped it." Thinking about it now, she realized it was a good thing she had.

Stephanie's brows flew up.

"It's fine. She was sweet." She flopped into her chair. "She wants it to be special."

"So why haven't I seen her before?"

"I've known her for a while, but this is very new." She smiled, wondering why she hadn't pursued Wynn before. "I think it surprised us both."

"I can see that." She went to the door. "Sorry I interrupted. I'll give you a couple more minutes to cool off."

"Thanks." She stared at the couch. What had she been thinking? She hadn't been thinking at all. The passion—the desire had taken her so quickly, she'd wanted to touch every part of Wynn at that moment. She would've had her if Wynn hadn't stopped them, and she would've regretted it. How was she going to handle the event tonight? Would the attraction be front and center? Would she be able to ignore it? *Get it together.*

A soft knock sounded on the door before Stephanie led the Baxters into the office. She stood, cleared Wynn from her thoughts, and crossed the room to greet them. She had work to do.

Chapter Twenty-four

Wynn tried to settle herself as she walked along the sidewalk to where she had parked her Jeep on the street. She hadn't expected Carly to respond the way she had. It was clear they were meant to be, but how to make that happen was still foggy. As soon as she got to her Jeep and slid into the seat, she called Suzanna.

"Can I come by and see you in a little while?"

"Sure. What's up?"

"I need your advice. My life is a mess."

"Seriously? Your life is never messy. It's always perfectly planned and in order."

That was true, she'd always been that way before, but that was before Carly entered the picture. "I did something super spontaneous this morning."

"What? Got a latte instead of a mocha?"

"I kissed Carly."

"Hold, please." She heard the muffled sounds of the kids in the background, then she said something to James, and complete silence after that. "Sorry. I can't have any distractions for this conversation. James is taking the kids to the park. How long 'til you get here?"

"Ten minutes, max."

"Hurry."

When she arrived, Suzanna was sitting on the porch waiting with two cups of coffee on the table beside her.

"I'm surprised you got them out of here that fast."

Suzanna handed her one of the cups. "James is pissed. He wanted to hear this firsthand."

"What the hell? Since when is my love life front-page news?" She took a sip of the coffee and burned her tongue. "Jesus. This is hot."

"It's news since you don't have one. Haven't for years." Suzanna blew out a breath. "I had such high hopes for you. That you'd get married and have kids someday. Lots of them for my kids to play with, but you're just like Jordan. Always at work. Driven by success."

"Yeah, well, I'm rethinking that situation."

"With Carly?"

She nodded. "Yes." She wanted *all* of that with Carly.

Suzanna slapped her hands together and rubbed them back and forth. "I've been waiting so long for you to wake up and see her." She picked up her coffee cup and held it in the air. "If it wasn't ten a.m. I'd open a bottle of champagne."

She clinked her cup against Suzanna's. "Why didn't you give me a push sooner?"

"I've been doing that for months. Do you really think I need your help at my events?"

"Oh. I thought you just liked hanging out with me."

"A bit dense, are we?" Suzanna laughed. "I do love you, sis, but I see you every Sunday at Mom and Dad's house." She sipped her coffee. "The kids love playing with you, by the way."

"Well, yeah. I still hold cool-aunt status."

Suzanna scrunched her nose. "Probably always will." She set her cup on the table and relaxed into her chair. "Tell me what happened with Carly. Don't you dare leave anything out. I want all the details."

Suzanna sat staring at her intently as she explained how she'd had dinner with Carly, how Carly had expressed her unhappiness with her marriage to Jordan, and how they'd kissed on the pier. When she'd woken up the next morning she'd somehow been transported in time to a year ago, the first time she'd kissed Carly on the pier.

Then she described how the day had repeated every day this week, and she'd gotten up every morning hoping time had moved forward and things were different. But they weren't.

"You didn't smoke anything, did you?" Suzanna pulled her eyebrows together. "This is a pretty unbelievable story."

"I know. It took me a few days to figure out what was happening."

"I can't believe you kissed Carly, and she ended up marrying Jordan."

"I thought she'd gone home with her. That's what Jordan led me to believe, anyway. Carly set me straight on that one. She *had* taken her home but only dropped her off. Nothing happened between them."

"She did that purposely to make you lose interest. A familiar *Jordan* tactic." Suzanna sipped her coffee. "She's good at that, always has been. I can't tell you how many times as kids she sent me on a wild-goose chase to get me out of the way. Remember the time she told me to go home to get Dad because she'd been bitten by a snake, but really hadn't?"

She nodded. "Dad was super-pissed."

"Right? We couldn't find her. Thought she was dead somewhere."

Wynn couldn't believe she'd forgotten how devious Jordan could be. "I totally fell for it—got out of her way, gave up all hope for something with Carly. Who was I to stand in her way if Carly wanted to be with her?"

"She's not the first one of my friends who's fallen for those charms. Jordan is super *suaveee*." Suzanna purposely mispronounced the word. "So how could Carly resist?"

"Exactly."

"But Jordan doesn't have an ounce of the compassion you do."

"I'm beginning to wonder whether I have any myself."

"Stop that. You've just been emulating the wrong sister."

She grinned. Suzanna was absolutely right. "I guess I have."

"But now with this time-loop thingy you're experiencing, you think things could be different?" Suzanna seemed to be understanding now.

"They have been for the past few days." She raised her hands in the air and let them drop to her legs and gripped her thighs. "I just can't get time to move forward. I must be doing something wrong."

"So you told Carly all this again this morning?"

"No. I just went there and kissed her."

"To her office? And she was okay with that?"

"Yes. She was more than okay. We almost had sex right there and then on her couch." She nodded as she stared into the yard.

"What stopped you?"

"I don't want it to be like that. I want it to be special because she's special." It had taken every bit of restraint she'd had not to make love to Carly this morning.

"Hmm. I think *you*, little sister, are in love."

"I'm sure of it. No doubt in my mind at all." She stood and paced the porch. "But is Carly in love with me?"

"Well, she's in something with you, because she doesn't sleep with just anyone."

"I know." She blew out a breath. "That's the only thing that gives me hope that this will work out." She flopped into the chair. "I've tried several different ways of doing things each day, and nothing seems to let me move forward."

Suzanna stared into her eyes with concern, as though trying to understand but didn't. "Tell me more."

"You don't believe me." Wynn shook her head and stood. "I shouldn't have told you any of it." She turned and shoved her hands into her pockets. "I know it's a crazy story."

"I'm really trying, but you have to admit it's far-fetched." Suzanna pointed her finger at her and moved it up and down. "I like that look you have today."

She'd chosen something more casual this morning. A plain white button-down covered by an army-green jacket along with black skinny jeans and white sneakers. It seemed to have fit the bill for Carly. I mean, who was she trying to impress? No one at work, that's for sure.

"It's never gonna happen. I just need to get over it—get over Carly."

"You absolutely will not. It will happen. Just keep trying."

"This isn't healthy. I think about her too much every day. I've changed everything at work, saved Shadow's mom, and been close to her so many times. I don't know if I can handle doing it again and then having it all fade away again. I want to wake up next to her—enjoy the sunrise—have morning sex." She raked her fingers through her hair. "I love too fucking hard."

"Hey." Suzanna popped to her feet and pulled her into a hug. "You go all in when it happens, and it makes my heart so happy seeing you like this. So captivated and in love." She backed up, squeezed Wynn's shoulders, and kissed her on the cheek. "It'll be all right. I'll help you."

Maybe Suzanna did believe her. "I just don't know what to do anymore."

"You're going to dazzle the fuck out of her like you did this morning." Suzanna chuckled. "That didn't come out quite right. No pun intended." She patted Wynn softly on the cheek. "I am officially your wingman for the night. I'll make sure Carly only has eyes for you."

She was relieved to hear that—to know that Suzanna didn't think she was crazy, that she knew Carly and she were destined to be together. Only time would tell whether Suzanna's help would make all the pieces fall into place. All she could do was hope.

After Carly finished counseling the Baxters, she immediately called Suzanna. "You're not going to believe what happened this morning."

"Really? What?"

"Wynn came to see me."

"Wynn? Really?"

She repeated in detail everything that Wynn had told her this morning except the throwing-herself-at-Wynn part. She'd kept that to herself for obvious reasons. Suzanna didn't seem surprised at all.

"You've talked to Wynn, haven't you?"

"Yeah." Suzanna dragged the word out slowly. "She just left."

"You just let me ramble on like an idiot? Why didn't you say something?"

"I wanted to hear your version."

"And?"

"They're pretty similar, but you left out a few details." She laughed. "Apparently, you were on fire this morning."

"Maybe a little."

"Really?"

"Okay, fine. I was like a nymph on pheromones. You know I'm not usually like that."

"I do, and I told Wynn that."

"I don't know how to explain it. I've always thought she was attractive. You know that." She took in a deep breath, trying to make sense of the emotions she'd been feeling. "It's just lately I can't get her out of my mind." Wynn's smile flashed in her head, and her stomach dipped "She does something unexpectedly crazy to me."

Suzanna's laughter came through the phone loud and clear. "The whole scenario is amazing. I mean, I've been trying to hook you two up for years, with no luck."

"What? When?"

"I'm going to tell you the same thing I told her. I have a full staff for events now—have for over a year. Neither one of you has actually been needed at any of them since I expanded the company." Voices sounded in the background. "Hang on." Suzanna's voice was muted, but she could still hear her tell James to take the kids outside. "For such smart, professional people, you two are both a little slow on the uptake. I say that lovingly."

"You think I should just go with it and let things happen?"

"Hell, yes." Suzanna's voice rose and then lowered. "You were going to have sex with her this morning. Why stop now? Clearly something's going on between you two."

"That's for sure." Heat burned the back of her neck. "Okay. Wynn is picking me up later, so I'll see you tonight."

"Yessss." The long *S* hissed through the phone. "You two are going to be so great together."

Suzanna was absolutely right. She *had* been willing to break all her rules to be with Wynn this morning. Why in the world would she run from another chance? Maybe all she needed was the courage to let it happen and a few glasses of wine.

❖

Wynn rushed into the coffee shop and picked up her order from the end of the counter, bypassing Sally by using the app on her phone again. She didn't have time for a wardrobe change.

"Hey." Sally came from behind the counter and rushed her way. "I thought I'd missed you."

She threw Sally a wave. "Sorry. In a hurry. Got a big thing at work." She spun and didn't look back. Her desire to make things work with Sally had dissipated the first time Carly had kissed her. She had no idea why she'd been stupid enough to get herself into that situation in the first place. Yeah, she did. Having the attention of a young twenty-something was flattering, at the least. Now, she just wanted to get this day over with.

She stopped at the security point at the entrance to fill in George on the plan to detain Davis, and he was all in. It was hard to believe a straitlaced security guard would be so excited about a prank.

She met Jack at Evelyn's office just like every day before, and they were both confused, as usual. "I brought coffee." She slid the tray of coffee onto the conference table and dropped paper copies of presentations next to it.

"Okay. I don't have a lot of time for chitchat today."

Evelyn's eyebrows flew up. "Who do you think you are?"

"The one who's going to save your job." She blew out a breath. "All of our jobs." She paced across the room and set up the easel and large pad. "And about a thousand more out there." She pointed to the door.

"I already have a plan for that."

"They're not going to accept your plan." She glanced at Jack. "They're not even going to look at yours because Evelyn's not going to present any of it because I didn't give it to her."

Jack drew his eyebrows together. "But you told me—"

Evelyn pointed at Wynn. "You're out of line."

"Yeah. Yeah. Tell me something I don't already know." She started sketching the new organizational chart on the pad. She took in a deep breath and turned around. "We all want to keep our jobs, right?"

"I have no plans to lose mine," Evelyn said, and Jack nodded.

"Okay. Then we have to work together. Davis is going to present a proposal to cut workforce. We have to locate him and lock him in a closet somewhere." She left out the part about her own strategy. This wasn't about redemption anymore, and that information would just make them trust her less.

"I knew he was a sneaky bastard."

"You'd be correct on both those counts. So we have to detain him until leadership buys in on our plan." She continued to write notes on the pad. "I've enlisted George in Security to assist with that task." She smiled. "Seems he likes pranks."

The meeting with leadership went exactly as she hoped. Only this time she'd secured a raise for Jack. He was taking on a whole lot more responsibility and totally deserved it. She'd said they could take it out of her salary if needed, and Evelyn had reluctantly said the same. Evelyn was gradually coming on board with Wynn's methods and management style. She seemed to be noticing that they made a difference. This had to go right today, or she would be at a loss.

On her way in, she had Evelyn's assistant schedule a meeting in the main canteen. An announcement there would eliminate everyone's fears. Wynn and Evelyn and Jack would present a united front and hopefully regain employee trust. It would take more than that, but it was a start.

All three of them strutted down the hallway in unison, like a scene from a John Grisham movie. Once they reached the main canteen, they greeted team members as they worked their way around the room to the microphones. There were three this time, rather than one. She scanned the room, and a feeling she couldn't quite describe filled her. The uncertainty that she was doing the right thing had disappeared. As she made eye contact with people's searching gazes in the crowd, she felt ready to put all these employees at ease. She wanted to let them know their jobs were safe and everything was going to be all right. That was her largest task for the day—the one that mattered most. She glanced at Evelyn, who smiled, and then at Jack, who couldn't seem to hide his happiness—and why should he? His plan had been an instrumental part of why leadership had agreed to take this path.

Wynn was slowly letting go of the protective shell she'd so carefully constructed. In the future all the people standing before her would become family. Isn't that what good leaders did?

A nervous silence blanketed the room, and everyone stilled, as they had before. It was the sort of silence that sucked the wind out of you, but that would soon be over, she hoped. She no longer wanted her presence to induce fear and uncertainty. She aimed to project a welcoming aura, where team members felt comfortable approaching her with greetings, ideas, and even issues occurring during their workdays. She calmed the shiver that came over her, a fantastic feeling this time. She glanced at Evelyn, who nodded. Today she got to deliver the good news rather than the bad.

"Thank you all for coming this morning. As you know, Sexton Technologies has faced several challenges in the past few months. We've had to cut contractors and temporary employees to the bare minimum." She started her speech exactly the same as she had on the day that now seem so far in the future. "I'm thrilled to say we will not need to reduce our workforce more, and all your positions are safe." Applause within the crowd erupted, and she paused a moment to take in the relief and joy on everyone's faces. Their suspicions had been debunked, their surprise evident. "You are all here because we..." she motioned to Evelyn and Jack... "wanted to tell you personally what a great job you all are doing. I'm now going to turn the floor over to Evelyn, your new chief operating officer."

Everyone clapped as Evelyn picked up her microphone and waited for the noise to settle. "And on that note, I'd like to announce that Wynn is our new chief information officer, and Jack is the new Director of IT." Everyone applauded again, and Evelyn waited for the noise to settle once more. "We all have a lot of work ahead of us to get this company back in the black. It won't be easy, but if we all pull together, it will happen much faster." She went on to tell them what was expected of them in the future, and that they would need to earn their raises and bonuses. Everyone seemed to be on board.

Wynn's mind checked out at that point. Knowing the outcome already, she let her thoughts wander to Carly and how things between them had escalated to warp speed earlier. She'd wanted to let it happen this morning so badly, but that hadn't been the right time or place to begin her life with Carly. She wanted to spend a lifetime making love to her, not just an hour on a couch in her office.

Chapter Twenty-five

Next up, Buttercup. Wynn didn't need to engage Jack with Buttercup. She had a plan to convince Maria to adopt Buttercup this time. She'd already called the shelter to make sure no one chose her in the meantime. Once home, if she succeeded, she would convince Maria that Buttercup was the sweetest dog, and that she would be a wonderful surprise for Jack.

After arriving home and changing into jeans and a T-shirt, and sneakers, Wynn went to the backyard, grabbed a shovel, and did some prep work for her plan. She created a crawl space under the fence just big enough for Shadow to get through. After scattering the dirt with her fingers to make it look more like Shadow actually had done the digging, she wiped small beads of sweat from her forehead. The task had been a little harder than she'd thought, considering a lack of rain the past month. She glanced up at the clear, blue sky. Where was the rain they'd had in one of the previous loops?

Now she was ready to put her plan into motion. She picked up Shadow and headed next door to Maria and Jack's house, hoping to convince Maria that all dogs weren't bad. After opening the side gate to her neighbor's backyard, she moved silently around to the back of the house and surveyed the yard. No pool or any other obstacles that could put Shadow in danger, and she didn't see anything she could get into trouble with either. Just a table and chairs set with an umbrella. She dropped a couple of small training treats in front of Shadow and instructed her to stay. Shadow ate one of the treats and moved to follow Wynn as she turned to leave the yard. She put up a hand, repeated the command, and hoped she would remain there for at least enough time to let Wynn get out the gate and to Maria's front door. She closed the gate, then ran up to the door and knocked rapidly in a panicked frenzy.

When the door pulled open, she widened her eyes at Maria. "My new puppy got out, and I can't find her. Can you help me search for her?"

Maria hesitated. "When did you see her last?"

"She was in my backyard. I always let her out first thing in the morning, but then I got distracted, and when I went to let her in, she wasn't there."

"How old is she?"

"I just brought her home last week, so about nine weeks."

Maria stopped and grabbed Wynn's forearm. "How big is she?"

"I don't know." She moved her hands up and down, trying to indicate her size. "Probably around fifteen pounds."

"Does she bite?"

"No. Not at all." She smiled. "She kisses a lot, though. She's the most lovable puppy ever." She tried to reassure Maria, but judging from the fear in her eyes, she wasn't sure if her effort was working.

Maria released her arm. "Okay. Let's check your backyard again first."

When they entered the backyard, Wynn purposely went straight to the other side, leaving Maria to find the spot she'd dug under the fence.

"I think she might be in my yard." Maria found the place right away and headed back toward the gate. "I hope she's okay. I don't think there's much there she can get into."

"I'm sure she's fine. Probably just confused. She might've forgotten how to get back home." That most likely wasn't the case. Shadow was very smart, a fact she'd found out quickly after she brought her home. She knew exactly how to get treats out of Wynn and did so often.

Wynn followed Maria into her backyard and spotted Shadow asleep in the same spot she'd left her less than a half hour before.

She stayed out of sight, just around the corner, watching as Maria came upon her.

"She's here." Maria immediately stopped when Shadow raised her head, then got to her feet and ran to her. She clutched her hands to her chest before she reluctantly put out her hand, and Shadow bathed it with kisses. Maria squatted to pet her. "And she's adorable." Shadow climbed onto Maria's knee and then fell backward. Maria sat, and the little black ball of fur was on Maria's lap before she knew what hit her.

"Wow. She really likes you. How come you and Jack don't have a dog?"

"I had a bad experience when I was younger. I've been afraid of them since."

"Nothing to be afraid of, right?"

"Seems not. Jack has always wanted one." She smiled as Shadow rolled to her back so she could scratch her belly. "I've been trying to overcome my fear. We go to the pet store occasionally to see them. My therapist says familiarity helps."

"Hey. I've got a great idea." She sat next to her. "Why don't you adopt one too? Then they could play together."

"I don't know. I've heard there's a lot of training involved with puppies."

"That's true, but I just found out that Shadow's mom, Buttercup, is up for adoption, and she's already trained." She looked at Shadow instead of Maria. "She's a puppy-mill rescue. I'd adopt her myself, but two dogs might be too much for me."

"Is she sweet like Shadow?"

"Sweeter." She stood and wiped the stray grass from her jeans. "Are you doing anything now? Why don't we go to the shelter and see her? You can make up your own mind."

"Nope. Nothing but this." Maria shook her head as she continued to pet Shadow. "Okay. I guess it couldn't hurt to see her."

"Awesome." She left Shadow with Maria and walked to the gate. "Just let me grab my keys and pull my door closed, and we can go." She'd already prepped the back of her Jeep with all the supplies they needed. She didn't want Maria to have any time to change her mind.

Maria met her at her Jeep and slid into the passenger seat. Shadow climbed across the console to see Wynn and back across it and settled in on Maria's lap.

She dialed the shelter as they pulled out of the driveway to let them know they were coming. She was trying to avoid any obstacles this time.

"So why hasn't Buttercup been adopted?"

"The girl at the shelter told me it's not uncommon for the mother to remain behind. Seems everyone wants a puppy rather than a full-grown dog."

"Why didn't you adopt her?"

"Honestly, I didn't know she was Shadow's mother, or her backstory, or I would have." She glanced from the road to Maria, who was gently petting Shadow. "As it is now, I can't give Shadow back."

"She is sweet." Maria rubbed her ear. "I hope Buttercup is too."

"Oh, she is. Trust me."

The sanctuary was set up with a main entrance and a chain-link fenced kennel area off to the side, where prospective adoptive families could walk an aisle between two large areas to view the pets. The kennel in the front was filled with a litter of what looked like hound puppies, the perfect sight to pull someone farther inside. They knew what they were doing here.

When they got out of the Jeep, Maria, still holding Shadow in her arms, stopped immediately at the sound of barking. "I can't go in there."

She could see the panic cross Maria's face. "Okay. That's fine. Why don't you stay here?" She led her to a picnic table near the front entrance. "I'll have them bring Buttercup to you." She raced inside and told the girl at the desk what she needed. She'd briefed her on the situation when she'd called earlier, and she seemed to be prepared. As the girl went to get Buttercup, Wynn raced back outside and took a seat next to Maria. Shadow roamed the ground, sniffing around the table legs.

When Buttercup came through the door on a leash held by the girl, Shadow ran across the dirt driveway and weaved through Buttercup's legs, almost tripping her.

"She's chocolate?" Maria seemed surprised. "Are you sure she's her mother?"

She nodded. "I'm sure." She'd forgotten to mention that detail and hoped it didn't make a difference. She'd explain the genetics to Maria on the way home.

Maria smiled widely. "They know each other."

Buttercup sniffed Shadow completely from head to toe before she gave her a lick on the nose. They played, going around in circles for a few minutes before the girl led Buttercup over to them. Buttercup took her cue immediately and sat directly in front of Maria, like she was a movie star playing the most important role of her life. She stared up at her with beautiful brown eyes. Anyone with a heart couldn't refuse this sweet girl.

Maria reached out and petted Buttercup gently, and when she stopped, Buttercup came closer and nudged her for more.

"I think she likes you."

Maria chuckled. "I think I like her too."

Exactly as she'd hoped. Wynn took a deep breath and smiled at the girl holding the leash. "Can we give her a little time to make sure?"

"Sure. I'll be inside. I've got the paperwork ready. All you have to do is sign." She handed the leash to Maria and went inside.

Maria raised her eyebrows. "You were pretty sure of this, weren't you?"

"I'm going to adopt her if you don't." She tilted her head. "I was struggling before, and I can't leave her now that I see this." Buttercup was lying at Maria's feet with Shadow curled up next to her.

"They can have playdates?"

"Whenever you want, and I'll be happy to look after her when you're away."

Maria drew her eyebrows together. "What if I can't handle her?"

"If that happens, I'll take her." She shrugged. "Make it work somehow."

Maria stilled and then took in a deep breath. "Okay. Let's do it."

After they got back home and Wynn had set up everything Maria needed for Buttercup, she headed back home. Maria was still a bit hesitant after they arrived, but by the time she'd left her house, she was all in and had agreed that Buttercup was a wonderful addition to their family and that Jack would love her.

She kissed Shadow on the head. "One task accomplished. You're a hell of an operative." She walked outside into her backyard for a few minutes and filled in the hole she'd dug under the fence. With Jack and Maria's approval, she'd have a gate put between the yards in the coming weeks to make the dogs' access to each other easier. Once Shadow was done with her business, Wynn went into the bedroom to get dressed. She chose something different to wear tonight, something softer—a pair of black skinny jeans, a white button-down shirt left untucked, and a casual gray cotton jacket. She settled on black, high-top Vans for shoes. Jordan would probably give her shit, but she wasn't going for best-dressed today. She wanted something more approachable.

She practiced her best smolder in the mirror as she brushed her teeth. She'd learned that habit from watching Jordan. Mimicking her sister had been a daily ritual when she was a kid. She'd idolized her growing up, but all those habits had to stop—now. She wasn't Jordan, would never be her, didn't want to be like Jordan anymore *at all.* She wanted everything Jordan didn't—the house, the picket fence, the family. And she wanted it all with Carly.

She rinsed the toothpaste from her mouth and spotted the trail of it that had landed on the front of her shirt. "Jesus, Ms. Butterfingers." She grinned at the name Carly had given her yesterday. "Why *not* start the evening out with a bang?" As she headed back to the closet to change her shirt, she hoped it went uphill from here.

As Wynn walked out the door to leave for the fund-raiser, she saw Mrs. P sitting on the porch drinking a glass of iced tea, just like every other day she'd experienced this week. She'd been so wrapped up in getting Maria to adopt Buttercup that she'd totally forgotten again to let Mrs. P know she had other plans tonight. She crossed the yard and took the seat next to her on the porch.

Mrs. P poured her a glass of tea. "I saw you and Maria come home with a new dog." Mrs. P grinned. "How'd you manage that? Maria's afraid of dogs."

"You can't tell her, but I kind of tricked her into it."

Mrs. P's eyebrows rose. "Do tell."

"I pretended to lose Shadow and engaged her help in finding her." She laughed. "She wasn't actually lost. I left her in Maria's backyard."

"That was sneaky." Mrs. P raised her glass. "Good job."

She picked up a glass and clinked it with Mrs. P's and then took a sip. She made the best iced tea. It was always perfect.

"You came home from work early today. You never do that."

"I had a big morning and just needed some time to take care of a few things." She rolled her lips in. "I'm sorry. I'm not going to be able to make dinner tonight. I have to help out at one of Jordan's events." She glanced at the time on her Apple watch and noticed the screen had dimmed. That hadn't happened before, had it? She shook her wrist and it brightened again.

"It's okay, although I'm not fond of being deserted because of your sister. She's a bit ungrateful, that one." Mrs. P patted her hand. "I'm feeling a bit tired tonight anyway."

"Did you get your nap in this afternoon?"

"Actually, no. I spent most of the day pulling weeds in the flower garden." She took another sip of tea. "Probably got a little too much sun."

"It's been pretty hot lately." She remembered her being dizzy the day before. She took out her phone and found Mr. P's number. "I'll call Mr. P. Maybe he should come home."

"No. Absolutely not. I need my time away from him as much as he needs it away from me." She frowned. "Retirement can give you all too much togetherness sometimes."

"I'll remember that." She chuckled. "You want to come with me? I'd love to escort the most beautiful woman to the ball."

"Nope. I'm sure you have someone waiting to be picked up." Mrs. P winked. "Planned or not." She drank another sip of tea. "If there's cake, bring some home for me. A big slice, not one of those dinky ones they cut nowadays. Cake used to be fun to eat. Now everyone just makes you feel guilty about it."

"Nope. You should never feel guilty about cake." She stood. "I'll bring you two huge pieces. I can get them before anyone else does."

Wynn heard Jack drive up and glanced over. She'd been hoping to see his reaction to their new family member before she left. The door flew open, and Maria stepped out onto the porch, followed by Buttercup. Jack stopped and grinned, then said something she couldn't quite hear to Maria. She nodded, and he ran up the steps and kissed her before dropping to sit on the step and pet Buttercup.

"That seems to have worked out well."

"It did, didn't it?"

Jack still had his job, Maria was happy, and Buttercup wouldn't have to spend any more time in the shelter. Everything was falling into place today. Now she just had to make sure she kept Carly away from Jordan.

Chapter Twenty-six

When Carly came out the front door of her townhouse, Wynn was speechless as she took in the gorgeous sight before her. Carly was even more stunning than she'd been the previous nights. She'd changed her choice of clothing to a V-neck, distressed-cotton dress that fell just below her knee at an angle. The colors ranged from black to white to tan. Her jet-black hair was draped to one side, exposing the loveliness of her collarbone, and a large drop-pendant necklace mixed with several small-patterned chains hung just above her belly. Everything she'd done had made the dress look absolutely elegant, yet still casual. She didn't know how, but they matched perfectly again, as though they'd planned their outfits together.

She jumped out of the Jeep and rounded it. "You look stunning." She pulled the passenger door open and took Carly's hand to help her into the seat, noticing that her tan, cork-wedge sandals brought her to the same height as Wynn.

"Thank you." Carly kissed her on the cheek and smiled as she got in. The best payment, ever. "I'm sorry about this morning."

She snapped her head to Carly. "You have absolutely nothing to be sorry for. I'm the one who should be sorry. I came to your office and kissed you without asking."

Carly took in a breath. "Indeed, you did." Her cheeks reddened. "Are you? Sorry?"

"No. Not really. It was the best morning I've had in a long time." She stared at the road and smiled as she glanced at Carly again. "It gave me something to look forward to tonight."

"Me too." The words were low and quiet as they came from Carly's lips. "I haven't been able to think about anything else since you left my office this morning."

She reached across the console and took Carly's hand in hers, then placed them together on her leg. The warmth that Carly's touch sent through her was amazing.

Carly's townhouse wasn't far from Waterbar, and it wasn't long before they arrived. Wynn pulled up in front of the restaurant and put the Jeep in park as they waited in line for the valet. She glanced at Carly and couldn't resist kissing her. Carly met her halfway, and their kiss made every part of her sizzle with excitement. She wanted to skip the party and take Carly home—make incredible, limitless love with her just as they had before. That wasn't possible, though. They had to be here tonight for this day to run its course. A whoosh of air entering the Jeep when the passenger door swung open startled them both. The valet stood waiting to help Carly out of the Jeep. His face was red, perhaps a little embarrassed that he'd just glimpsed a private show.

"Sorry. I couldn't resist."

Carly trapped her bottom lip between her teeth and smiled. "Promise me you'll never be sorry again about kisses like that."

"I promise." Goose bumps covered her skin as the feeling of happiness rushed through her. Carly made the rest of the world disappear. She wanted to throw the Jeep into gear and drive to absolutely nowhere, until the wheels fell off, just to spend more time with her without anyone else around. Instead, she watched her take the valet's hand and slide from the passenger seat. A huge lump formed in her stomach at the thought of that never happening. She sucked in a deep breath and got out of the Jeep. Tonight had to be the night for everything to come together.

They made their way inside and found Suzanna at the bar reviewing her checklist.

Suzanna turned and smiled widely. "You two made it." She gave each of them a hug and then took Carly's hands. "You're absolutely gorgeous tonight." She let one of Carly's hands drop and took Wynn's. "I say you both forget about work tonight and enjoy yourselves."

Carly suddenly seemed confused. "Oh, my. I forgot my clutch in the Jeep." She glanced at Wynn and broke into a sexy smile. "I got distracted."

"Good distraction?" Suzanna asked.

Carly didn't take her eyes from Wynn's. "I'd say more like spectacular."

Wynn was beginning to enjoy the heat that burned her cheeks as she grinned. "I'll be right back."

Suzanna took her by the arm. "Hang on a minute. We don't have the bottle of Louis XIII."

"It's on its way. I pulled in a favor from a friend of mine who owns a liquor store. Her name's Jean. Introduce her to Jordan when she gets here, will you? I think they'll get along well."

"It'll be my pleasure." Suzanna whispered in her ear, rubbing Wynn's shoulder as she said, "I'm really proud of you for making this move, sis."

"Thank you." She left Carly with Suzanna and made her way across the room to the door and then outside. After she retrieved her key fob from the valet, she headed to the usual spot where her Jeep was parked. She glanced at her watch—only a few more hours to make this day end right. The date on her Apple Watch grew lighter, then darker, just like it had earlier. What the hell was wrong with it? Something about the date was familiar. A siren in the distance made her freeze. *Mrs. P.* A chill swept up her spine as the memory hit her. How could she have forgotten—just blocked it out. She had to leave. *Now*. A rush of panic flashed through her as her adrenaline spiked. Mrs. P was in trouble. She sprinted to her Jeep, jumped in, and sped out of the parking lot, hoping she wasn't too late.

She hit the button on her phone for Mrs. P and waited. After several rings it went to voice mail. She called again. No answer.

She looked at her watch again. It wasn't even eight o'clock yet. She cancelled the call and hit Mr. P's cell number.

He answered after two rings. "Hello."

"Hey, Mr. P. I called Mrs. P to ask her something, and she's not answering."

"What? I can't hear you, Wynn." She heard bowling pins crashing in the background. "I'll call you back when I finish my game."

She ended the call and tried Mrs. P again. Still no answer. She hit Jack's number, and he answered immediately.

"Hey, Boss. What's up?"

"Are you at home?" She heard loud chatter in the background and knew he wasn't.

"Sorry, no. We're out celebrating. All three of us. We found an outdoor micro-brewery and brought Buttercup along with us."

Fuck. "Did you see Mrs. P before you left tonight?"

"Nope. She must've already gone inside."

She glanced at her watch again. "Thanks."

"Hey. Maria and I love Buttercup. Thanks for taking her to pick her up, and thanks for everything you did today."

"I'm glad everything worked out the way we planned." Her concern lulled briefly as the nice feeling of doing something good for someone took over. "Sorry. I gotta go. I need to check on Mrs. P."

She made it to the house in under thirty minutes, a drive that usually took forty-five to sixty in traffic. She hugged the curb as she sped up to Mrs. P's house and then threw the Jeep into park—it bounced as she launched out of the driver's seat and across the lawn to the front door.

She knocked. "Mrs. P, are you in there?" No response. She reached for her keys before she remembered they'd installed a new electronic deadbolt and had given Wynn her own code to gain access. "What the hell is the number?" She sucked in a breath to calm her scattered thoughts. "My birthday." She keyed in tomorrow's date, and the door unlocked.

She rushed through the house, finding Mrs. P collapsed next to the bed with her phone in her hand as though she'd been trying to call for help. Wynn immediately called nine-one-one before she dropped to the floor next to her and felt her forehead. She was flushed and hot to the touch.

"Nine-one-one, what's the emergency?"

"I found my neighbor unconscious. I think she may have heat stroke."

"What's the address there?"

Wynn rattled off the address, and the emergency dispatch operator repeated it back to her.

"Why do you think she has heat stroke? Does she have any history of heart attack or stroke?"

"She was complaining of dizziness earlier after she'd been working in the yard. Damn it. I should've noticed."

"Calm down. What time was that?"

"Maybe two hours ago." She tried to calculate the time in her head, but her brain wasn't letting her.

"Is she out of the heat now?"

"Yes. She's inside. I found her on the floor in her bedroom."

"Is her breathing regular?"

She leaned over Mrs. P's mouth felt her breath on her cheek. "Seems to be."

"That's good. The EMTs are on their way. Is the front door open?"

She thought for a moment. She hadn't closed it. "Yes. Should be wide open."

"Here's what I need you to do until the EMTs get there. Are you listening?"

"Yes."

"Find a cloth of some kind, wet it with cold water, and apply it to her neck and wrists."

"Okay." She ran to the bathroom, found a few washcloths, wet them, ran back to Mrs. P, and did as the operator instructed.

"Any change?"

"No." Mrs. P didn't move. The coolness of the compresses didn't seem to affect her at all.

"Just keep cooling the cloth and reapply it."

"That's what I'm doing." A shiver ran through her. "Oh, my God. She can't die." *Not again.* She heard voices in the hallway, and two people dressed in uniforms appeared, moving her out of the way.

"How long has she been down?"

"I don't know. I called when I found her. She was complaining of dizziness a couple of hours ago."

One EMT covered Mrs. P with a cooling blanket, while the other started breaking and shaking ice compresses. After the fourth compress, which was placed between Mrs. P's legs, she seemed to shiver.

"Okay. Let's load her up."

After the EMTs had Mrs. P all settled, she hopped into her Jeep, fired the engine, and waited to follow them. Once the Bluetooth connected to her phone, she hit the button for Mr. P. and took a few calming breaths while she waited for him to answer.

"Mr. P, I need to talk to you. It's an emergency."

"Wynn. Hang on. Let me get someplace where I can hear you." The sounds of bowling balls hitting the alley grew faint in the background. "I'm sorry. I forgot to call you back."

"I don't want to alarm you because Mrs. P seems to be all right, but she's on the way to the hospital."

"You're taking her?"

"No. She's going by ambulance. I found her unconscious and called them. They think it's heat stroke."

"I'm on my way." The line went dead. He hadn't asked which hospital, but they were taking her to the one closest to the house, and he would figure that out. She hit Carly's number next. She'd left without saying a word to her about where she was going. A sound came from the floorboard. *Shit.* She'd gone to the Jeep to get Carly's clutch. She called Suzanna next because she wasn't about to call Jordan. The phone rang a few times and then went to voice mail.

"Hey, sis. I had an emergency and had to leave. Mrs. P has heat stroke, and I called an ambulance. I'm following it to the hospital now. Call me when you get this, and please let Carly know, will you?" She hit the hang-up button on her steering wheel.

Once they arrived at the emergency room, Wynn was directed to the waiting room without any information. She'd called Mr. P from the car. He should be there soon.

Mrs. P hadn't survived last year, and everyone in the neighborhood had felt the loss. Mrs. P was truly loved and was like a second mother to Wynn. Mr. P hadn't been the same since. She couldn't believe she'd forgotten about this tragedy each time the day had repeated. She'd been selfishly wrapped up in her own life. She didn't deserve to be happy, and she'd suffer with living without Carly in her life as long as Mrs. P made it through okay. Living the day over again had exhausted Wynn. She couldn't keep her eyes open. If the day repeated again, taking care of Mrs. P would be her first priority. She would clear her schedule and spend the day with her to make sure she stayed out of the sun, to make sure she was safe.

Chapter Twenty-seven

A familiar voice shook Wynn from her drowsy state. She opened her eyes and glanced around the emergency room. Everything was sideways. She was lying on the couch with her head on someone's thigh. Had Suzanna shown up last night? She didn't remember seeing her.

Someone brushed their fingers through her hair. "It's okay, baby. We haven't had any new information yet. Go back to sleep."

Carly? She twisted to look up at her. "You're here?"

"Of course I'm here, silly. I wouldn't let you wait here alone while they work on Mrs. P. Thank God, she's going to be all right. She really needs to stay out of the sun."

"How did you know?" Had she told Carly that today? She didn't think so.

"What? That Mrs. P's going to be all right? The doctor said so. They're hydrating her now, and she should be able to go home in the morning." Carly smiled. "But you wanted to stay and make sure."

"I did?" She sat up. "I mean. I did." She looked at Carly's clothes—a tropical dress with a sweater covering her shoulders—then at her own—Bermuda shorts and Hawaiian shirt. Casual… totally different than what they'd been wearing at the fund-raiser.

"Sorry it took me so long. I had to get the kids settled."

"You have kids?"

Carly looked at her strangely. "I was talking about Shadow and Lucy." She touched her belly. "But soon."

She blinked a few times and closed her eyes. This was a new ending to this day. “We have two dogs and a baby on the way?”

Carly put the back of her hand to Wynn’s forehead. “Are you okay? What did you have to drink tonight?”

“What’s today’s date?”

“August twenty-first. Tomorrow’s your birthday. You really are shook up, aren’t you?”

“I’m fine. I think.” The sparkle of Carly’s wedding ring flashed in her line of sight. She was back in present time, and Carly was *her* wife, not Jordan’s. “This whole thing has just put me into a spin.” She wasn’t just talking about Mrs. P’s health. “You left the fund-raiser?”

“You mean your birthday barbecue? The one you’ve been planning for weeks?” Carly touched her cheek, then glanced around the waiting room. “Maybe we should have you looked at too.”

“No. I meant our party.” She clasped Carly’s hand. “I’m just glad you’re here with me.” She kissed her to make sure it was all real.

Carly pulled her eyebrows together. “Of course, silly. I sent everyone home. Suzanna said she’d clean up and check on the pups in the morning, if we’re still here.” Carly squeezed her hand. “I don’t want you here alone. I know how special Mrs. P is to you.” She smiled. “I honestly don’t know what I’d do without her either. I need her gardening advice in that huge yard of ours.”

“Jack and Maria are on their way.”

Suddenly the memories she couldn’t seem to find played in her head like a movie hitting each frame in fast-forward, only she knew every scene—every line. The wedding, the honeymoon, the day they’d found out Carly was pregnant. Everything was there in high definition like it had happened only yesterday, and she’d experienced it all. She actually felt the joy and happiness it brought her. She couldn’t control the tears that sprang from her eyes.

Carly wrapped her arms around her. “Aw, honey. Everything’s going to be all right. I talked to the nurse. Mrs. P has heat exhaustion, but she’s going to be fine.” She shook her head. “She just needs to learn to stay out of the sun. That’s all.”

“Tell me about how it all started again.”

"She looked a little flushed when she got to the party and seemed to get worse. When she passed out, you called an ambulance and rode with her to the hospital since Mr. P was bowling."

"No. Not that." She stared into Carly's eyes as she scrunched her eyebrows together. "How we started."

"You don't remember?"

"I do, but I think hearing you tell me might calm my nerves."

Carly smiled as she relaxed into the couch and took her hand. "It was just your average, ordinary day. I remember having a full schedule, but you sent me a text out of the blue and wanted to have breakfast and talk to me about something." She laughed. "I had no idea what it was about. Then you showed up, came into my office, and kissed me with such intent, I couldn't resist you." Carly sighed. "We ended up on the couch, and I wanted to do all the things with you I wouldn't let myself do with anyone else."

"But?"

"You wouldn't let me, and I was ridiculously embarrassed." Another sigh. "But then you said you wanted our first time to be special. I think you captured my heart right then. You convinced me to let you escort me to Jordan's fund-raiser."

"You said yes." She smiled.

"I did, but you went back to the Jeep to get something."

"Your clutch." She remembered it ringing on the floorboard.

Carly nodded. "And you just disappeared. I was heartbroken. I thought I'd done something to scare you away." She laughed. "I mean I practically threw myself at you before we got out of the car, but I thought the feeling was mutual."

"It was." It was like a scene in an out-of-focus movie getting clearer by the moment.

Carly smiled as she ran her fingers through Wynn's hair. "The party was over, and I'd gone outside, walked far down the pier when Suzanna tracked me down and told me why you'd left."

"And then?"

"I grabbed the first cab I could find and went to the hospital to be with you." Carly smiled. "I think that's when I actually fell in love with you."

"You came for *me*? I thought you and Jordan were—"

"Jordan? God, no. It was never Jordan. It's always been you." Carly brushed a strand of hair from Wynn's face, stroked her cheek with her thumb. "I had to come. Suzanna told me how close you are to Mrs. P, and something told me you needed me." She swallowed hard. "Honestly, I needed you too." She brought Wynn's hand to her lips and kissed the back of it. "You made me realize how much I'd been ignoring in my life, how much fuller it could be with you in it."

They heard rapid footsteps coming down the hall, and Jack and Maria rushed into the waiting room. "How's she doing?"

"Mrs. P is good." Carly glanced at Wynn. "I'm more worried about this one right now. She's pretty shaken up."

"I'm okay." She grinned, scooted closer to Carly, and put her arm around her. "Everything's perfect now. As long as you're here with me." And it was. Her life had finally continued. Her heart was filled with so much joy, but she couldn't explain it to anyone, and wouldn't. She was surrounded by her wife and friends, and knew Mrs. P would recover. She glanced at the baby-bump just beginning to show in Carly's belly. Life was only going to get better.

Epilogue

Wynn rubbed her eyes as she woke, enjoying the familiar soft hum that sprang into song when Carly remembered the words to the sweet lullaby. It was the pure sound of happiness, and Wynn couldn't care less whether Carly knew the words to the song or made up her own. She reached down beside the bed and felt the soft fur of Shadow's head. Lucy immediately licked her hand. A cocker spaniel, she was the smaller of the two and always needed more attention.

Carly peeked her head around the corner from the bathroom entrance. Wynn's breath caught in her throat at the sight of her. She was more radiant than she'd ever been.

"Wake up, sleepyhead, or we're going to be late."

"What? Where?" She must've sounded like an idiot.

"Are you okay? If you aren't feeling well, I can go by myself. I think Jordan and Jean will be there." Carly moved into the room.

When their daughter, Destiny, came into view on Carly's shoulder, tears sprang from Wynn's eyes. She couldn't believe how wonderful her life was. The past year or so she'd spent with Carly since the day stopped repeating had been the best days of her life.

"Oh, honey." Carly rushed to the bed, plucked a couple of tissues from the box on the nightstand, and blotted the tears from Wynn's face. "It's okay. You can stay home if you don't want to go to your parents' house." She sat on the edge of the bed and laid Destiny across Wynn's chest. "But your daughter and I are going to enjoy the last bit of nice weather while the pool's still open."

She kissed the top of Destiny's head, took in the sweet baby scent, and basked in the wonder of it all. "No. I'm fine. I want to go see Suzanna and the kids, and Mom and Dad will be upset if they don't get to see Des." Her parents loved their grandchildren, had arranged their lives around enjoying them, watching them grow. She swiped at her cheeks, wiping away the remaining tears. "It's just that you're both so beautiful, and I love you so much. I never thought my life would be this perfect."

Carly's lips spread into a wide smile. "I love you too, but I'm not coming back to bed. I've already fallen for this ploy once this week."

"I mean it." She placed her hand on Destiny's back and patted her gently. "You're even more beautiful since you had Des." She'd been radiant throughout her pregnancy, but motherhood looked wonderful on her.

"Keep talking that way, and I just might call and tell them we're not coming." Carly took a deep breath and kissed her.

Wynn immersed herself in the kiss, tugging Carly closer, wanting to feel every part of her pressed against her. "Promise me something?"

Carly slid into bed next to her, gazed at her through hazy eyes, and pulled her lips into a soft smile. "Sure."

"Promise me you'll kiss me like that every day for the rest of our lives."

"I will. I promise. Just like this." Carly covered her lips with light kisses before she took hold and let her tongue glide slowly into Wynn's mouth. It was the most wonderful kiss in the world.

THE END

About the Author

Dena Blake grew up in a small town just north of San Francisco where she learned to play softball, ride motorcycles, and grow vegetables. She eventually moved with her family to the southwest where she began creating vivid characters in her mind and bringing them to life on paper.

Dena currently lives in the southwest with her partner and is constantly amazed at what she learns from her two children. She is a would-be chef, tech nerd, and occasional auto mechanic who has a weakness for dark chocolate and a good cup of coffee.

Books Available from Bold Strokes Books

Death Overdue by David S. Pederson. Did Heath turn to murder in an alcohol induced haze to solve the problem of his blackmailer, or was it someone else who brought about a death overdue? (978-1-63555-711-4)

Entangled by Melissa Brayden. Becca Crawford is the perfect person to head up the Jade Hotel, if only the captivating owner of the local vineyard would get on board with her plan and stop badmouthing the hotel to everyone in town. (978-1-63555-709-1)

First Do No Harm by Emily Smith. Pierce and Cassidy are about to discover that when it comes to love, sometimes you have to risk it all to have it all. (978-1-63555-699-5)

Kiss Me Every Day by Dena Blake. For Wynn Jamison, wishing for a do-over with Carly Evans was a long shot, actually getting one was a game changer. (978-1-63555-551-6)

Olivia by Genevieve McCluer. In this lesbian Shakespeare adaption with vampires, Olivia is a centuries old vampire who must fight a strange figure from her past if she wants a chance at happiness. (978-1-63555-701-5)

One Woman's Treasure by Jean Copeland. Daphne's search for discarded antiques and treasures leads to an embarrassing misunderstanding, and ultimately, the opportunity for the romance of a lifetime with Nina. (978-1-63555-652-0)

Silver Ravens by Jane Fletcher. Lori has lost her girlfriend, her home, and her job. Things don't improve when she's kidnapped and taken to fairyland. (978-1-63555-631-5)

Still Not Over You by Jenny Frame, Carsen Taite, Ali Vali. Old flames die hard in these tales of a second chance at love with the ex you're still not over. Stories by award winning authors Jenny Frame, Carsen Taite, and Ali Vali. (978-1-63555-516-5)

Storm Lines by Jessica L. Webb. Devon is a psychologist who likes rules. Marley is a cop who doesn't. They don't always agree, but both fight to protect a girl immersed in a street drug ring. (978-1-63555-626-1)

The Politics of Love by Jen Jensen. Is it possible to love across the political divide in a hostile world? Conservative Shelley Whitmore and liberal Rand Thomas are about to find out. (978-1-63555-693-3)

All the Paths to You by Morgan Lee Miller. High school sweethearts Quinn Hughes and Kennedy Reed reconnect five years after they break up and realize that their chemistry is all but over. (978-1-63555-662-9)

Arrested Pleasures by Nanisi Barrett D'Arnuck. When charged with a crime she didn't commit Katherine Lowe faces the question: Which is harder, going to prison or falling in love? (978-1-63555-684-1)

Bonded Love by Renee Roman. Carpenter Blaze Carter suffers an injury that shatters her dreams, and ER nurse Trinity Greene hopes to show her that sometimes hope is worth fighting for. (978-1-63555-530-1)

Convergence by Jane C. Esther. With life as they know it on the line, can Aerin McLeary and Olivia Ando's love survive an otherworldly threat to humankind? (978-1-63555-488-5)

Coyote Blues by Karen F. Williams. Riley Dawson, psychotherapist and shape-shifter, has her world turned upside down when Fiona Bell, her one true love, returns. (978-1-63555-558-5)

Drawn by Carsen Taite. Will the clues lead Detective Claire Hanlon to the killer terrorizing Dallas, or will she merely lose her heart to person of interest, urban artist Riley Flynn? (978-1-63555-644-5)

Every Summer Day by Lee Patton. Meant to celebrate every summer day, Luke's journal instead chronicles a love affair as fast-moving and possibly as fatal as his brother's brain tumor. (978-1-63555-706-0)

Lucky by Kris Bryant. Was Serena Evans's luck really about winning the lottery, or is she about to get even luckier in love? (978-1-63555-510-3)

The Last Days of Autumn by Donna K. Ford. Autumn and Caroline question the fairness of life, the cruelty of loss, and what it means to love as they navigate the complicated minefield of relationships, grief, and life-altering illness. (978-1-63555-672-8)

Three Alarm Response by Erin Dutton. In the midst of tragedy, can these first responders find love and healing? Three stories of courage, bravery, and passion. (978-1-63555-592-9)

Veterinary Partner by Nancy Wheelton. Callie and Lauren are determined to keep their hearts safe but find that taking a chance on love is the safest option of all. (978-1-63555-666-7)

Everyday People by Louis Barr. When film star Diana Danning hires private eye Clint Steele to find her son, Clint turns to his former West Point barracks mate, and ex-buddy with benefits, Mars Hauser to lend his cyber espionage and digital black ops skills to the case. (978-1-63555-698-8)

Forging a Desire Line by Mary P. Burns. When Charley's ex-wife, Tricia, is diagnosed with inoperable cancer, the private duty nurse Tricia hires turns out to be the handsome and aloof Joanna, who ignites something inside Charley she isn't ready to face. (978-1-63555-665-0)

Love on the Night Shift by Radclyffe. Between ruling the night shift in the ER at the Rivers and raising her teenage daughter, Blaise Richilieu has all the drama she needs in her life, until a dashing young attending appears on the scene and relentlessly pursues her. (978-1-63555-668-1)

Olivia's Awakening by Ronica Black. When the daring and dangerously gorgeous Eve Monroe is hired to get Olivia Savage into shape, a fierce passion ignites, causing both to question everything they've ever known about love. (978-1-63555-613-1)

The Duchess and the Dreamer by Jenny Frame. Clementine Fitzroy has lost her faith and love of life. Can dreamer Evan Fox make her believe in life and dream again? (978-1-63555-601-8)

The Road Home by Erin Zak. Hollywood actress Gwendolyn Carter is about to discover that losing someone you love sometimes means gaining someone to fall for. (978-1-63555-633-9)

Waiting for You by Elle Spencer. When passionate past-life lovers meet again in the present day, one remembers it vividly and the other isn't so sure. (978-1-63555-635-3)

While My Heart Beats by Erin McKenzie. Can a love born amidst the horrors of the Great War survive? (978-1-63555-589-9)

Face the Music by Ali Vali. Sweet music is the last thing that happens when Nashville music producer Mason Liner, and daughter of country royalty Victoria Roddy are thrown together in an effort to save country star Sophie Roddy's career. (978-1-63555-532-5)

Flavor of the Month by Georgia Beers. What happens when baker Charlie and chef Emma realize their differing paths have led them right back to each other? (978-1-63555-616-2)

Mending Fences by Angie Williams. Rancher Bobbie Del Rey and veterinarian Grace Hammond are about to discover if heartbreaks of the past can ever truly be mended. (978-1-63555-708-4)

Silk and Leather: Lesbian Erotica with an Edge edited by Victoria Villasenor. This collection of stories by award winning authors offers fantasies as soft as silk and tough as leather. The only question is: How far will you go to make your deepest desires come true? (978-1-63555-587-5)

The Last Place You Look by Aurora Rey. Dumped by her wife and looking for anything but love, Julia Pierce retreats to her hometown, only to rediscover high school friend Taylor Winslow, who's secretly crushed on her for years. (978-1-63555-574-5)

The Mortician's Daughter by Nan Higgins. A singer on the verge of stardom discovers she must give up her dreams to live a life in service to ghosts. (978-1-63555-594-3)

The Real Thing by Laney Webber. When passion flares between actress Virginia Green and masseuse Allison McDonald, can they be sure it's the real thing? (978-1-63555-478-6)

What the Heart Remembers Most by M. Ullrich. For college sweethearts Jax Levine and Gretchen Mills, could an accident be the second chance neither knew they wanted? (978-1-63555-401-4)

White Horse Point by Andrews & Austin. Mystery writer Taylor James finds herself falling for the mysterious woman on White Horse Point who lives alone, protecting a secret she can't share about a murderer who walks among them. (978-1-63555-695-7)

Femme Tales by Anne Shade. Six women find themselves in their own real-life fairy tales when true love finds them in the most unexpected ways. (978-1-63555-657-5)

Jellicle Girl by Stevie Mikayne. One dark summer night, Beth and Jackie go out to the canoe dock. Two years later, Beth is still carrying the weight of what happened to Jackie. (978-1-63555-691-9)

Le Berceau by Julius Eks. If only Ben could tear his heart in two, then he wouldn't have to choose between the love of his life and the most beautiful boy he has ever seen. (978-1-63555-688-9)

My Date with a Wendigo by Genevieve McCluer. Elizabeth Rosseau finds her long lost love and the secret community of fiends she's now a part of. (978-1-63555-679-7)

On the Run by Charlotte Greene. Even when they're cute blondes, it's stupid to pick up hitchhikers, especially when they've just broken out of prison, but doing so is about to change Gwen's life forever. (978-1-63555-682-7)

Perfect Timing by Dena Blake. The choice between love and family has never been so difficult, and Lynn's and Maggie's different visions of the future may end their romance before it's begun. (978-1-63555-466-3)

The Mail Order Bride by R Kent. When a mail order bride is thrust on Austin, he must choose between the bride he never wanted or the dream he lives for. (978-1-63555-678-0)

Through Love's Eyes by C.A. Popovich. When fate reunites Brittany Yardin and Amy Jansons, can they move beyond the pain of their past to find love? (978-1-63555-629-2)

To the Moon and Back by Melissa Brayden. Film actress Carly Daniel thinks that stage work is boring and unexciting, but when she accepts a lead role in a new play, stage manager Lauren Prescott tests both her heart and her ability to share the limelight. (978-1-63555-618-6)

Tokyo Love by Diana Jean. When Kathleen Schmitt is given the opportunity to be on the cutting edge of AI technology, she never thought a failed robotic love companion would bring her closer to her neighbor, Yuriko Velucci, and finding love in unexpected places. (978-1-63555-681-0)

Bold Strokes Books
Quality and Diversity in LGBTQ Literature